Wellspring

Janice Holt Giles

Wellspring

HOUGHTON MIFFLIN COMPANY BOSTON

Portions of this book have appeared in *Good Housekeeping,*
Woman's Day, McCall's, Kentucky Writing, and *Deep Summer.*

Library of Congress Cataloging in Publication Data

Giles, Janice Holt.   Wellspring.

CONTENTS: Rhythm in writing.—Kinta: The edge
of the world. The picnic. The gift.—Kentucky:
The minor miracle. Kentucky. Wilderness road.
According to his lights. When the 'lectric come to
the ridge. Tetch 'n take. Dear sir.—[etc.]
    I. Title.
PZ3.G3929We [PS3513.I4628] 813'.5'4 75-15989
ISBN 0-395-20731-2

Printed in the United States of America

w 10 9 8 7 6 5 4 3 2

CONTENTS

SPOUT SPRINGS

INTRODUCTION

A BOOK EDITOR can know no greater satisfaction than to be associated, over a long period of years, with a literary craftsman like Janice Holt Giles. This has been my good fortune — and that of my colleague Anne Barrett — throughout a large part of Janice's writing career. The obvious danger in such a relationship is that at some point one begins to take such competence, such steady productivity, for granted. I like to think that this was never true with Janice. Each book was a new venture. As she tells us in her charming memoir, *Around Our House,* there were false starts, there were technical hurdles to be surmounted and new devices to be tested before she could achieve her major ambition. This was to create a series of novels about the opening of the American West that would combine the drama and personal involvement of fiction with scrupulous adherence to historical fact.

She began with the first real frontiersmen, the Kentuckians, contemporaries of Daniel Boone; men and women who crossed the Appalachians through Cumberland Gap and hacked out their farms in what Vachel Lindsay called "the spirit-haunted forest

... stupendous and endless," west of the mountains. From her studies of old diaries and records, she came to know these frontiersmen so well that she had no trouble in telling a story from their point of view. There is warmth, an intimacy, about her writing that bridges two centuries and makes her characters seem almost contemporary. And in portraying Hannah Fowler, her daughter Rebecca, and later Savannah, she helps us to understand, as few writers have, what a pioneer woman's life was like — how she felt, how she survived.

Janice had a firm plan from the start. As the series developed, the scene moved westward to include the Arkansas Territory (now Oklahoma, where she herself grew up), the Santa Fe Trail and the far west; it re-created the romantic era of the stagecoach and the old steamboat days on her beloved Green River.

Janice Giles has also written a number of books outside the historical series. There are her first novels, beginning with *The Enduring Hills* (recently reissued) about her adopted country of Kentucky. There are several works of nonfiction and an autobiographical novel, *The Plum Thicket,* in an entirely different vein: a penetrating exploration of her own childhood and of the society into which she was born.

All this did not come easily. To be sure, the early books (with the exception of the first) had, in her own words, just "rolled out." She recalls telling me, when we first met, that she felt guilty about taking money for doing something that was so much joy and so little work. I do not remember the conversation, doubtless because I knew that her sense of guilt about the ease of the work would all too soon be assuaged. Like most writers, she would occasionally find herself blocked in midstream, and would go through periods of despair before she found her way back into the main current. But she always managed, eventually. In the end the writing of each book turned out to be, as it always had to be for her, a labor of love.

The short pieces presented in this volume give some idea of the versatility, the wide range, and the authenticity of Janice Giles's work. Each is related in its own way to one of her books. There is a great variety of mood and setting; one of her greatest strengths as a writer is her sense of time and place. When she uses dialect to evoke a period or a locality, it is always convincing. For other writers, the first chapter in this volume will be a particular joy. Janice Giles knows that an effective style depends no less on a sensitive ear than on a discerning eye. She knows that the rhythm of a sentence can be as important as the choice of words. A craftsman as well as a scholar, she has always had respect for what Winston Churchill called a "noble thing": the structure of the ordinary English sentence.

— PAUL BROOKS

Rhythm
in
Writing

RHYTHM IN WRITING

"Once a book gets well begun, my ear takes over. It makes me know, for instance, that this is the wrong word and it has at least one syllable too many and I must, if necessary, spend and hour or two trying to think of, or find in my dictionary and thesaurus, the right word."

Around Our House

THE DIFFERENCE between good writing and mediocre writing is frequently a matter of rhythm and euphony. Often, indeed, rhythm is what makes a writer's style, and always it is what gives him pace. There are many kinds of rhythm in writing. One of the most important is simply the melody of words and their proper balance in a sentence.

Words can give you sound effects that heighten the meaning of your sentences simply by the way they sound. The English alphabet is very versatile. Take the letter *s* for instance. Its sound can be used to denote evil, hatred, disgust, loathing, in such words as snake, sin, serpent, disease or hiss. Or we can use it to denote tenderness and gentleness in words like sweet, soft, shadow, lissome, still, sorrow and sadness.

F is a quiet, muted sound that barely breathes. "Full falls the fading light upon the glen" is an example of horrible alliteration but is a good illustration of the muted, quiet effect of the *f* sound. Hard *c* and *g* have a brittle, crackling sound, as does *k*. Listen to crack, cataract, cough, cut, gravel, gust and gullet. *T*, *d* and *p*, are explosive sounds and may be effectively used to express disgust, anger or bitterness, as in "Bitter is the brown of death, black and dark and dull."

3

Anyone knows how to put words together to make sense, but the writer must learn to use words to add to his meaning by their very sounds. If he wants a quiet mood, he must make a stream murmur or sing, not bubble or chuckle; the breeze must sigh or sough, not blow; the sky must be pale or luminous, not bright and clear. If he wants to describe a thunderstorm, he must rattle around a bunch of *r*'s and some *d*'s, as in "The ragged edge of clouds rimmed round the hills, and thunder threatened rattlingly." I use these exaggerated alliterations to show you the effect. If he wants to build a mood of tenderness and love, he will throw in lots of *l*'s and *v*'s and soft *sh*'s, with long, open vowels — "Lashes curled lovingly over soft, deep eyes."

That is the melody of writing. But beyond melody must lie a deeper rhythm. Rhythm is the very pulse of writing, its balance. The simplest rhythm is in the cadence of sentences. They must sing and flow, or chop and crackle, or meander gently, or sizzle with heat and anger. A good writer can handle all of them equally well, and knows almost instinctively when to change his pace. A good writer also writes sentences that will scan almost as easily as poetry, not of course rhyming, but with a stress and balance that handle well.

In addition to capturing the attention of the reader, the first page of a book is usually where an author must set his pace and style, form his rhythms. I began *The Plum Thicket* with this sentence: "Last summer I went back to Stanwick." It stood alone, paragraphed, by itself. I could have said, "I returned to Stanwick last summer," which would have been much less emphatic. Generally the simplest, the shortest words, put together with simple stress, are the best for emphasis. The sentence was meant to stand out, stark and emphatic. It was also meant to imply forthrightness, which is actually a false implication, for the novel is a psychological suspense story, and nothing about it

4

is forthright. It reads like an innocent summer idyll, but there is always an undercurrent of dark tones. But the first sentence, or at least the first paragraph, of a novel must grab the interest of the reader or only the most patient or loyal reader will wade through the remainder of the novel. There is a hint of the hardness in *The Plum Thicket* in the use of the word "back" and the "Stanwick" in the first sentence.

I began *The Kentuckians*, which is a historical novel, with the sentence: "I have a wish that those who come after me should know the truth about our troubles with the Transylvania Company, and the truth about those first hard years in the settling of this country." Immediately the reader knows, from the length and the wording of this sentence, that it is going to be a folksy kind of story, told by a man who had a part in the trouble and struggle. The reader knows, furthermore, that he is an earnest, brave and candid man. He wants the truth to be known. The memoir style, rhythm and pace is set, and the reader follows easily along as the man remembers and tells his story in his own way.

The books of the ridge trilogy, *The Enduring Hills*, *Miss Willie* and *Tara's Healing*, are written in a ballad style, with singing, strongly cadenced descriptive passages, with characters and incidents that would fit into such folk songs as "Fair Ellender" or "Lord Randall" or "Black is the Color of My True Love's Hair." There is melodrama, grief, violence, birth and death, and to balance them there is joy and happiness and gentleness and goodness. They are as sentimental as the old folk songs themselves, and fitting because the old folk songs are still sung in the region of their setting.

That is rhythm in style. There is also rhythm in the structure of a book. All the chapters must lead toward the final climax, but that must be a long flowing rhythm, like the shoreward swells of deep water. There are, however, waves within

5

that long, swelling rhythm, which crest and then recede. They are sometimes divisible into chapters; sometimes they are longer and more intense, building up over several chapters. They are the ebb and flow of the scenes and the dramatic action that make up the plot, but they must never be so strong as to dwarf the final, surging climax. They lead toward it, sometimes almost touch it, and then slowly subside to start building again.

There is still another kind of rhythm that may be used to strengthen a book. Ernest Gann had the copilot in *The High and the Mighty* whistle a small tune almost abstractedly. The repetition of that tuneless whistling gave a tied-in, tight rhythm, not only to the character, but to the whole structure of his book. E. M. Forster does the same with Beethoven's Fifth Symphony in *Howard's End*, the very plot of the book paralleling the alternating movements of the symphony, from peace to panic and emptiness. Proust does it with a scrap of the sonata, Vineuil's "little phrase," which recurs several times in his long *Remembrance of Things Past*.

It does not have to be done with a musical phrase, however. It may be very successfully done with a habit of a central character. My Hannah Fowler had heavy black hair that was forever falling forward and that she brushed back constantly. She brushed that hair back on the first page of the book, and the gesture is repeated often enough that it becomes a fixed, connected rhythm between the character and the reader. A bird song, heard at certain seasons, recurring, gives a rhythmic feeling. *Miss Willie* is a rhythmic cycle. It begins with the song of a thrush, which is not repeated until the end, when the book finishes with the song of a thrush. My book *The Kinta Years* begins with my first memory, a little girl named Corinne Moore. The book ends when my family moves away from Kinta, Oklahoma, and I tell Corinne goodbye, my heart broken at leaving her.

6

Willa Cather uses light in the same way in *The Song of the Lark*. The book is suffused by light, sunlight, moonlight, starlight, and the light, bright joy of song. She does the same thing with houses in *The Professor's House*. There are at least a dozen houses in the book. In my first book, *The Enduring Hills*, I made use of the appearance of the hills to give a framework for the plot, a blocked, rhythmical structure. Forster uses a wisp of hay in one of his books. The word "hay" occurs time and again. Virginia Woolf uses the passing hours, as tolled by Big Ben, in *Mrs. Dalloway*. Any such thing, repeated with discretion, becomes rhythmic. It must not be overdone or it becomes monotonous, but if skillfully handled it is like the *leitmotif* in a symphony, or counterpoint in harmony. It provides a rhythmic undertone.

The names of characters have a special rhythm of their own, either because of their euphony or because of their fitness to the characters. I think I have never done better than to choose "Hod Pierce" for the young ridge boy in *The Enduring Hills*. The name "Hod," with its association with hard work, indicated his long, withering toil, as well as the simplicity of the boy's character. And I liked the use of "Pierce" as I thought of the boy thrusting, piercing his way out of his environment.

"Miss Willie" is almost perfect for a spinster schoolteacher, as well as the simplicity of the name. There is an element of masculinity in all old maids. "Willie" is also a rather endearing diminutive of William and Miss Willie had a kind of pixieish quality, which made her very lovable. The name fits her like a shoe.

"Hannah Fowler" is another good name. I wanted the name of a woman who was strong and enduring. The old-fashioned name of Hannah suggests that quality. She had to be strong, physically strong, because she had not only to endure the hard

7

work of life on the Kentucky frontier of those early days, but she had to live through her Indian captivity.

I went dreadfully astray in the choice of "Tara" in *Tara's Healing*. If the title originally chosen, however, which was *Scarlet Ribbons*, because Tara's love for Hod Pierce's ailing mother made him bring red bows of ribbon to brighten her hair and give her moments of joy, had been used, it would have been perfect. Tara was originally an artist. He was also Irish. I was asked, on the assumption that the public does not like to read about artists, to change him to a doctor. I should have changed the name with the vocation, but I did not sense the flaw until the book was in print. *Tara's Healing* is also a good example of a bad title. It had nothing to do with healing, except in the sense that love is a healing thing. He did learn to love and serve people.

"David Cooper" is, I think, a good, sound name for the frontiersman in *The Kentuckians*, solid, simple, plain: and his wife's name, "Bethia," is good, but I made her rather a weak person without intending to and spoiled the Cooper family for much further use in the historical series.

"Katie" was a good choice for the little girl in *The Plum Thicket*, and "Aunt Maggie" was all right. There were lots of Kates, Lizzies, Maggies, Lucys and Emilys around the turn of the century, which is the time of the book, and in the South, which is its setting.

Girls' names, as a rule, should be more musical than boys', and the most musical have at least four syllables or five. With a one-syllable last name, the first name should have several, such as my daughter's name, Elizabeth Moore. Then there are Catherine Wells, Margaret Mann, Jane Montgomery, Sue Maloney and so on. I have a niece whose name is Joan Holt, which is atrocious from the musical standpoint. The assonance of the two *o* sounds is bad, and with her one-syllable last name, her first namc should have had at least three syllables. Joann would not have been bad.

My own name, Janice Giles, two *j* sounds together, is too short, and this is one reason why I use my maiden name with it. Janice Holt Giles is a little better but still not good. Janice is simply not a musical name, with its short *a* and *n*. I should have used my middle name, which is Meredith. Meredith Holt when I was a girl, or Meredith Giles since I married, would have been great.

Book titles, aside from telling something about the book, should, if they are to have sales value, be euphonious and rhythmic also. As a rule, I like a short, descriptive title. I like one the customer can easily remember. And I like it to mention the name of at least one character because people like to read about people. *The Enduring Hills* is an excellent title, though for the sake of euphony "The" should have been left off. It has a psychological value — it is like a magnet drawing people to something safe and secure and enduring. *Miss Willie* was fine; the combination of "Miss" and "Willie" was intriguing. *Tara's Healing* couldn't have been worse. *40 Acres and No Mule* was, on the surface, too long, but it was taken from a familiar saying of Civil War days when the freed negroes were promised 40 acres and a mule. I thought its familiarity would save it.

The Kentuckians is a good title, exactly right for a novel about early Kentucky. *The Plum Thicket* is good, thicket indicating a maze or tangle, which, psychologically, was what the book was about. *Harbin's Ridge*, which was my husband's book, was originally titled *Faleecy-John*, after the central character, and I still think it is much the better title. The softness and rhythm would have, I believe, interested people. But the book did well anyhow. Good titles certainly help make good sales and it is well to give considerable thought to them. But publishers have a way of either suggesting or arbitrarily changing titles on you, as they did in *Harbin's Ridge* and *Tara's Healing*.

Another example of a changed title was my book *The Land Beyond the Mountains*, originally called *The Glory Road*. But Bruce Catton had just a few years earlier brought out a book titled *Glory Road*, and I changed my title to *The Land Beyond the Mountains* in order to avoid confusion. The book did well, because once again it was about the Kentucky mountains, which always appeal to readers.

A good way to watch the rhythms in a book is to read the sentences aloud. This will frequently tell you if they are badly balanced or do not handle well. And a thesaurus is invaluable in helping you to choose words. Personally, I never consciously weigh and balance, but I had a good musical background and before I ever began to write fiction I had written a good bit of poetry, so I think cadence and rhythm are probably inherent in my make-up. My musical ear tells when I am off.

Many writers seem to have a natural ear for rhythm, but since English is naturally a stressed language it seems to me anyone can learn, with discipline, to write lucid, well-balanced sentences and paragraphs. And, happily, I think most writers do have something of a talent for it or they wouldn't be writing at all. Take a little talent, add discipline and hard work, and you can come up with a much better quality of writing.

Kinta

THE EDGE OF THE WORLD

"The edge of the world looked so near. If only Mama would let me go just once I was certain I could reach it in a very short time."

The Kinta Years

HIS FULL NAME was Stonewall Jackson Breckinridge. Inevitably he was called Stoney. He lived in Beaver Creek, population three hundred and fifty, in the Indian Territory, which was not yet Oklahoma. His father, whom everyone called "Professor," was principal of the school. His mother was a musician and an artist. He was an only child. He was six years old.

With frowning concentration he was trying to master the art of riding, pushing and guiding his new red wagon all at the same time. One knee was doubled into the bed of the wagon. The other leg pushed. One hand braced against the wagon frame, the other gripped the tongue. He went up and down the short strip of sidewalk, sometimes managing to stay on the walk and straighten the wagon out. He went back and forth, back and forth, until his doubled knee began to ache; then he brought the wagon to a stop at the fence corner where the sidewalk ended and sat to rest a moment.

The professor's house was the last one before the prairie began. The dusty road bent around its white paling fence and then straightened out to unroll flatly across the land until it met the sky in infinity. The boy sat with his shoulders drooping, his thumb in his mouth where it strayed when he felt bored or lonely or unhappy, his eyes following the road.

He thought that where the sky and the road met was the edge of the world. He had watched cowhands race their ponies out the road until they were lost to sight, only a swirl of dust marking their trail. He had seen the buckboards of the ranchers sweep around the corner of the fence and head into that long, level, white road. He had seen the Indians spurring their horses into the dust, the blankets that a few of them still wore making a strange, flowing garment in the wind.

But he was not allowed to go out on the road. "The prairie is wild and wide," his mother had said. "You'd get lost. There are wolves and gypsies out there." He had heard the wolves himself, on frosty winter nights, and he knew that bands of gypsies frequently camped on the fringe of the town. His mother didn't say there was also the edge of the world over which you might fall, but he knew it was there, too.

He wondered what happened when all the people who rode the road came to the edge of the world. How, for instance, did one ride a horse down that steep other side, or drive a wagon or buckboard over it? How did the red-covered gypsy wagons ascend it? And he wondered if the other side of the world was anything at all like this one. He never told anyone what he thought or wondered, and he never asked. This was something he wanted to keep to himself.

Sometimes when he looked out across the prairie it was so big and so wide, so empty and limitless, that he felt himself shrinking in size like Alice in Wonderland. He could feel himself growing smaller and smaller until his blouse hung loose around his shriveled chest. He became the tiniest speck of humanity on the face of the earth, no larger than a mote of dust in a sunbeam. Then he was afraid. At other times, when the wind blew in his face, he felt as big and as wide as the prairie itself, capable of holding all its vastness, filled with all its space. He became a giant, able to stride across it in seven-league boots, daring and venturesome. That was when he ran the hardest, laughed the loudest and sang the song his mother sometimes sang when she played for him at night:

> Follow the Romany patteran
> Sheer to the Austral Light,
> Where the besom of God is the wild
> south wind,
> Sweeping the sea-floors white.*

"What," he asked his father once, "is a Romany patteran?"

"Romany means gypsy," his father had said, "and a patteran is a kind of marked way, you might say, like a blazed trail."

"Oh, a gypsy road?"

"Well, that's near enough."

"And what is sheer to the Austral Light?"

His father had laughed. "Clear to the edge of the world, to the end of time, to the beginning of heaven."

Stoney's eyes had widened. The edge of the world was right out there! He shivered with excitement. "Tell me about gypsies."

"They're wandering, roving, wild and free, following wherever the road leads. They love music and dancing and laughter, and some of them, if you cross their palms with silver, can tell your fortune, marvelous things about the future."

"I wish I could see a gypsy, up close."

His father had tucked the covers more tightly about his neck. "Sometime," he promised, "we'll visit one of their camps. Maybe this summer, if any come."

Stoney sat humped on his little red wagon and looked out across the prairie. It was always there: broad, flat and level, stretching limitlessly on all sides. He thought that from where God sat a prairie town such as Beaver Creek must look like a

* From "The Gypsy Trail" by Rudyard Kipling.

tiny pimple on the flat belly of the wide, wide earth. He sighed. He wished just once he could follow the road. "When you're a little older," his father had said, "you can have your own pony and ride on the prairie. But it's too big for such a little boy now. You don't even know east from west yet." And he echoed his mother's words: "You might get lost."

But anybody could follow the road. You didn't need to know east from west to do that. You just went where the road went and came back when you got there.

He left his wagon and ventured timidly beyond the end of the sidewalk onto the road. It went so straight. He couldn't possibly get lost. He took one step and then another, stopping to look back, listening for his mother's call. But it didn't come, so he kept on taking one step and then another. Suddenly he felt full of excitement, swelling as wide and as big as the prairie. The besom of God was blowing, the south wind, full in his face. He stretched out his arms and began to run. It was all right, he knew. He would go to the edge of the world, just once, sheer to the Austral Light. He would peek over and then he would come straight home again.

It was a long road and his legs grew tired, but he was no-where near the Austral Light yet. Straight ahead of him it lay, looking as far from where he was as it had at the fence corner. But all you had to do was keep going to get there. He amused himself by watching the dust plop up between his bare toes, by walking pigeon-toed and looking at the queer tracks he made, by walking on his heels, by making a zigzag path from one side of the road to the other. Once when he looked back it frightened him a little. The town was just a splotch in the distance and he felt cut loose from its safety. So he didn't look back anymore. He grew tired and he grew hungry, but he kept doggedly trudging on.

He came, finally, to a place where the road dipped down into a dry wash. In the bed of the gully a wagon, with a big red-canvas top, was camped. A lean dog scratched fleas beside a lazy fire, and a white horse munched from a feedbag hung from his head. A man sat leaning against a wheel of the wagon, a battered hat cocked on the back of his head. He wore a red-checkered shirt, and black suspenders held up a tattered pair of pants. He was playing a concertina. His eyes were closed and he sang softly. The music was plaintive, wistful, yearning.

Stoney's heart pounded. There had been no gypsies this summer, but here, surely, was one, close up. He shuffled the sandy dirt under his feet and waited politely until the song was ended. Then he called out, "Tell me, sir, are you a gypsy?"

Unstartled, the man opened his eyes and looked up at him. He laughed. "Aye, you could call me a gypsy, lad."

"Where are your friends?"

The man waved an arm widely. "Oh, here, there, yonder."

"I thought gypsies traveled in bands."

"Sometimes they do, sometimes they don't. Just depends."

"I see." Stoney waited a moment and then in a small voice, which he tried to make large, he said, "Could I come down there and listen to your music?"

The man made another sweeping gesture with his arm. "Come and welcome. It's a vast place, this prairie. I've no claim staked out on it."

Stoney slithered down the gravelly bank of the gully, hunkered by the man. "I've never seen a gypsy close up before."

"You've not? And where have you been keeping yourself all your life?"

"Back there." Stoney pointed. "In Beaver Creek."

"So you live in Beaver Creek. I suppose you've a father and a mother."

"Oh, yes. My father is the professor."

The man nodded. "I've heard of him. Spouts Greek and Latin poetry at the drop of a hat. You've wandered off the range a little, haven't you?"

Stoney considered the matter gravely. "I expect I've come ten thousand miles already."

The gypsy squeezed his concertina and a small catlike sound sighed out of it. "You must be pretty tired."

"My legs are tired," Stoney admitted, "but the rest of me isn't."

"Legs," the gypsy said and nodded knowingly, "have a plaguey way of getting tired before the rest of you does." He fingered his instrument and a little tune took form.

Stoney felt the back of his neck tingling.

"Is this road," he asked finally, when the tune didn't seem to be going anywhere, "is this road the Romany patteran?"

"Well, now," the man said, squinting one eye, "it might be at that."

"Being a gypsy," Stoney said, "I thought you'd know."

"And so I do, lad. But gypsies have many roads, you know."

"Oh."

The tune started again.

"But this is the one," the boy insisted, "that leads sheer to the Austral Light?"

The gypsy's fingers danced on the stops and a waterfall of notes cascaded into the air. "Sheer to the Austral Light?"

"You know, the one in the song. Follow the Romany patteran sheer to the Austral Light."

"Oh, that light. Sure, sure, this is the one."

Stoney laughed softly. "I knew it! I knew it!"

The little tune played between them, like a dancing veil of light. "You were starting to the Austral Light, were you?" the gypsy asked.

Stoney nodded. "Just once I wanted to see it, you know; just peek over the edge of the world and see what it looked like."

A deep, rich chord embellished the small tune. "Just once?"

"Yes. You see, ever since I was very small I've seen other people go out this road, clear to the edge of the world. It's out there, you know." He pointed. "Exactly where the road runs into the sky."

The gypsy's head bobbed.

"Are you," Stoney asked, anxiously, "going there yourself?"

The tune broke off and the gypsy shifted his concertina and shoved his old hat farther back on his head. "Well, you see, lad, I've just come from there."

"Oh." It was a small sound of disappointment.

There was a silence and the boy looked up at the rim of the gully. "I thought, maybe, if you were going that way I could ride with you and get there quicker. I have to be home by dark."

"Going to push you a little, isn't it?" the gypsy asked. "It's getting on toward sundown now."

Stoney stood up in panic. "Oh, no," he said quickly, "it's not much farther. I can get there and home again by dark if I hurry."

The man shifted his feet. "Well, now, I tell you, sonny, I was heading in the other direction, but I'd just as soon make another turn around the Austral Light as not. Why don't you just sit here a spell and I'll cook us a little supper and then we'll go together. It's farther than you think."

Stoney thought about it. "You're sure you don't mind?"

"I'm sure. Matter of fact, I always hate to see the last of that Austral Light. It's something to see, now, and no mistaking."

The boy sighed with relief. He had been a little worried. "All right. If you're sure it won't be any bother."

"No bother at all. I'll just chunk up the fire and open a can of beans and fry a little meat and we'll eat first. You hungry?"

"Awful hungry." Stoney grinned.

"I thought so."

As the man went about fixing the meal, Stoney followed him, helping where he could. "My father," he said, "told me that gypsies could tell your fortune, if you'd cross their palms with silver."

"So they can. You want your fortune told?"

"I don't have any silver."

The gypsy looked thoughtfully in the fire. "Well, there's one kind of fortune don't need any silver. Just needs some tea leaves."

"Is it as good a fortune as the other?"

"Better, in my opinion."

"Do you have some tea?"

"I have. And I'll be fixing it right now."

When the tea was made, the gypsy poured a cup, drained it off, then showed the boy how to swirl the leaves. "Now, let me have a look." He peered into the cup.

"Is it a good fortune?" Stoney asked, finally, a little anxiously.

The man fingered his chin. "I'd say it's one of the best I ever looked into. Now, let me see. You're going to grow up to be a fine, big man."

"Like my father?"

"Like your father. And this here little doodad means you're going to be very happy. And you're going to travel all over the world and make a lot of money."

"Where does it show I'm going to travel?"

"See these wide spaces between the leaves? That's the seas you'll be crossing, probably to Africa and India and China."

"And the money?"

"Well, that's this little pile over here in the corner."

"Am I going to get married?"

"Oh, yes, to a girl as beautiful as a fairy princess. And have six children."

"Six!" Stoney was aghast. "Do you think I'll be able to take care of that many?"

"And why not, with all that money?"

"Would it be enough to pay for each one to have his own pony?"

"Plenty, and enough left over for licorice sticks every Saturday night." The gypsy set the cup down and stirred up the fire. "Well, there's your fortune, laddie."

Stoney sighed happily. "It was a very nice fortune. Thank you for it. You're sure it will come true without the silver?"

"Silver don't matter much to tea leaves. It's just palms that get itchy for silver." The man stirred the beans.

"You didn't play much music yet," Stoney reminded him.

"Been talking too much. You want to hear some music now?"

"Yes, sir."

"Just settle yourself comfortable, then, while the supper's finishing."

He picked up the concertina and propped himself once more against the wagon wheel. He pushed and squeezed on the instrument and wonderful sounds came from it, chords and trills and little rippling, flowing notes. He sang about the River Shannon, and about the lakes of Killarney, and about something called the Blarney Stone, and about a girl named Kathleen, and about a town called Dublin. He sang so many songs the meat almost burned and he had to throw aside the concertina and snatch the pan from the fire. "Like to ruined our supper," he grumbled.

"Oh, I shouldn't have minded," Stoney told him. "My father was right. Gypsies do make wonderful music."

It was while they were eating that the boy approached the subject he most wanted to hear about. "How," he asked, "how ever do you manage to drive your wagon up the other side of the world? I mean, the edge of the world must be so steep. How can horses and buggies and wagons go up and down it?"

"Well, now, it takes some managing," the gypsy admitted. "In some places it's so steep you have to get out and scotch the wheels to keep from sliding back."

"You do?" The boy's eyes widened. "But don't the horses slide, too?"

The gypsy took a swallow of tea. "Sometimes they do. But there's kind of little steps, like, and if they're real sure-footed, they can walk up or down all right."

"Doesn't that make your wagon bump a lot?"

"Not as much as you'd think. They're awfully little steps."

Stoney ate his beans. "What is the Austral Light like?"

The gypsy took a long breath and let it out. "It's hard to tell about it, lad. It's like nothing you'd ever expect to see in this world. It's all pearly and rosy and a little cloudy, and there's rainbows chasing around in the clouds, and there's a kind of dim, far-off music playing all the time, like harps maybe. And there's a sweet smell like wild roses . . ."

"And the south wind."

"The *south* wind?"

"The besom of God, you know."

"Oh, sure. Sure there's the south wind. It blows all the time."

"But not very hard."

"Oh, no. Just a breeze; just enough to make the music swell and send the wild-rose smell all over."

"And to feel on your face."

"And to feel on your face."

"Never anything but the south wind?"

"Not ever. Never a west wind, or a north wind, or even an east wind."

Stoney ate the last of his beans. "It must be beautiful." He lifted his face earnestly. "You're very good to take me there."

The gypsy cleared his throat. "Well, I kind of like the place myself." He scraped the plates out for the dog. "We'd better be starting, I expect."

Stoney helped him back the white horse into the wagon shafts, helped him load the food stores. The back of the wagon was crowded with bedding and odd-looking tools. "What is all this stuff?" he asked.

"Well, a gypsy has to live on the road, you know, and turn his hand to whatever comes handy. I sharpen knives and scissors and things for people, and mend pots and pans."

"Oh, in your spare time."

"Yes. When I'm not visiting the Austral Light. Climb up, laddie."

He boosted the boy into the wagon's seat and climbed up himself. He took up the reins, clucked to the white horse, and the wagon slowly pulled up the far bank of the gully. The sun had set and a red and purple haze hung over the horizon, shot through with bands of gold. "There," Stoney pointed. "That's where it is."

The gypsy nodded. "That's where it is, all right."

The white horse ambled slowly, very slowly it seemed to Stoney, for suddenly he felt sleepy. At home he would have had his bath by now, and soon would be going to bed. His eyes drooped and his head nodded. He jerked it upright from time to time but each time it drooped further and his eyes stayed closed longer. The gypsy watched him, and finally, smiling, he drew the small head over on his knee. Stoney sighed and settled comfortably. The gypsy pulled the horse around, then, in a wide circle, and headed for Beaver Creek.

He met the search party about a mile outside of town. He pulled up the horse and they played their lanterns over him. "Are you looking for the professor's boy?" he asked.

"Why, it's Tim O'Hara, the tinker," one of the men said. "Yes, the boy's lost on the prairie, Tim. Have you seen anything of him?"

"I've got him here. But keep your voices down. He's asleep."

The professor rode up alongside, shone his lantern over the sleeping child. "Thank God! His mother is frantic. We were following his tracks on the road, but were afraid he might have wandered off as night came on."

Tim laughed softly. "He came up on my camp in the Flat Red gully. He was following the Romany patteran, sheer to the Austral Light."

The professor chuckled. " 'Where the besom of God is the wild south wind, sweeping the sea-floors white.' "

"That's it. He said it was a song. Maybe I ought to have brought him straight on in, Professor, but it seemed terrible important to the lad to see this Austral Light. He thought I was a gypsy and could take him there. It didn't seem right to disappoint him. He's had his supper and he's come to no harm."

The professor lifted the little boy into his arms and looked thoughtfully down into the face of his son. "You never know, do you, what a child thinks and feels? They let you know so little of what goes on inside. No, we've been anxious, but I'm glad you didn't disappoint him." He looked at the tinker. "Did he get there, Tim? Sheer to the Austral Light?"

The tinker grinned. "Not exactly sheer, Professor, but he got pretty close."

"I'll bet he did. Thank you, Tim, for being a good Irish gypsy."

"That's all right, sir. He's a fine little lad."

Ruefully the professor smiled. "Pretty much of a gypsy himself, isn't he? But aren't we all? I'd better take this one home to his mother, now, though."

He wheeled to ride off. The tinker called after him. "Professor? What in tarnation *is* the Austral Light?"

Over his shoulder the professor answered. "The grass in the next pasture, Tim, the other side of the mountain, the coast of the farthest seas, the beckoning finger, the throne of grace, the radiant mystery." His voice faded and died away and there was only the soft sloughing sound of horses' hoofs in the heavy dust of the road.

Slowly, the tinker gathered up his reins and followed.

(This story was published originally in *Woman's Day*, November 1965.)

THE PICNIC

"Lucy McGraw and John Holt were married on Saturday evening in the parlor of the family home."

The Kinta Years

MAMA ALWAYS SAID that Papa just swept her off her feet. "Like that," she used to say, making a swift motion with her hand. "He just wouldn't take no for an answer."

Mary and I had visions of Papa, young Lochinvar come out of the West, sweeping Mama off her feet, literally scooping her up and running away with her. It wasn't at all difficult to think of Papa as a dashing young cavalier. He was still a tall, slender, very winsome man. We thought he must have been almost beautiful, when he was younger and had more hair.

But Aunt Sallie spent the summer with us once. "Nonsense," she said. "It wasn't that way at all. Lucy set her cap for Mr. John the minute she laid eyes on him. And she went to a right smart trouble to get him, too."

Mr. John was the new principal of the school. He was fresh from the university, had a smart new cutaway buggy and a fast young mare, the sweetest tenor voice anyone in the town had ever heard, and his way with a fiddle was little short of wonderful. He was twenty-five years old, and he wasn't married.

There wasn't a girl in town who didn't sigh when he drove smartly past her house and wish, hopefully, she might be the lucky one he invited to drive out with him. What a feather in

26

a girl's cap that would be, to drive out with the new school principal! Each one wanted to be the first. How envious it would make all the others.

Lucy was the only one who didn't sigh, who didn't admit she would be thrilled speechless to be asked. She was seventeen, and she was gay, high-spirited, proud and lovely. She had light brown hair that sparkled with little red glints in the sun, skin so white it was milky, and light, merry blue eyes. She wore her hair up, of course, and her five petticoats properly swept the ground. But she could still lift her petticoats and beat any of her brothers in a foot race when she wanted to. "I think he's stuck-up," she said, tossing her head. "He's just a showoff, with his stiff white collars, and his new buggy and his fast horse. He just wants everyone to notice him. I wouldn't accept, even if he asked me."

"You wouldn't?" said Laura, her best girl friend.

"Indeed, I wouldn't. I should simply decline the honor."

"Well, I wouldn't," Laura said firmly. "I'd jump at the chance!"

"You would!" Lucy said scornfully. "He doesn't impress me at all."

Both girls were silent then. It was a beautiful, mild day in late September and they were sitting on the back porch of Lucy's house, stringing the last of the garden beans. "I wonder," said Lucy, then, "if he's going to the picnic."

"Everyone else is wondering the same thing. And who he'll take, if he goes," Laura said.

Lucy felt a little ripple of excitement. That meant he hadn't asked anyone yet. Laura would know, if anyone did. She had three older sisters and between them they knew everything that happened almost as soon as it happened. Laura would be the very first to know when he asked someone.

The picnic on the last Sunday in September was an annual affair with the young people of the town. It was a kind of last goodbye to the long, happy, lazy summer, which they had spent boating on the river, going on long, moonlit hayrides, gathering on front verandahs with guitars to sing, going picnicking in the hills. It was always held at Cold Springs, a lovely place on top of the one mountain that poked itself up higher than the surrounding hills. They never went there on their other picnics. Cold Springs was always saved for the last Sunday in September.

"Who are you going with?" Laura asked.

"I haven't decided yet," Lucy told her.

Laura sighed. It must be wonderful, she thought, to be able to pick and choose the way Lucy could. She had to depend on her faithful swain, Charlie. But Lucy always had her choice of the boys. But, then, Lucy was the prettiest girl in town. It was only natural the boys should swarm after her like bees in clover. "I may," Lucy said then, "not go with anyone. I may just go with the girls."

Laura gasped. There were always a few girls who didn't get asked by any of the boys, who went together in the hay wagon and clung together on the picnic. No one who could have an escort at all would ever have gone with the girls. "You wouldn't!" she said.

Lucy flung up her head. "I'm tired of all those silly boys. I think it might be fun not to be stuck with one of them all day."

Laura shuddered. Charlie bored her sometimes, but she'd rather be bored than appear without an escort. It practically stamped you as a wallflower. "I don't," she said honestly. "What will everybody think?"

"I don't care what they think," Lucy answered. "I'm just of half a mind to do it!"

She didn't tell Laura that she had met Mr. John at the post office one evening last week, that he had bowed courteously, spoken to her, engaged her in conversation. "You're keeping well, I hope, Miss Lucy," he had said.

"Very well, thank you, Mr. John," she had replied, twirling the handle of her parasol.

He had spoken then of the weather. "Very mild, for late September, don't you think? Or is it always this warm here in the fall?"

"Oh, it's usually fairly warm until October. We count on the warm weather lasting until after the picnic." She thought she had inserted that very cleverly.

"The picnic . . . yes. Bill Herndon told me about the picnic."

"You're going, I suppose?" she had asked, very casually.

"I hope to, yes."

"It's usually quite an enjoyable affair," she had said primly.

"I understand it is." He had said a very bold thing, then. He had laughed and said, "I'll have to find a young lady for the occasion. Could you suggest one, Miss Lucy?" And he had looked at her meaningfully.

"I shouldn't dream of doing such a thing, Mr. John," she had answered, and then, as bold as he, she had said, "but you shouldn't have any difficulty." It was as good as telling him that if he asked, she would accept. But, disappointingly, he had changed the subject then, said something about the mail being very late and he didn't think he'd better wait any longer, and he had bade her good day. He meant to call, though, she was certain.

As the week of the picnic came and the days wore on the phone rang often enough, but it was always one of the boys. "May I escort you on the picnic, Lucy?"

Pleasantly, she declined each invitation. She was positive Mr. John would call. Lucy McVay was going to be the first young woman to drive out with him. But as the days passed and Mr.

John didn't call, as the other boys became committed to taking other girls, she began to be a little nervous and fidgety. She had turned down six invitations. Surely he would call today!

But Saturday came and he hadn't called, and along toward the middle of the morning Laura burst into the kitchen. Lucy was ironing a voluminous petticoat. "You'll never guess," Laura panted, collapsing into a chair, "who Mr. John is taking on the picnic!"

Lucy's heart sank. "Who?"

"He's taking Lizzie Walters!"

Lucy's iron was poised over the bottom ruffle of the petticoat. She looked at Laura unbelievingly. "Lizzie Walters! I don't believe it!"

"Well, he is. Lizzie is so excited she's lost her spectacles."

"That I can believe. She's always losing them."

Lizzie Walters was fully twenty years old, a tall, skinny girl, very plain, awkward, mousey, who peered nearsightedly through steel-rimmed spectacles. Everyone liked her, but no one ever asked her for a date. She always tagged along with the other unasked girls.

Bitterly, Lucy draped the petticoat over the back of a chair and put the iron on the stove. It was the last straw. She had turned down six invitations to give Mr. John his chance, and he had ignored her for Lizzie Walters! She had never intended to be stuck with the crowd of girls, but now she had no alternative except not to go at all. She thought about developing a sudden illness. No . . . Laura would have spread the news that she had done it deliberately. Her face was saved to that extent, at least.

But it would be an unbearable day, watching the boys and girls paired off, taking pictures of each other, having fun, she, for the first time in her life unescorted, stuck with the crowd of plain, unasked girls. It made her squirm to think of it. Her pride came to the rescue. Well, nobody would know it if she didn't have fun!

Just the same it was dreary, crawling into the hay wagon with the rest of the girls while the buggies, holding the paired couples, lined up, ready to race to be the first on the long, straight road out of town. Mr. John and Lizzie seemed to be in high spirits, Lizzie holding on to her flat sailor hat, laughing, Mr. John fresh, as usual, in a high white collar, his whip poised over the little mare. Lucy watched them start off, saw Mr. John's buggy wheel perilously near the others, pass them and take the lead, dashing off in a cloud of dust. He *did* have a very fast horse there, she had to admit, and her envy rose bitterly inside her. She would have given anything she possessed to be sitting there beside him. Then her chin came up. She was going to have *fun* today, she reminded herself.

She settled down in the hay and deliberately set herself to be her gayest, happiest, lightest-hearted self. She succeeded so well that she kept all the girls laughing the whole way, and they piled out at the Springs, gathering around her, still laughing. Without a glance at the others, she said, loud enough for all to hear, "Let's leave the sissies here to fix the lunch. Let's go explore the cave."

It was always the unescorted girls who fixed the lunch, but with Lucy leading them they daringly left it, followed giggling and laughing where she led. Laura watched them disappear over the side of the cliff. She wondered about all that fun and laughter.

The boys and girls wandered about, in pairs, holding hands, posing to have their pictures taken, clambering over the jutting rocks, the girls squealing and having to be helped, drinking from the icy spring, gathering the scarlet sumach branches, until finally they grew hungry. "Do we build a fire?" Mr. John asked then. He had been an impeccably gallant escort to the beaming Lizzie.

"Oh, yes. We always build a fire to make coffee."

The boys gathered wood, the girls delicately unable to carry more than twig at a time, but valiantly insisting upon helping. When the picnic cloths were spread and the food laid out, someone said, "We'd better call the girls now, hadn't we? Wonder where they've got to. I haven't heard them for a long time, come to think of it."

"Oh, if they're in the cave you couldn't hear them from here," someone else answered.

Mr. John had wandered over to the edge of the cliff. "How do you get down to the cave from here?" he asked.

"There's a crevice in the rock, there, and a little path."

They began to shout for the girls, and at first there was no answer, then several of them came scrambling up the path. "Come quick," they called. "Lucy's got her foot hung in that crack at the back of the cave. We can't get her loose!"

The boys headed for the path, Mr. John in the lead, the girls trailing behind. At the edge of the cliff one of the boys turned. "You girls stay here. We don't want anyone else hurt."

Obediently, the girls stopped. They chattered excitedly, wondering how it had happened. "Maybe a rock rolled under her foot," one said.

"Or maybe she fell," another offered.

Laura stood, listening and thinking. If Lucy McVay was stuck in that crack it was a seven-days' wonder. She knew that whole cave like the palm of her hand. Laura thought she was beginning to see what Lucy was up to. She was certain of it when Mr. John appeared at the top of the path, carrying Lucy, the rest of the boys following, single file.

Laura spread a blanket and Mr. John laid Lucy gently on it. "She fainted," he explained, "when I had to free her foot. She must have been suffering greatly." Lucy's long skirts trailed gracefully, covering entirely her feet and ankles.

The girls fluttered about, their starched skirts rustling as they moved. The young men built up the fire hurriedly. Mr. John stayed by Lucy's side, chafing her wrists. Lucy lay with her eyes closed, pathetically limp and exhausted. Laura watched her. Lucy McVay had never fainted in her life. It was her boast that nothing could make *her* faint. And Lucy had the most beautiful long eyelashes of any girl in the crowd. She would know exactly how lovely and fragile she looked, her face palely white, her lashes curling on her cheek.

Mr. John stripped off his coat and made a pillow for her head. Lucy sighed when he lifted her head, then gasped as if in pain. "She's coming to," Mr. John said. "Quick, get a cup of water, someone." One of the boys dashed off for it. Mr. John continued to rub Lucy's wrists.

Slowly she opened her lovely blue eyes, looked directly up into Mr. John's face, then looked around her as if bewildered. "Where am I?" she asked, in a small, feeble voice.

"Don't try to talk, Miss Lucy," Mr. John told her. "You're safe now. You stepped into that crack at the back of the cave and turned your ankle." He leaned back as if to rise. "One of you girls will have to examine her ankle." It was unthinkable, of course, that a man should see a lady's ankle, much less examine it.

Laura stepped forward. "I'll look at it."

Mr. John moved back and spoke to the others. "Don't crowd around her. She needs the air." Obediently they made way.

Laura knelt beside Lucy and bent over her. "Who do you think you're fooling, Lucy McVay?" she whispered.

Lucy opened one eye. "The whole dratted bunch, I hope," she hissed. "And if you give me away, Laura Spencer, I'll never speak to you again!"

Laura sniffed. "I ought to." But she knew she wouldn't. The habit of loyalty to Lucy was very strong in her. She turned the skirt back a little from Lucy's ankles. As she expected there wasn't a thing wrong with either one. But Lucy moaned realistically when Laura probed and pressed on the left one. Laura turned the skirt back down, stood up. "We'll have to take her home quickly. Her ankle may be broken."

No one doubted it; no one questioned it. Promptly and decisively Mr. John took charge. "Two of you fellows make a pack-saddle and carry her down the mountain. I'll run on ahead and make a bed for her in my buggy."

No one disputed his authority. He had proven he had the fastest horse.

Lucy was carried down the mountain, gently, and deposited just as gently in Mr. John's buggy. He stepped in beside her. "I'll have you home in no time, Miss Lucy," he promised. Then he remembered Lizzie. "Oh," he said, turning, "Miss Lizzie . . ."

"Don't give me a thought, Mr. John," Lizzie said gallantly. "I'll come on in the wagon with the rest of the girls."

"And that," Aunt Sallie said, "was the way your mother *really* managed to get your father."

"I don't think she was very kind to Lizzie," Mary said, her seven-year-old eyes sad over Lizzie's fate.

"Well, dear," Aunt Sallie said, comfortably, "there's an old saying that all is fair in love and war."

"And she really didn't hurt her ankle at all?" I asked.

"Not at all. It wasn't the least bit hurt. But she had to pretend it was. She walked around on crutches for a month. Mr. John, of course," she added dryly, "called every day to ask about her, brought her flowers and candy, took her driving in his buggy, was very solicitous."

"And then they got married," Mary said.

34

"Well, not for another year. But your mother had him where she wanted him from then on."

Papa came around the corner of the house. "What have you been telling my girls, Sallie? I heard the last of it. Who had whom where she wanted him?"

"Lucy had you where she wanted you, Mr. John," Aunt Sallie said, laughing.

"Oh," Papa said airily, "that!" He dropped down onto the top step and gathered Mary and me between his knees. He nuzzled his chin on Mary's hair. "I knew all the time she hadn't hurt her ankle that day."

Mama had evidently been eavesdropping. She slammed the kitchen door behind her as she came out onto the porch. "You knew it all the time?" she asked, incredulously.

"Of course," Papa said. "Your skirt didn't *quite* cover your ankle when I first got to you. There wasn't a thing wrong with it, and I knew it. You stepped down very gently into that crack, and your foot came free without any difficulty. You could have walked out of that cave just as easily as I did."

"Well, of all things!" Mama said. "You didn't let on!"

"Oh, no. I didn't want to spoil it for you. And besides," he added, looking slyly at her out of the corner of his eyes, "I felt pretty flattered you'd gone to so much trouble to get my attention."

"How did you know," Mama snapped at him, "it wasn't for one of the other boys?"

"Well, you'd turned all them down. I couldn't figure you'd go to so much trouble for someone you'd turned down. It had to be for my special benefit."

"Humph," Mama sniffed. Then she turned on Papa. "You mean to tell me you pretended for one solid month to believe my ankle was really hurt? Took me driving? Brought me flowers and candy, and all that? You just pretended?"

"Well, you were pretending, weren't you?"

"Of all the mean things, Mr. John!" Mama said indignantly. "You didn't care at all."

Papa laid his hand on her knee. "Oh, yes, I did. I cared terribly. You were the prettiest girl I ever saw, and the most popular one. I fell in love with you the first time I saw you, but I didn't think an old bachelor would have a chance with you. I would have given my right arm to take you to that picnic, but I was scared to ask you."

"So you took Lizzie Walters!"

"Well, if I couldn't take you, it didn't matter whom I took," Papa said gently.

"I still think," Mary said, looking mournfully at Mama, "you were mean to Lizzie."

"We were," Papa agreed solemnly. "We were very mean to her."

"Well," Mama said tartly, "you needn't grieve for Lizzie, Mary. She married the richest man in town the next year. All I got for my pains was a poor schoolteacher."

But I noticed that when she leaned forward to brush an ant off Papa's collar her hand lingered a little longer than it needed to. I didn't think Mama would have traded her poor schoolteacher for the richest man in town. I thought she was very glad to make Lizzie welcome of him.

Thinking about it, though, it *did* seem to me that if anyone had been swept off his feet, it had been Papa. Mama, I decided, had just forgotten how it was.

THE GIFT

"When I was about six or seven years old I fell in love with a young man who occasionally did some work around our place."

Around Our House

NEARLY EVERY DAY she went out to the big gate and waited for him to come swinging home across the prairie. She climbed to the post and sat there patiently, her hands folded in her lap.

She was a round, apple-cheeked little girl, not very tall for eight. But when she waited for Jeff to come home, she felt slender and tall and fair like a princess. She waited like a princess, quietly and decorously, in her tower atop the gatepost.

If he had been to the lower range, he would come into sight on the rim of the prairie straight out of the west, the sun behind him like a golden chariot wheel, both he and his piebald pony gilded with its fire.

If he had been to the upper range, he would come from the north, out of the foothills of the Winding Stair Mountains. She would not see him as quickly then, for the darkness of the mountains would hide him until he came out of their shadows.

She could never decide which direction she would rather he came from, and she never knew which to expect, for he left home long before she was awake in the morning. If he came from the west, she saw him sooner, but it took longer for him to reach home. It sometimes seemed like an eternity before he grew from a speck on the horizon to a man on a horse. If he came from the north, he emerged suddenly from the shadows into full view, and it was no time at all until he was riding up to the gate, smiling at her, lifting her solemnly from her perch to the saddle in front of him.

She liked the suspense of not knowing. She liked sitting there waiting, facing the west but turning to the north from time to time, trying to guess where he would come from. Sometimes, when she thought she had seen him, she slitted her eyes to make him small and almost invisible again, to prolong the suspense a little longer, to fool herself that it wasn't he. Those were the days when she was aware of the shortness of time, when she knew, profoundly, that the time of waiting was really the best, that once he had reached the gate and lifted her onto his horse, all too soon they would reach the corral and the moment for which she had waited would be over.

He never waved to her from the prairie, and she never waved to him from the gatepost. She simply waited, and he rode toward her. When he reached the gate, he would smile at her. She knew, truly, that that was the perfect moment, for her love would swell inside her until she felt big with its swelling. She sometimes could not bear to see his lean, dark face lifted toward her, the smile parting his lips until his teeth showed white. She sometimes could not lift her eyes higher than his thin hands holding the reins for fear the swelling love inside her would burst. She felt strangely aquiver then, achey and shivery.

He would smile and say, "Hello, Sallie."

She would reply, returning his smile, "Hello, Jeff."

He would open the gate, ride through, close it, and then he would sidle his horse up close to the post and lift her down. He never asked her if she had been waiting long, if she were hot, what she had been doing all day, if she had been a good girl. He never talked foolishly to her at all. Instead he walked the horse slowly to the corral, sometimes never saying a word, sometimes telling her the most beautiful things. "I saw the big brown trout in Beaver Creek today."

"Was he in the big pool?"

"Yes. He was lazy and sleepy today, just lying there in the water, down close to the bottom, hardly moving at all. I watched him for an hour, and he didn't move more than a few inches in all that time."

She knew, then, he had eaten his lunch on the bank of the creek, in the shade of the cottonwood tree, and that he had lain on the grassy bank and watched the trout in the clear, shallow waters of the big pool.

Another time he would tell her the beavers had finished their dam, and she would know he had been working the ravine where the creek flowed small and narrow and fast between the sides of the mountain, and while he talked she could see the beavers, their brown sides glistening with water and sun, their broad tails slapping, their slim, flat heads nosing twigs and branches and mud into place.

Once in the mountains he had seen an eagle. "He was a golden eagle, as gold as the sun, and he sailed down the canyon not more than six feet away from me where I stood. Not a feather on his wings moved, he sailed so stilly, and the sun glinted off his head like a mirror."

If he had been to the lower ranch, far out on the level prairie, he might tell her, "There was a lizard on a rock today, just sitting there, sunning himself, and a fly came by, and quicker than you can tell it, the lizard's tongue flicked out and the fly was gone."

She could see it, the lizard blue-flamed in the sun, the rock gray beneath him, waiting motionlessly until the fly flew past. She could see the incredibly rapid flick of the stiletto tongue, and the settling back, then, into immobility, of the lizard. "Did he go away then?"

"No, he waited for another fly."

And she knew that Jeff had eaten his lunch in the shade of the rock, and that he had sat, shoulders propped against the granite surface, watching the lizard catch flies.

He never told her that he had been branding calves, that he had been rounding up cattle, that he had been mending fences. She knew that. He was hired to do that, and it was unnecessary for him to tell her. He told her instead what he had seen — a big brown trout, beavers at work, an eagle sailing down the canyon, a lizard catching flies. And when they reached the corral, he slid out of the saddle and lifted her onto the ground. Politely, then, knowing he must take care of his horse, she thanked him and told him good night.

Sometimes she did not have to wait for him. When he worked about the place, he was there all day, and she followed him around, her pink sunbonnet shading her face, her yellow braids swinging beneath it, her short, sturdy legs tireless behind him. She held the staples for him while he nailed wire fencing in place. She held a piece of lumber while he sawed it in half. She held the oilcan while he worked on an old motor. Her father would say, "Jeff, don't let Sallie get in your way."

And Jeff would slant his eyes at her under the brim of his hat and smile and say, "She never gets in the way."

Her father would laugh and pull one of Sallie's braids. "You like Jeff a lot, don't you, baby?"

And she would be ashamed of him, for his foolishness and his childishness. She did not like Jeff. She liked dozens of people, but what she felt for Jeff was so different it was as if she herself were a different person with him. She loved Jeff, dearly, wholly, utterly.

Depending upon her mood, he was sometimes a prince, sometimes a knight, sometimes quite satisfactorily just the foreman of her father's ranch. She never told him or anyone that she planned to marry him when she was grown, or that she planned to grow up very fast to make it possible. She never told anyone that when she waited on the gatepost so patiently, or followed at his heels about the place, she was in training to be his wife.

When her aunt had been planning to be married, she had overheard her mother tell her, "In this country a wife has to do a lot of waiting for her husband — a lot of waiting while he's off seeing to things, and she has to be a help to him. Remember that, Susan, and don't be impatient with Jim."

Sallie remembered it, and she set herself to learn to wait patiently, to hold staples and oilcans and pieces of lumber helpfully. She meant to be a good wife to Jeff when the time came, and it was inconceivable to her that it should not come.

But she never told him so.

There came a day, in the early fall, when she had to say to him, "I am going away to school next week."

"I know," he said. "Your father told me. You're going to stay in town with your aunt and go to school."

He was cleaning his rifle, and she was holding the gun grease for him. "I expect," he said seriously, "you will do well in school. You have got a good mind, Sallie."

She was pleased that he thought so. "I expect I will," she said.

He rubbed thoughtfully on the gun barrel with an old cloth. "Books are a fine thing to know."

She nodded. "My father says so."

"I never got to know enough about books, myself. I've always wished I had."

"Why didn't you?"

"I had to go to work."

"But you know a lot of things that aren't in books."

"Yes, but it would help me, though, to know more that's in the books. I'd be a better man, I expect."

Although she did not know in what way Jeff could be better than he was, she did not argue about it. If he said so, it must be true. "I intend to study real hard," she told him. Since he thought so highly of books, she must apply herself to them.

"You do that. Not everyone has the chance for an education. You must make the most of it."

As the last days went by, she was conscious of restlessness in herself, not being able to settle happily to any play or task. The impending change hung over her, making her wander about. She came to each familiar chore and thing with the knowledge it was going to be left behind, and she stored up its familiarity to take with her into this new world.

She came finally to the last day and to her goodbye to Jeff. They rode into the corral, and he lifted her off the horse. "I am going tomorrow," she said.

"Yes." He did not tell her to be a good girl; he did not remind her again of her duty to the books. He held out his hand, as if she were another man. "I will miss you," he said.

She took his hand, felt its hard, calloused palm, and for the first time felt tearful and afraid. A lump choked her throat, and she had to swallow twice, very hard. "I will miss you, too," she told him.

He squatted beside her then, and she looked directly into his eyes, which were now on a level with hers. Wonderingly, she noticed there were little gold flecks in them and that there were fine, weathered wrinkles at the corners. Then he smiled at her, and she wanted terribly to fling her arms about his neck, hang on to him, and let the stinging tears she was holding back have their way. Instead, she continued to search his eyes. "You will be here when I come back?"

"I will be here."

She sighed. In nine months she would be back home, and he would be here. But then *he* would be waiting, and *she* would be riding toward him. From the corner of her eye she saw her father coming. Hurriedly she murmured, "Goodbye now," and went away into the house.

If he said goodbye, she did not hear him. Her ears were stopped by the beating of her heart.

The nine months were long, but she did not pine or dream overly much. She had always the confidence of her knowledge. They would pass and she would be going home and Jeff would be there. She studied dutifully. She made friends with the other schoolchildren, and played their games with them at recesses and during the noon hour. She helped her aunt with the housework and minded the new baby for her.

But with her whole being she knew that she was faced toward home. She moved through the day and the months with the inner knowledge that she made progress by walking backward. She moved with time, but with her face turned away.

She did not expect to see Jeff during that long time, but twice he came to town. He came in October, when he was taking a shipment of cattle to market in Kansas City, and again at Christmas.

When he came in October, he seemed strange to her at first, dressed as he was in a dark suit and with shirt and tie such as her father and uncle wore. He sat across the room from her on the small sofa by the fire and talked to her uncle about the cattle market, about the hurried ways of the city, about trains coming and going. Gradually, as he talked, the strangeness wore off, and when he spoke directly to her, and smiled at her, he became himself again. "The leaves are beginning to turn," he told her, "in the mountains. The old cottonwood by the big pool on Beaver Creek is yellow already, and so many leaves have fallen on the water that the whole top of the pool looks like a thick yellow carpet. You'd think you could almost walk on them, there are so many."

He asked her if she wanted any special thing from the city. "I don't know," he told her seriously, "how good I'd be at picking out something for you, but I could try."

Feeling unaccountably shy before her uncle and aunt, she refused to name anything, but her aunt spoke up. "She's been wanting some red slippers. There's a pair in the mail-order catalogue she's been wishing for. I'll show you."

She brought the catalogue, and Jeff studied the picture. Then he nodded and had her stand on a piece of brown paper while he drew the outline of her feet. "So I'll be sure and get the right size," he told her.

She did not know when he came back from the city, for he must have gone directly home to the ranch without stopping in town, and nothing at all was said of the red slippers. Sadly, she thought he had forgotten, but without effort she forgave him. He'd been very busy, she told herself.

At Christmas, though, he came with a message and gifts from her parents. The message said they were sorry they could not come to spend the holidays in town with her as planned, but her mother was ill. The gifts were loving and thoughtful ones — a beautiful new doll (for they did not know she was too old for dolls), a plaid taffeta dress and a soft, silky fur muff and cap. Jeff gave them to her, and when he had admired them with her, he handed her another package, which he had laid on the table when he came in. "Mine looks kind of skimpy alongside your folks' presents, but I thought you might like it."

He had wrapped it clumsily, in red paper. Slowly she took off the wrappings, her heart beating suffocatingly up into her throat. It was a small chest he had made her from cedarwood, just big enough for ribbons and handkerchiefs, and he had carved her name, "Sallie," in the top. She put her nose down to smell the sweet, fresh smell of the wood, and rubbed her hand over its satiny top. She could see him working on the chest, evenings maybe, in the bunkhouse, choosing the pieces of cedar, careful to select those with both red and yellow in them, whittling out each piece, fitting it to the next one, sanding them down to this soft smoothness, and then finally, with his knife, perhaps, cutting her name in the top. She could see his hands, thin, brown, holding the knife. The chest made every other gift seem small and insignificant. She touched it gently, as she felt she always must.

"Aren't you going to open it?" he asked her then.

Surprised, she looked up at him. "Is there something inside?"

He nodded, and when she lifted the lid, there were the red slippers, a little crowded, but he had managed to wedge them in. It was too much that he should have made her a cedarwood chest. The tears almost came, but she blinked them back. He came to her rescue. "Try your slippers and see if they fit."

He busied himself to give her time, drawing up a chair and settling a cushion for her to rest her feet on. The slippers fitted exactly, and as she swung them, eyeing their twinkling toes, her mood shifted, and she felt as bubbly and light as the slippers. Jeff looked at them, his head cocked on one side. "Looks to me," he said, "as if those were dancing shoes. I don't know if they'd stand up to trudging around the ranch much."

"They're for Sunday best," she told him. "I only mean to wear them on very special occasions."

He nodded. "That's what I thought they were for."

Then he swung up his hat and put it on rakishly. "I've got Christmas business of my own," he confided. He looked at her, his flecked eyes larky and happy. "Merry Christmas, Sallic."

She could not at all find the words to tell him thank you. All she could say was, "Merry Christmas, Jeff."

At the door he turned and spoke again. "I saw wild turkeys

in the canyon yesterday. A whole flock of them. I almost didn't see them, they were so near the color of the leaves, brown and speckled. But the old tom gobbled and gave himself away."

Thus he added one more gift to her merry Christmas.

Those were the two times that broke the long winter. In May her father came for her, and when they headed home for the ranch, her turnabout feeling left her, and she felt as if for the first time since she had left it she was faced in the right direction.

She asked questions eagerly, about her mother, about the house, about the cows and horses. She circled all around the subject she most wanted to hear about, knowing she did not really want to hear about it until she could hear it from Jeff himself. Several times she came near the edge of a question concerning him. "Has the herd at the lower ranch wintered well?"

"Fine. There'll be a good shipment this year."

"Has there been enough rain this spring to bring out the pastures on the upper range?"

"Plenty. Beaver Creek has been running full all spring."

Once her father started to say something of his own accord. "Jeff has —" he began, but she forestalled him. "Oh, look, there's a prairie dog."

She did not want to hear. It was her old game of suspense, not knowing, waiting a little longer for the perfect moment. He would be there, waiting. Not on the gatepost as she had waited, but there, somewhere about the place, and she would soon see him, and he would smile at her and say, "Hello, Sallie." She smoothed the folds of her plaid taffeta dress and bent forward to see the tips of her red slippers. He would know, when he saw them, that this was a very special occasion.

He was there at the gate, waiting, to open it for them. And he smiled at her, and at the sight of the smile on his dark face her love swelled up, as always, making her heart feel tight and ready to burst. He said, "Hello, Sallie," and he helped her out of the buggy. He saw the red slippers, too. She saw his eyes drop to them, and when he looked back up at her, his smile widened.

He did not say anything before her father, though, as if he knew he must not. The red slippers were just between themselves.

Instead, he went to help her father with her trunk, and she stood, waiting, looking about at the familiar buildings, glad and happy to be at home again. At the back of the orchard, then, she saw a new building, a small frame house, painted white. "What is that?" she asked.

"That's Jeff's new house. He's going to get married next week. Couldn't have him bringing a bride home to the bunkhouse."

In the short years of her life, nine of them, she had known what it was to be cold, for on the prairie the wind and snow blew icy cold straight out of the north, unimpeded. But never before had she felt the kind of cold that froze into her bones at that moment. It was as if the cold started in the marrow of her bones and spread slowly into her flesh, congealing it and turning it hard as stone.

She could not move, and so she stood, frozen, and waited as her father and Jeff, laughing together now, carried her trunk into the house. She saw the rough bark of the locust tree under which she stood, and she heard the bees humming among the blooms. She smelled the heady sweetness of the blooms, and she felt the bulk of the house behind her. She saw the sun lying blindingly bright on the grass beyond the shade of the tree, and she saw the fences and felt an ant crawling on her ankle. But she really saw only the small frame house in the orchard, and she really felt only the coldness between her shoulders.

She heard the screen door slam, and in a moment Jeff was

standing beside her again. She found that she could move, then, and she squared around to face him. "You said you would be here when I came back," she accused.

"I am here," he said quietly.

"No," she told him.

"But I am," he insisted.

"No," she repeated.

He squatted beside her as he had done when she told him goodbye. He put his hands on her shoulders, and she could not bear them. She twisted away. "Sallie, what is wrong? Have I done something? Aren't we friends anymore?"

She looked at him strangely. "We weren't friends. We weren't ever friends."

"I thought we were. I thought we were good friends."

His eyes still had the small golden flecks in them, and with anguish she thought of this woman he was going to marry, who would all her life look into them, and at whom he would smile, and whom he would tell about the brown trout and the eagle and the lizard. "Why are you going to be married?" she burst out angrily at him. "How could you be? *I* loved you! *I* was going to marry you!"

His face sobered suddenly, and he looked away from her, one knee going down to the ground to brace himself. He did not say anything for a long, long time, and, waiting, she tried to regain her composure. It shocked her that she had burst out at him and confided those hopes to him. She had never meant him to know until the time came, but she had blurted them out, in her pain, and it outraged her to be so betrayed by her own feelings. She waited, not knowing what he would say, or if he would say anything, not knowing why she waited, except, perhaps, from habit of waiting.

When he spoke finally, he did not remind her that she was only a little girl, that she did not know the meaning of love, that someday she would grow up and meet a fine boy her own age and marry him and be happy forever after. He did not tell her she would learn to love his wife, that she must visit them in the new house. He did not say to her, laughingly, that she would forget all this, or that if she did remember it, in time, she would laugh at the memory. He said none of these expected and wholly untrue things to her. Instead he said, "I love you, too, Sallie, and if things were different, I would feel very honored to have you marry me. I love you so much, Sallie, that even though I am going to marry someone else, I will never love her in quite the same way. All my life you will be my dearest love, my unobtainable love."

He turned to face her then and gathered her very close in his arms. She felt the hard strength of them tight about her, and the roughness of his cheek against hers. She cried, then, not stormily as a child cries, but quietly, as a woman cries, and he allowed her tears for a long time. Then he spoke again. "You see, Sallie, you are a princess, and a princess can never marry a commoner. A princess can only marry a prince."

"You are a prince to me."

"That's only because you love me. I am the commonest sort of commoner."

His analogy was just reasonable enough to be nearly believable. Dimly she understood that because she was her father's daughter and would someday inherit all these vast lands and herds, and because he was a cowhand, rough and unlettered, there was a likeness to the princess in the storybooks. He loved her, but he could never marry her. She clutched him tighter, wanting to believe. "But you do love me? You always have and you always will?"

"I do love you. I always have and I always will."

"The most?" She whispered it.

"The most."

Gently, tenderly, and even proudly he denied his deepest love and presented the denial as his finest gift to restore a small girl's sense of dignity, to heal a small girl's sense of treachery.

She wiped her eyes on his shirt sleeve and drew away from his arms. She looked at him, the dark, sober face, the flecked, troubled eyes. And she recognized the denial for what it was. Sadly she knew she had compelled it. He loved this woman he was going to marry, for he would not be marrying her otherwise. She guessed that his Christmas business, which had made him so gay, had been with her.

But instinctively she recognized also the splendor and the kindness of his denial. And since she had willed it from him and her pride was restored by it, she must not now, she saw, do him the dishonor of refusing it. She must not shame him by unbelief. Gently, then, tenderly and bravely, she received it. With pain still shining in her eyes, with coldness still chill between her shoulders, she took his face between her hands and kissed him sweetly on the forehead. "We will always love each other," she told him, "but we must always hide our broken hearts."

He closed his eyes at the touch of the cool, soft young lips, and when he opened them she was walking away, the red slippers, forgotten, twinkling in the sun. With a strange sense of loss he watched her, feeling oddly that at that moment, for him as well as for her, it was very nearly true.

(This story was published originally in *Good Housekeeping,* January 1957.)

Kentucky

THE MINOR MIRACLE

"I was secretary to the dean of the Louisville Presbyterian
Theological Seminary."

40 Acres and No Mule

OLD MR. FORBES stood just inside the great door and beamed
happily on the members of the congregation as they entered the
church. He had stood exactly there on practically every Sunday
for fifty years, and he always beamed. Today was special,
though, and the beam, if possible, was a little beamier than usual.
He was delighted that it was such a fine day and that so many
of the congregation had come to hear the new preacher's first
sermon.

The people of New Hope were fond of saying that old Mr.
Forbes looked just like Winston Churchill, and he was accustomed to hearing them say it. His mirror told him that he did
possess the same cherubic countenance and portly figure, but the
Churchillian likeness ended there, for instead of the bulldog jut
of the jaw, Mr. Forbes's face wore simply the benign look of
eternal good will.

Fervently Mr. Forbes hoped that Mr. Churchill did not have,
either, his own trouble with his upper plate. Long familiarity
with its propensity for dropping down had made automatic his
habit of speaking through two fingers pressed gently against his
upper lip, and, as an actor would have said, throwing his lines
away. His voice always issued downwind, so to speak, for once
(horrible memory) his plate had dropped when he was making

53

a speech at a Rotary dinner. It had been so unnerving, as well as frightening, for he had almost swallowed the teeth whole, that Mr. Forbes had never tried to make a speech again, and to guard against any further such embarrassment he had developed the aforementioned habit.

It served him very well, though it led to some misunderstandings occasionally, such as the time old Mrs. Martin had called to ask about her bank balance and had understood him to say nine hundred dollars, when he had actually said five hundred, and feeling wealthy she had gone on a spree of riotous spending. Mr. Forbes had felt obliged to cover her widestrewn checks.

As executive vice-president of the Bank of New Hope, and after fifty years of service, Mr. Forbes's salary was exactly two hundred dollars a month, and the shock of having to make good four hundred dollars' worth of Sallie Martin's bad checks had almost, but not quite, driven him to trying Grippo, the adhesive powder so widely advertised for slipping dentures.

Of course, he had eventually got the four hundred dollars back, along with a lecture from Sallie about stupid old men with ill-fitting teeth, but he did not like to recall the feeling of loss and insecurity at withdrawing such an amount from his savings. Mr. Forbes put money *in* the bank. He rarely drew it out.

Because he had never married, the bank and his church were the anchors of Mr. Forbes's life. The congregation referred to him as "a pillar of the church," and, in truth, his Sabbath presence was as certain and as predictable as the stone structure itself. For thirty years he had been treasurer of the church, it being the unanimous opinion of the congregation that no one was more eminently fitted to handle their funds than the vice-president of the bank. Mr. Forbes had given the finances of the church the same careful and scrupulous attention he gave to the affairs of the bank, reporting conscientiously each month to the board.

In addition to being treasurer, he had willingly and happily served in many other capacities. He was always, for instance, chairman of the Every-Member Canvass to raise the annual budget. He had labored long and diligently on the Committee to Shingle the Parsonage Roof, and saved the congregation nearly one hundred dollars thereby. The women of the church had never ceased to be grateful to him when he had rescued them from the mire of their entanglement over the church carpeting, they having failed to multiply the length by the breadth correctly.

Mr. Forbes was also an inveterate delegate to all conventions and conferences, along with the minister. Once, trailing clouds of glory, he had even been sent to a *national* conference, and although it had been twenty years ago he still liked to tell of it. "When I attended the national conference . . . ," he often prefaced quite casual observations.

But where Mr. Forbes really shone was on the Committee to Call a New Minister. It would never have occurred to the church to leave him off that committee, for one of the stars in Mr. Forbes's crown was his personal acquaintance with the president of the seminary. Mr. Forbes had gone to college with President Hughes and, in private at least, was privileged to call him John.

Only six times in fifty years had it been Mr. Forbes's pleasure to advise and counsel with a Committee to Call a New Minister, for the New Hope church was in the habit of keeping its ministers a long time. But each time the procedure had been the same. "Why don't you get in touch with President Hughes, Mr. Forbes?"

And with becoming modesty Mr. Forbes had always accepted the commission, reporting to the committee afterward, "President Hughes says this young man is one of the best students the seminary has ever had. He says we could not go wrong to call him."

That usually ended the matter, for it was assumed that between President Hughes and Mr. Forbes the New Hope church could call only the best young men. Of course, anyone graduating from seminary was a good man, and it was simply one of those fortunate dispensations of Providence that through Mr. Forbes's friendships with President Hughes they were always able to get the best of the good men.

So it had happened that once again, after fifteen years of a quiet and satisfying ministry, the pulpit being empty, Mr. Forbes had approached President Hughes. A young man had been found. Alfred Snowden his name was, and President Hughes had spoken of him affectionately as Alf. "He's a real live wire," he had told Mr. Forbes. "He'll do you a good piece of work."

It was typical of the New Hope church that they never insisted on hearing a ministerial candidate. Mr. Forbes took care of all that, and when Mr. Forbes said a young man would make them a fine minister, it was good enough for them. So no one had yet heard young Mr. Snowden preach. This was his maiden sermon before them, and proudly and happily Mr. Forbes greeted them as they came in. Once again he had been able to serve his people well.

The organ prelude began quietly. Mr. Forbes closed the great door and slipped into his place in the back pew. He liked to sit there because he could hear late-comers and meet them, with admonishment for silence if the pastoral prayer had begun or if the congregation was in the middle of a hymn, and keep them waiting until the appropriate time for seating.

The organ sounded the processional and the choir solemnly filed in. Young Mr. Snowden entered from his study. Mr. Forbes blinked. The young man did not wear the academic robe as he was entitled to. Instead he was dressed, quite decently, of course, and unobtrusively, in a dark business suit. But New Hope ministers always wore the Geneva gown. It had been freshly cleaned and pressed and hung handily on the hook back of the door. Mr. Forbes made a mental note to remind the young man.

With decorum the new minister took his place in the huge carved chair at the back of the pulpit and bowed his head in silent prayer. Then he led the congregation in the familiar call to worship, the recitation of the Creed and the Gloria. Mr. Forbes nodded approvingly. The young man made a fine appearance. He was tall, quite handsome with his mop of black hair and his voice was splendidly resonant.

It was time, now, for the first hymn. On the order of service it was listed as "A Mighty Fortress is Our God," and the riffle of pages accompanied the congregational search for the correct one. But suddenly young Mr. Snowden waved aside the order of service, smiled winsomely down on his people and said, "I think we need a more stirring hymn this morning." He turned to the organist and asked, so all could hear, "Do you know 'There's Power in the Blood'?"

She nodded, momentarily bereft of speech, and uncertainly shifted the stops in front of her and played the opening bars. Mr. Snowden smiled happily. "This hymn isn't in the hymnal, but I'm sure you all know it. Shall we stand? And let's all sing out joyously. Let's put some power in it! Let's make the rafters ring!"

The rafters of the New Hope church were not used to ringing and they failed to respond to the weak efforts of the congregation. In fact, Mr. Snowden seemed the only one to know the words of the song and his rich baritone had almost to carry it alone.

At its end he motioned for the people to be seated. "I'm sure," he said, "that we all revere the good old hymns of the Presbyterian church, but some of them are about as full of life as a funeral dirge. We need more joy in our music, more life, more surge and power. We shall sing at least one of the more lively songs each Sunday from now on."

Heads turned in the direction of Mr. Forbes. He met their concentrated gaze bravely, but privately he was terribly dismayed. How could this young man have attended seminary three long years without learning the basic facts of hymnology — that good music and good poetry were both essential? What had John Hughes sent them in Alf Snowden?

The sermon that followed was all right, as far as it went. The young man properly read the entire chapter of Scripture from which his text was taken, adhering to the tradition of not lifting a few verses out of context. But actually it amounted, when he began to talk, to little more than a prospectus of what Mr. Snowden proposed to do. "We must reach the youth of our church," he insisted, "and Mrs. Snowden and I have outlined a program of vital activities for our young people. Some of us," he smiled benignly, his young, cheerful face belying his own inclusion, "are getting older, and the mantle of services must fall on younger shoulders. We want, now, to invite all the young people of the church to a get-together at our home this evening. There will be no night service, therefore . . . and it is my hope that the congregation will seriously consider doing away with it altogether so that we may stress the evening activities with the young people."

Once again heads turned toward Mr. Forbes. It was true that the night service attracted only a handful of elderly people, all of whom had been at the morning service also, but to abandon it altogether was little short of heretical. Mr. Forbes felt a sinking in the pit of his stomach. This live wire of President Hughes's might prove to be a little too live, he thought. New Hope was, after all, a very small town.

No one knew quite what to say when the service ended. Loyally, Mr. Forbes took his place beside the young minister to introduce him to the families of the church, and as the young people streamed by, mostly they contented themselves with a bewildered look at Mr. Forbes and a thin smile and word of welcome to Mr. Snowden. Mr. Forbes didn't blame them. Never had President Hughes sent them so revolutionary a character as this young man. He must have a word with him.

When the last of the people had left he turned to the young man. "Mr. Snowden, you're new here and there may be a few things you'd like to know about our church. This church is over one hundred years old. I've been a member here since boyhood . . ."

The preacher waved his remarks aside. "Yes, I know, Mr. Forbes. I know this is an old church, and it's almost a dead church. I'm going to put some life into it."

Mr. Forbes, in turn, ignored the minister's remarks. "Now, about the robe, Mr. Snowden . . ."

"I don't believe in wearing the robe, Mr. Forbes. I am a man, a very common, ordinary man, and I do not wish to be lifted up above the congregation." Mr. Snowden said this very earnestly.

"But the minister *should* be lifted . . ."

"No, sir . . . the minister should be down where his people are!"

Mr. Forbes laid two tremulous fingers against his lip. "And no night service, Mr. Snowden!"

"I explained how I felt about that in my sermon," the young man said. "I want to stress the young peoples' program."

"But we've always . . ."

"That's just the trouble with old churches," the young man went on. "They've always done things in the same old way. What this church needs is some new blood. It needs a charge of dynamite, to tell the truth."

Mr. Forbes did not recall ever having been so disturbed, but he drew himself up to his full height. "Just be careful, sir," he warned, "that you don't blow it sky-high with too big a charge."

"Oh, never fear. I'll be careful, all right. And call me Alf. I'm just a hail-fellow-well-met sort of guy, you know."

Never in his life had Mr. Forbes called his minister by his first name. The dignity of the ministry prohibited it. It would, in his opinion, be like saying "Old Buddy" to God. "I will *not* call you Alf, Mr. Snowden," he said with conviction. "You may be hail-fellow-well-met all you please, but you are the servant of God in our midst and I, for one, intend to remember it."

He went home, trembling for the future.

But if Mr. Forbes did not call the new preacher Alf, everyone else in town did. In no time at all he could walk around the square and be hailed on all sides with, "Hi ya, Alf . . . Hey, Alf, when are you and the missus coming over for supper?"

The townspeople liked him, there was no mistake about it. He went around in sneakers and an old sweat shirt on weekdays, played first base on the softball team with professional efficiency and wrangled with the umpire as mercilessly as any other member of the team. He was in great demand as a speaker at all the community affairs, and he held an audience helpless with laughter with his fund of funny stories. He was in the middle of every civic enterprise, tireless in organizing benefits, heading up the Red Cross drive, sparking the fund for the new swimming pool, and dozens of times a day Mr. Forbes listened to the delighted comments of his friends and neighbors. "Say, that new preacher you've got is a humdinger. He's all right. He's really waking this little old town up!"

In the church he was rousing a few things, too. After the initial shock had worn off most of the congregation rallied around him, and the young people were crazy about him. Never had the church had so vital a youth program. On all sides Mr.

Forbes heard them talking. "Alf says . . ." "Preacher wants . . ." "The parson told us . . ." and so forth. There were fish frys, wiener roasts or hay rides almost every week and Sunday night had been duly given over to their interests. They had a basketball team, a bowling team, and Alf was even teaching them to square dance.

Little by little Mr. Forbes began to feel as if he were a stranger in a strange world. The roof of the church did not fall in, but frequently he wondered why it didn't. He still, however, had his post as treasurer. He could still watch over the temporal affairs of his straying people.

Even that came to an end, however. One night at a board meeting, gently but firmly Mr. Snowden recommended his replacement by a younger man. He put it well, but nothing could ameliorate the dismissal. "Mr. Forbes has served the church long and faithfully. It is time he had a rest. It is time younger shoulders took up the mantle of service."

In the silence that followed, broken only by the roar and pounding in his own ears, Mr. Forbes thought how fond Mr. Snowden was of that phrase — the mantle of service on young shoulders. In Mr. Forbes's opinion, young shoulders were often too impatient to carry such a mantle, and too inexperienced and unwise. Older shoulders, accustomed to the load and devoted to it, usually found it easier to carry. And a church wasn't something to play around with.

The men of the board looked uneasily at him. With dignity he spoke. "Mr. Snowden is probably right. I have served in this post too long, perhaps. I shall be glad to step aside."

It was not true, of course. He could never be glad to step aside, and he would be lost without this compelling concern. But there wasn't much else he could say, and some element of fairness in him made him say, even to himself, "Maybe I *am* too old. Maybe we older ones *are* too old. Maybe we *do* need to step down and step aside. Maybe, even in religion, we need to move with the times."

Nothing, however, could have kept Mr. Forbes from being in his pew on Sunday mornings. Preachers might come and go, the order of service might be altered, but the New Hope church went on forever, and Mr. Forbes went on with it. After his resignation as treasurer, however, he no longer arrived early and stood within the great door to greet the congregation. He somehow hadn't the heart any longer. But he was always in his pew.

He suffered through the rousing, lively opening hymns, much better sung now that Mr. Snowden bought new hymnals. He took little comfort from the social gospel that the young minister so zealously preached, but there was at least the reading of the Scripture and the age-old affirmation of the Apostles' Creed. When the young preacher decided to omit the recitation of the Creed from the service, Mr. Forbes even tried to admit that perhaps it, too, in its archaic language, was outmoded. But he always said it to himself at the appropriate place. And valiantly he defended the minister against any small criticism that riffled the surface, such as that over the square dancing in the church basement. Mr. Snowden was his minister. No one should criticize him in his presence. "There's nothing wrong with square dancing," he maintained stoutly, "in the church basement or anywhere else. It's just a kind of singing game, a sort of play party game."

It was perhaps six months after Mr. Snowden had been called that it became generally known that his wife was expecting a baby. The jokes Mr. Forbes heard addressed to the young preacher after that sometimes made his ears burn, but he told himself not to be an old fogy. Young people nowadays talked about anything, freely and openly. But he remembered with heartache how delicately their former pastor had handled the birth of each of his six children. No one had dared to call coarse and vulgar things to Mr. Johnson. Privately, Mr. Forbes could not help feeling that there were *some* things too personal for open discussion.

It was Mr. Forbes's habit to eat his lunch in the Best-Food-in-Town Grill. Strangers were wont to say that if that was the best food in town they'd hate to eat the worst, but it did very well for Mr. Forbes. He was sitting on his usual stool one day, the third one from the front, and the proprietor had just brought his plate lunch, the Blue Plate Special — roast pork and gravy, mashed potatoes, peas and carrots and cole slaw. With a good appetite Mr. Forbes attacked it. The proprietor leaned an elbow on the counter. "Say, Mr. Forbes, what about this young preacher of yours saying the miracles in the Bible are just a lot of hogwash?"

Mr. Forbes laid down his fork and took a sip of water. "I'm sure he never said anything of the kind, Pete. You know how these things get exaggerated." But his stomach was fluttering and his appetite was gone. It sounded just like Mr. Snowden.

"He sure did . . . right here at this counter . . . just yesterday. I heard him myself, so it's not exaggerated. Said if Jesus really healed anybody it was because he knew something about medicine and disease. Said Jesus wasn't really resurrected from the dead, either. Not in his body. Said it wasn't possible. Said nobody believed in such things anymore because they just weren't possible."

Mr. Forbes slid off the stool and drew himself up. "I believe in them, Pete, and I have not yet joined the ranks of nobody!"

He stalked out of the restaurant. Anger raced through him. The preacher had gone too far. He remembered, too late now, that they had not examined Mr. Snowden on his orthodoxy. It had not seemed necessary. It could be assumed that any young man, examined by seminary and admitted as a candidate for the ministry, further schooled for three years, would be sound theologically. But somewhere along the line something had gone wrong with this young man. Mr. Forbes intended to set it right.

Thirty minutes later, in Mr. Snowden's living room, Mr. Forbes heard the young man repeat his heresy. Once again he was gentle. "Mr. Forbes, belief in the miracles is not necessary to the faith. Actually, they tend to weaken the faith of modern young people. They *know* such things could *not* happen. They go against all the laws of nature. It's like insisting the world is square when it has been proven round. Religion must keep pace with the times. We must discard those old ideas. The spirit of Christ, not the Christ of the miracles, must be our message today."

Mr. Forbes took his hat and prepared to leave. "The miracles of Christ *were* his spirit, Mr. Snowden, and Christ crucified and risen is still his most divine message."

Mr. Snowden patted his arm. "Now, Mr. Forbes, perhaps we don't see eye to eye on the details of this, but I think we both mean the same thing."

Mr. Forbes shook his head. "No, sir, we don't. Mr. Snowden, I've sung your rousing songs and learned to like some of them right well. I miss the recitation of the Creed, but I can always say it to myself. I wish you would wear the robe, but I can see that it is not necessary, and no one in the church has been happier than I over your work with the young people. But don't try to take the miracles out of the Gospels, Mr. Snowden. That's not keeping pace with the times. That's taking the divine heart out of your message and your faith, and when the heart is gone, there's nothing left."

Mr. Snowden smiled. "Well, keep your miracles, too, Mr. Forbes. As for me, I can do without them."

Mr. Forbes left, needing four fingers to keep his plate in place. He pondered what to do. He could, of course, and perhaps should, take the problem to the church authorities, for it was, after all, a matter of heresy. But he shrank from doing so. In the first place, the New Hope church had never wrangled with a minister, and he hated to see it get involved. In the second place, and he confessed it wryly, he hated to admit he had erred in recommending the man. But neither of these was as important as his sudden reluctance to see the young preacher hurt. His life's work would be ended were he to be brought to trial before a church court. Remembering the love the townspeople felt for the young minister, the devotion of all the young people, the tireless zeal with which Mr. Snowden labored in good works, Mr. Forbes did not see how he could be the instrument to deal him such a death blow. Lord, he prayed finally, humbly, Thy will be done.

It was two months later that Mrs. Snowden's time came, and the whole town knew of it, of course. They also knew that she must have a Caesarean section. Gaily, on the appointed day, Mr. Snowden drove her to the hospital, acknowledging all the good wishes called to him with a wave of his hand and a good-natured grimace at the bets on the sex of the child. Then the town settled down to wait for the good news.

Toward the middle of the morning Mr. Forbes was in his office, pondering an application for a loan, when the proprietor of the Best-Food-in-Town Grill stuck his head in the door. "Hey, Mr. Forbes, have you heard? The preacher's wife is pretty bad off!"

"How bad off?"

"Well, something went wrong and they say she hasn't got much chance to pull through."

Mr. Forbes reached for his hat. His place was beside his pastor at such a time as this.

He hurried to the hospital and was directed to a small hall outside the operating room. Mr. Snowden was pacing the floor, his hair rumpled, his old sweat shirt pulled down from his throat as if to give him more air. He grabbed Mr. Forbes's hand. "Pray, Mr. Forbes! If you've *ever* prayed in your life, Mr. Forbes, pray now!"

"I *am* praying, Mr. Snowden," Mr. Forbes said, but he went to his knees automatically and closed his eyes.

He stayed there, unconscious of the passing of time, hearing a sobbing breath from the minister now and then, hearing his footsteps take up the relentless walk back and forth, hearing him plead aloud, "God, I can't lose her . . . I *can't* lose her. Please, God, don't take her away!"

It may have been an hour, it may have been two, but the doctor finally came. Mr. Snowden started up, thinking he was being called for the last moments with his wife, but the doctor gripped his hand and smiled. "She's all right, Mr. Snowden. She's come through and she's safe now." He untied the mask, which he had slipped down, and stood fingering it, shaking his head. "It was a miracle . . . literally a miracle." He looked up at Mr. Snowden. "She died right there on the operating table. Her heart stopped beating and she had no pulse, and there was nothing we could do. We tried everything. We had given her up. Then for no reason we could understand, the heart started beating again, the pulse strengthened and before our very eyes she started living again. Simply a miracle, I tell you."

"A miracle!"

The doctor nodded. "There is no other way to explain some of the things we doctors see occasionally, Mr. Snowden. Your wife died, and no skill of ours brought her back to life. What happened in that operating room was a resurrection from the dead." Briskly, then, he spun on his heels. "You may see her in about thirty minutes." And he walked swiftly off down the hall.

The minister looked at Mr. Forbes. Still awed he said, "I was the one who could do without miracles!"

"None of us can," Mr. Forbes said gently. He put his hand on the young man's shoulder. "Our human intelligence is so meager compared to the Great Intelligence that governs us all that it is barely on the fringe of understanding, son. Sometimes we think we have learned everything, but all we can ever know is but a drop in the vast sea of God's compassionate wisdom."

"But miracles!"

"They don't make sense, do they? But do you truly believe that human experience and wisdom are all of experience and wisdom?" Mr. Forbes smiled. "I had a course in logic in college, and I learned there that *everything is possible*, both scientifically and logically. How much more possible it is in faith. Just because something happens outside the realm of ordinary experience doesn't mean it *can't* happen. Why, life itself doesn't make sense. We don't know whence we came, or why. On the face of it, life is impossible, and there is no greater miracle. Why should we wonder at the miracles of healing? With God, nothing is impossible."

Mr. Snowden took a deep breath. "Mr. Forbes . . ." He hesitated a moment, then plunged on. "I feel as if just now I am being called to the ministry . . . to the real, divine ministry."

Mr. Forbes put on his hat and pushed tentatively at his upper plate. He smiled through his two fingers. "Perhaps you are. Perhaps you are. God works in wondrous ways, and a minor miracle often accompanies a greater one." He took the minister's hand in both of his. "When you see your wife, give her my love."

Mr. Snowden's eyes misted. "Yes, sir . . . I will."

Mr. Forbes hurried out the door, his own eyes misted and his heart singing within him. There was a spring in his heels as he

67

bounced down the long hill to the town square. He knew he would be able to recite the Apostles' Creed aloud next Sabbath, and he thought Luther's hymn might open the service. Young Mr. Snowden might even wear a robe, now . . . but these things were as nothing. The exultation in Mr. Forbes's heart had nothing to do with them. It had to do with the brush of angels' wings hovering over a human life, and with the holy privilege of witnessing the call of a disciple. He had seen beyond all expectation the Lord's will being done.

He came to the town square and bent his steps toward the bank. At the Corner Drug he stopped before a crowded display in the window. He contemplated the display a long, long time, then, squaring his shoulders, he marched firmly through the door. "Jim," he said, "give me a tube of the Grippo, will you?"

Only the Lord could pass a major miracle, but Mr. Forbes could achieve a minor one himself. He was going to stick his teeth in tight and quit that foolishness of talking through two fingers!

KENTUCKY

"I don't know how to tell you of its indescribable beauty."

40 Acres and No Mule

"HEAVEN MUST BE a Kentucky sort of place." Legend has put the words in the mouth of that trapping man, Daniel Boone. Let it stand.

But Kentucky was a fable. It was the land we hadn't come to yet — that far place of dreams where meadows were fair, forests were noble, streams were overflowing. It was always the land beyond — over another mountain, across another rolling river. It was the land God made just right and put in exactly the right place.

It was the Bluegrass and the Cumberland, the *Belle Rivière* and the Chenoa. It was the wide Missouri and the Sweetwater, the High Plains of Nebraska and the Grand Tetons. It was Oregon and the golden horn of Yerba Buena. It was San Xavier and the City of Angels. All of it was Kentucky, dream-haunted, fabulous, utopian. If we could only get there, it would be the Garden of Eden.

The swells of the Pacific brought the dreams to an end. They said Kentucky is not a place. It cannot be found. Kentucky must be built. It must begin with man in harmony with nature, and man at home in the human community.

Very well. Begin with a piece of country shaped like that eternal symbol of work — the moldboard plow. Make it a natural reservoir with mountains on the east and a broad water

69

highway on the north. Let the basin be fertile and rich, so that it will grow bluegrass and golden tobacco and tall corn and fat cattle. Let the plow go to work.

Then spill over the mountains and down the water highway into the great basin and heartland every kind and type of man. Stir and mix them all together. In the bluegrass land lay out broad streets and build a college called Transylvania and call the town the Athens of the West — Lexington.

In the middle of the rich basin, in a double log cabin, call ten statehood conventions and birth a state. Call it Kentucky. Build another college and call it Centre. And call the town of the double log cabin Danville.

On the lovely Chenoa, lay out another town. Put the state capital there. In its jeweled cup of hills and bending river it will look like a vineyard town in the Belgian Ardennes, but call it Frankfort.

Begin with the land and the great diversification of men. Add the plow. Add education and law and order and the legislative process. Join with fourteen other states to form a more perfect union. Add churches and homes.

And for a long, long time the result was very nearly the Kentucky of fable. The great basin and heartland breathed with the seasons and produced richly, intellectually, physically and materially. The people lived by the rhythms of the land, and there was a time, and there was a rich warp and woof to life.

Even when the rest of America was jolted by the industrial revolution at the turn of the century into a faster and faster pace, the heartland of Kentucky — from Somerset to Shelbyville, from Winchester to Bowling Green — continued to live by the rhythms of the land. It stayed unhurried, rich, fertile, and the inner clocks of its people remained geared to the pulse and beat of the land.

Then something happened and there began to be a shift in

mood and a change in rhythm. There was another war, a different war, a bigger war, which began to bring a shift in mood and a change in rhythm. There was another war, a different war, a bigger war, which ended with the Bomb and Hiroshima. And when it was over, time seemed to be running out, and the breathing of this great heartland was suddenly too slow and its people had a rhythm that was too slow.

Suddenly the emphasis was no longer on the land. The great tobacco belt, the fine bluegrass land, the land of corn and fat cattle must step up, must make progress, must grow and expand and become bigger and bigger. It must catch up, it must keep up, it mustn't fall behind. It was all very well for Switzerland to be the jewel of Europe; Kentucky could not afford to be the jewel of America. It must not be last of the fifty states.

Almost overnight Progress was no longer related to the richness of human life and the stature of men in the human community. We forgot that Progress is an unthinkingly accepting notion that can sanctify crime if necessary, and we let Progress become industry and big business and superhighways and more and more construction, and we geared education to pressures.

We have this now in the heartland. We have great industrial complexes that sprawl and belch, and the people, with their inner rhythms disturbed, can now stand at an assembly line. Every little town and city in the area has its industry, small or big, to boast about, and fights for more. Close out the farms and move the people into industry. Progress.

We have the broad ribbons of superhighways, and more and more are yelled for. People who no longer know the rhythms of any land must be always to-ing and fro-ing, going nowhere in particular, but going, and they always go faster and faster. Planned death. Progress.

We have dams and lakes and soon there will be no living water left. Some of them are wise and useful, for the storage of water in a land that has unwisely diminished its water sources. But some of them are pure pork barrel. Close out the farms and put the people on water skis.

We in Kentucky are out of rhythm. We have lost the beat to which our inner clocks were geared and have not yet found another to which we can step confidently.

History proves that man is greatest when all his capacities are developed harmoniously. Our greatest problem in the heartland of Kentucky is to rediscover the old dream of a Kentucky sort of place. We must build, but we must do it providently, carefully, thoughtfully, and we must keep the harmony and the rhythm of man in his total environment as its central purpose.

(This chapter was printed originally as a special feature in the Louisville *Courier Journal*.)

WILDERNESS ROAD

"I wanted to deal with the opening of the West in such a way as to make it vivid, real, dramatic and so authentic it could be taught as history."

Around Our House

"Pa says there's not room for e'er other thing. I don't know if we can get your feather bolster loaded on."

"The feather bolster will not take such a heap of room, James. Make a place for it."

Rebecca Boone knew it was not Daniel who had objected to the feather bolster. James had been strung as tight as a fiddle string since the day his father had named his intention of taking them to Kentucky, and now that the time had come to leave he couldn't hide his pleasure to be going at last, or his impatience at the tedium of loading the pack animals. Give James his way and he would have ridden off with nothing but a horse and a gun, no bothering with womenfolks and young ones and house furnishings.

Like father, like son, she reckoned, remembering the times without end Daniel had so ridden off. In a way it was a pity that James had been too little to go along on most of Daniel's great specks, and that this, his own first great speck, had to be cluttered with women and children. A man liked an unhampered speculation. It was a pity for James, but it had been a great comfort to her. It was bad enough to have Daniel away in the woods for months on end without one of the boys being gone with him.

She went about quietly, packing a slat basket with food left from their last home-cooked meal. It wouldn't last long, but it would be a waste not to take it and she had never had rations enough to waste anything.

From the corner of her eye she watched James struggling with the feather bolster. She knew what he was thinking by the way he tugged and jerked at it. Feather bolster! Feather bolsters in Kentucky, where a man would have all he could do to stand off the Shawnees with one hand and clear him a piece of ground with the other! It went the foolishest, the things women had to have. He laid the bolster on the floor and folded it over three times, but before he could tie it into a neat, compact bundle it escaped him into fat, puffy sausages of air and feathers. He grunted and sweated and laid it out again. He pushed and pulled and mumbled down in his throat and grumbled. More so than need be, Rebecca thought, and she paid him no mind.

It was not seemly for a woman to look with favorance on any one of her young ones over the rest, but she misdoubted there was a mother living but had a special tenderness for her oldest son, her first-born. Time and again as the lad was growing up he had twisted her heart until it was hard to be stern with him. He had been so clever and quick, and so given to lightheartedness. Daniel's sandy hair and her own black, combined, had turned out a sort of goldy-red in James. It had always pleasured her to look on that bright head. But she knew well enough that did she ever allow him to take an inch he would take a mile, so risky were all young ones, so she had oftentimes steeled herself against him. And he need not think, sixteen though he was now, that she could be talked out of taking her feather bolster to Kentucky, either.

Daniel's shadow darkened the door. "You about ready?"

She folded a linen square over the basket and slung it on her arm. "Soon as James gets my feather bolster tied on. Seems it would of been a heap easier to tie it on back somewhere so's one of the least ones could ride on it."

"You want it should get tore into bits by the briars and thorns?" His frustration made James speak scornfully of her woman's lack of knowledge.

Undisturbed either by his scorn or by her lack of knowledge, she followed Daniel out into the early sun, speaking softly to her son in passing. "No, I shouldn't want it to get tore into bits by briars or thorns, or e'er thing else. See it's packed good so's it won't be, if there is aught to be uneasy of."

James would learn in good time that while women might lack the kind of knowledge men had, they had a kind of knowledge of their own, which men, for the most part, made a poor shift of doing without. She knew what would be required of her in the wilderness, and she knew to what uses the feather bolster might be put to ease those requirements. But no need to say. The young had to do their own learning.

The train of pack horses strung out along the trail, each animal loaded heavily. It was a good train, well disposed and well loaded. Daniel had seen to that. There was a place on a good, steady horse for each of the least ones to ride, and a place for her handy to them. The men, Daniel and James, would walk and lead the train. The oldest of the younger ones would drive the milch cows and the three hogs. Daniel pulled her horse around for her and helped her to mount. She arranged her skirts and steadied the basket in her lap.

She was taller than common, Rebecca Boone. She could look Daniel straight in the eye, and though Daniel wasn't extra-heighted, it made of her a tall woman. She was not a woman often given to laughter or to gaiety of spirit, but she had the name among the settlements on the Holston of being steady and sure in her ways, quiet in her speech and high-hearted in bad times. She was stout and skilled in all the ways a woman in the western country had need of being skilled.

She could shoot, though not as well as Daniel, for once when she was aiming at a deer she had misfired and killed her own riding mare. They had laughed at her over that, down on the Yadkin, but they did not forget either that the same winter, because of Daniel's being gone on a long hunt for skins, she had killed and dressed out enough meat to feed her family well and have some left over to serve Daniel when he came home in the spring.

She had always made out better than most women when her man was away. She asked no help in tending her crops, but set to and tended them herself, plowing and planting and gathering, all. Whatever she turned her hand to, man's work or woman's, she did well. That is what people on the Yadkin said of Rebecca Boone.

James came out of the cabin with the feather bolster tied into a roll and, peering around it, made his way clumsily down the slope of the yard.

"Go back and pull the door to," Rebecca called to him.

In disgust James flung the bolster on the ground and turned back.

Daniel chuckled mildly. "What difference, Rebecca? You are leaving of this place for good and all. What difference whether the door is shut or not?"

"I wouldn't like to think of the weather blowing in and making a ruin of the house," she replied quietly.

She looked down the string of pack horses. Eight of them, there were. Daniel had done well in his trading for the animals. They were smaller than most men would have wanted, but Daniel said you needed small, fast, sure-footed animals on the trail going into the Kentucky country, and he had reason to know, the times he had been there. She wished, though,

there had been a way to take more of the house-plunder. Not
that she questioned Daniel was right. The trace was no more
than a path, and steep and ledgy in places. No wagon could
go over the trace, he had said. Still and all, it was a wrench
to leave her beds and her tables, her chairs and the dish dresser
Daniel had made for her. It came hard to leave them, but the
worst was having to leave her loom. How she was going to
manage without it, she had no notion. Likely Daniel would
get around to building her another one but, knowing Daniel,
she knew it would be a time and a time before he got to it.
She sighed, but not in real distress. It was mostly a sigh of
habit. In twenty years of being married to Daniel Boone she
had sighed and given up many things, but mostly without too
much regret.

It was what a woman had to expect if she married up with
a restless, wandering man. And most men in this western country were what you would call wandering. Wasn't much to be
done about it. You married your man, had his children for
him, fed him, made his clothes and oftentimes his crops, tended
his home when he had one, worried over him when he was
gone, which he mostly was, never knowing whether he would
come home dead or alive, or even if he'd come home at all. You
made out, one way or another. And when he got restless and
began looking past the corn rows toward the woods and mountains, you sold out and crawled on the back of a pack horse and
went toward the west with him, for it was always the west that
pulled him. To the east were people, and comforts and an
easy way of life. All the women in the western country thought
with longing of the east. But they never looked in that direction, for they knew better. No man who ever got as far west
as the undermountain country turned his eyes east again.

"Well, it's shut, for all the good it'll do," James told her,
coming up the near horse and laying the feather bolster across

its back. "It's closed and bolted. I took the trouble, seeing you wanted it shut."

"Yes," Rebecca said. "You done good."

The lad took thongs and cinched the bolster down tight, making certain, for all his impatience with his mother for taking it, that it would be safe on the trail. She watched him, thinking how well Daniel had taught him. It pleasured Daniel for James to be so near grown now. He had been, you might say, waiting for it a long time. So they could be menfolks together. A man set such a heap of store by his sons.

Daniel took his place at the head of the train of animals. He looked back. "All set?"

James sent a proprietary glance down the line. "All set!" he called; then he stepped up and took his place by his father, topping him by a good inch. They turned their faces up the trail, and the horses fell into line behind them.

Rebecca did not mean to look back. It did no good, she had found. In spite of her intentions, however, she found herself twisting her body around to take one more long look at this last home she was leaving. Men, she thought, hadn't the feeling for places a woman had. A man wouldn't likely know what she meant when she said she left a little piece of herself behind each time she moved away from a house that had sheltered her and her brood, but there wasn't ever a woman who had left a place that wouldn't know. Whatever of yourself you had put into a place, you generally left behind you with it, so that no matter how puny a place it was, there was a sadness when it came time to turn your back on it. Likely it was but natural for a woman to want to stay put, to build fences and set out an apple tree and a rose bush . . . to know that the sun of an evening was going to set over the same place it had risen of a morning. A woman was so natured she liked a sameness. She felt better when she knew she could gather the corn in the fall she had planted in the spring. With a man it was different. Men were poured from a different mold. Ever moving, they were, like water seeking the sea.

She had known this time was coming almost from the day she had married Daniel Boone, for even then, as long ago as twenty years, he had talked of little but the land over the mountains, the Kentucky land. It was during Braddock's War, in 1755, before ever they were wed, that he had met up with John Finley who had been a trader among the Indians on the Ohio. When Daniel was home from the war and they were wed, he had remembered all the things John Finley had said, and he had told her, it was untelling the times, "It must be a fine country, Rebecca. John says there is an abundance of game of every kind. He told of seeing buffalo in such herds as to be uncounted, coming down to the salt licks. And deer and elk and bear. Pigeons and turkeys so thick they make a cloud over the sun. And the land. He told how the land was richer than any he'd ever seen, good land, well watered and prime. I have a great desire to see that land, Rebecca."

Mile by slow mile he had moved them toward it, each new shift and change taking them ever westward. He had seen the country, too, for he had gone hunting there, and when he had come home in the spring of 1776, after two eternally long years spent hunting out skins for his stake, when she had not known from one good day to the next but what he was scalped and his bones left bleaching in the elements — when he had come home, she had known the time had come. "I've got my stake," he told her, "and there's forts there now, Rebecca. There is other folks."

He had begun gathering together the families to go with him to make a stand in Kentucky. Forty head of folks all told.

79

In a way, she thought, easing the leg thrown over the saddle horn, it was a relief to have it over and done with, to be shut of it, all the talk and the speculation, and to be leaving out.

They made slow time to the Powell Valley, but if it fashed Daniel she couldn't tell. Driving milch cows and hogs on the trail was a tedious thing, although the children did as well as could be expected of them. They just naturally dallied and had to be put up with. It seemed like the horses were always rubbing the packs loose against things, too — rocks, or limbs or stumps, and time was lost having to stop and straighten them. Making camp of an evening took time, too, with the young ones to see to and the cooking to do. Even so, they reached the meeting place where they were all to come together in plenty of time.

It was a good thing to see the other womenfolk and to hear woman-talk again. Some took it in good part, this moving to Kentucky with their men, but some took it ill. "We'll never see our homes again," mourned old Mrs. Donohue, watching the sun set that evening behind the craggy cliffs that marked the gap to Kentucky. "We'll all be killed by them heathen varmints. I misdoubt we'll ever see the land itself. They'll be laying in wait for us ere we step foot on it. You mark my words!"

"The way I see it," a younger woman said, shielding her face from the heat of the fire with her arm crooked over her eyes, "Indian trouble is Indian trouble where'er it is. We've had it in good measure on the Holston. Don't see as it could be much different in Kentucky."

"My John says," another spoke up, "the land is worth the trouble. He says if enough of us go and stick together we can stand off the Indians." She was a bride and she blushed as she spoke of her John.

"What do you say, Rebecca?" they asked, turning to the wife of their leader.

She turned the browned hoecakes out onto a flat shingle of bark. "Why, what's there to say? If your man has got to see what's on the other side of the mountain, he's got to see, is all."

"And you think it's right for them to go dragging us women and young ones out there so far from home?"

Rebecca Boone's dark eyes were steady on the woman who asked. "Where is home," she said, "except where your man is."

They took a few days to get the cumbersome and now fully assembled train repacked and loaded, places and duties assigned, livestock rounded up and belled, last-minute preparations done and last-minute ructions and misgivings settled. Daniel checked and rechecked their own provisions. "I wish I'd brung along that least anvil I left at Billy Russell's," he grumbled. "And I'd like it a heap better if we had more flour and salt. Be a time till we get more out there."

Colonel Russell's station was the last place one could buy such necessaries. They had passed it two days before. "Well, it's too late now, Dan'l," Rebecca said, sensibly.

"Yes. We'd best be moving. The season's getting late."

It was September and the nights were already chill. They had to get where they were going and make some sort of provision for the winter before cold weather set in. They had taken what care they could, and there was nothing for it now but to move on out beyond, break the last ties that bound them to the settlements and go it on their own hook. They left at sun up the next morning, well ordered and well organized, guarded front, flank, and rear by Daniel's own picked riflemen, as safe as caution and experience could make them.

The first day was bound to be slow, Daniel told them when they camped that night a bare twelve miles from where they had started. They would get the hang of it in a day or two, he said. "Make camp and get your rest tonight whilst it's still safe."

He couldn't get to sleep himself, however. Rebecca felt him turning and twisting beside her. "You wearied, Dan'l?"

"No. But I'm going to send James back to Billy Russell's for that anvil tomorrow. I know in reason there'll be need of it and I can't rest for thinking of it. I'll have Billy send some more flour and salt, too."

"You aiming on waiting here?"

"No, we'll move on. He can catch us up easy, him alone that way and us moving slow."

His mind made up, he slept. It was Rebecca who was restless now. She wished Daniel would wait for the boy, but doubtless it wouldn't be fair to the others. And James was good at taking care. She had to stop thinking of him as a little fellow. He could do his part the same as the rest. It would pleasure him to be sent on the errand . . . make him feel big to be so trusted. She composed her thoughts and finally slept.

The next morning she saw to it that the boy had a good breakfast while Daniel explained what it was he wanted him to do. "Take the little sorrel mare," he concluded. "She's fast. And don't tarry. Don't lose no time. You'd ought to catch us up the day after tomorrow."

After he was mounted Rebecca walked toward the boy. Impatiently he pulled up the mare and waited. She had it on the tip of her tongue to tell him to mind out and take care, but she bit the words off. It would shame him in front of the others to be so cautioned. "Best get me another little awl," she said instead. He nodded and gave the mare her head. Rebecca watched him until he was out of sight back down the trail, the mare traveling swiftly, James's goldy-red hair bent over her neck.

The party moved slowly on westward, ever nearer the overhanging cliffs and the dark breastwork of the mountains. On the evening of the third day Rebecca caught herself listening and looking back. He ought to be turning up any time now, she thought.

When he had not come by the time they camped she felt a deep uneasiness, which she tried to hide, going about her cooking quietly as usual. The stock tethered and guards set, Daniel came up to eat his meal. "Doubtless," he told Rebecca as he ate, "Billy Russell has furnished him a heavier load than I thought, and he's made slower time. He'll be up with us in the morning."

"Yes," she said. No need dwelling on it, but Daniel had not dispelled the uneasiness.

Camp had been broken the next morning and the animals loaded when Billy Russell himself rode up, his horse lathered and breathing hard, and Billy as distraught as a man can be and still talk sense. Throwing himself off his horse he yelled for Daniel. "Daniel! Daniel Boone!"

Daniel came running.

"Daniel, a terrible thing has happened! Your boy, and mine . . . ambushed last night! They're killed. Indians! Shawnees! A big party of them!"

"Your boy?"

"I sent him along with James, and two workmen. One of the workmen had just got back from Williamsburg with a load of powder and I thought you'd welcome some extra. I came on behind and just overtook them . . . what's left of 'em. I made sure they would catch up your party yesterday, or I would never have . . ."

"Where?"

"Back down the trail. Not more than five miles. They must of camped there last night." Colonel Russell groaned. "Dan'l, they tortured 'em. Pulled out their fingernails. Stuck splinters in 'em and burned 'em and slashed 'em. Skulped 'em. They're burnt and cut till a body . . ." He broke off, his face twisted and white.

It was too late. Rebecca had come up and heard. A slow shudder, beginning in her stomach, ran over her body and ended in a weakening of her knees till she could barely stand. She felt as if her breath was being choked off in her throat. Last night, while they slept unawares, James was being hurt so . . . Her hand reached up and pushed at the knot lumping in her throat. But her voice came clearly. "They are dead now?"

The colonel swept off his hat. "Yes, ma'am." His mouth trembled and his voice shook. "I am sorry, Miz Boone."

Daniel turned quickly, his jaw tight. "There are these to think of!"

Indians! Indians! The word swept like a flame over the people and set them shaking. Daniel gave hurried orders and the party scattered down the narrow ravine in which they were camped. The women and children were herded under an overhanging bank where the roots of giant trees had hollowed out a shelter. "Stay here," they were told. "Don't move, no matter what."

They were barely hidden when shots back down the trail told that the attack had begun. Daniel gathered his men and posted them at the mouth of the ravine. "Wait till they come nigh," he warned them, "and make sure you've got a good shot. Make ever' one count."

There was no time to see to the cattle and the horses and they were immediately stampeded, crashing off into the woods in all directions. Soon the ravine was filled with the hideous yells of the Indians and the clatter and crash of gunfire. It was made more awful by the crying and moaning of the women

84

and children. Rebecca went about among them. "Hush, now,"
she soothed. "Hush. It does no good to cry. Feed the least
ones these hoecakes, and you girls — that gravelly bank looks
like there was a spring underneath. Dig there and see. We'll
all be thirsty ere long."

She went about among them fearlessly because there was
nothing in her to feel fear. There was only a deadness that
hung like a heavy weight about her neck. Nothing was real
to her, not the gunfire, nor the savage yells, nor the babies
crying. All that was real to her now was the thought of James,
lying yonder stiffened and still, his bright head shorn, his hands
gashed and cut and his tormented body mutilated. She soothed
the babies and encouraged the frightened women and there was
no break nor tremor in her voice, because she did not know
what she was doing or saying. Habit was serving her, for inside
her heart was squeezed and bleeding, crying over and over,
"My son . . . my son."

The day, in all its fear and awfulness, wore on. The Shawnees did not keep up a sustained attack. After the first great,
almost overpowering, surge they fell back; then slowly they
vanished into the woods, taking cover behind the trees and
bushes and logs, firing from hidden places that were hard for
Daniel's men to discover.

Fearing to be surrounded and besieged in the narrow cove,
Daniel fanned out his men, thinning them along the front but
covering the sides and rear. The men hid as best they could,
behind rocks, a bank of earth, a felled tree, and they fired at
the smoke of the Indians' guns. That a shot told now and then
was evident when a painted Shawnee fell, twisting, from behind a tree, his last scream drawn harshly and quaveringly
from his throat.

There would be periods of silence, lasting sometimes an hour
or more, silence so complete as to make the men wonder if the

Shawnees had crept off. But if a man grew careless, or rest-less, a shot rang out, echoing down the ravine, bouncing off the rocky ledges and dying out in a fading rumble. There would be other times when it seemed as if every Indian fired on signal, and the woods rang with the noise and filled the ravine heavily with sound and smoke. From one moment to the next, it was impossible to know what to expect.

When she had done what she could for the women and children, Rebecca went to stand where she could see. So it happened she was watching when a bullet glanced Daniel's skull and sent him reeling. She was beside him in a moment, her hands feeling, his blood staining her arms and the front of her dress. "It's but a scratch, Dan'l," she told him then, tear-ing at the hem of her dress. "I'll bind it so's the blood won't blind you."

"Knocked me down," Daniel said, "but it don't hurt much."

"No. Did you see where the shot came from?"

He shook his head. "I was loading."

Rebecca's hands finished with the bandage. "He's up there behind that biggest beech tree. Near the rim of the hollow."

"I'll get him."

But when he reached for his gun he staggered. Rebecca took it from him. "You set here a minute. I'll shoot for you till you feel able again."

He allowed her to take the gun. "I come over dizzy all at once."

"Yes."

Slowly she lifted the gun and rested it, readied it for firing. Daniel coached her. "Wait till he shows hisself. He'll not be able to keep from looking out to see. He'll edge hisself out a mite. Wait till there's enough of him to kill, then fire."

Rebecca nodded, laid her cheek along the walnut stock and waited patiently.

86

First she saw the smallest movement along the tree trunk, no more than a shadow darkening the far side. Then she saw a shoulder bulge a little larger. Her finger tightened. Boldly, then, the Indian peered out and as he did something swung loose from his chest and hung, swaying, glinting goldy-red in a shaft of bright sunlight. Rebecca's thighs quivered. She made the new scalp her target and squeezed the trigger. She saw the Indian spin and stagger, heard him yell, watched him fall heavily to the ground. She handed the gun to Daniel, and vomited sickly at his feet.

Daniel watched her, puzzled. When she lifted her head he said, "You got him."

She nodded. "He had James's scalp on him."

She walked slowly back to the cavelike shelter of the women and children and sat down on a rock. Little by little the nausea, the oily bile of her sickness, passed. She kept seeing the goldy-red scalp, swaying with the movement of the Indian, and an ague took her, shaking her achingly for a moment. That, too, passed, and when one of the least ones came up whimpering for comfort she took it on her lap, cradling it gently. "There, now. It's all right. Hush, now, there's nothing to harm you."

Toward the middle of the afternoon the firing became desultory and then it stopped entirely. The men waited. An hour passed. The men grew restless, and then one deliberately poked his hat on a long stick up above a log. It drew no fire. "They've left out," Daniel said. "They've headed for the Ohio."

Cautiously the men reconnoitred, but there was not an Indian to be found. As suddenly as they had come, they had gone, stealthily taking their wounded and dead with them. Slowly the people gathered in the mouth of the ravine and the women and children, freed, formed knots about their menfolk.

The party was not without its casualties. Isaac Cooper was bad hurt, a shot through his stomach. He would die within a matter of hours. James Goodwin was also badly hurt, his leg being broken, but he had a chance to live. Robert Whitney had a flesh wound in his shoulder, and Daniel had his skull creased. Only one man had been killed outright. They had been lucky, they felt. It could have been so much worse.

As the tension of the fighting eased and the talk grew louder, however, there were hysterical overtones in the women's voices. "Lord have mercy," they wept, "but it was terrible."

"We'll have to turn back now. We can't go on. We're too bad hurt."

"This is just the beginning — this near the settlements, too. We'd best turn back while we can."

And higher and more hysterical than all the others was old Mrs. Donohue's voice. "I said it! I warned you! I said they'd lay for us. It's going against the will of the Lord to go on, I tell you! I'm crossing no mountains! I'm going back to my home!"

Apart from them sat the young bride, a widow now, the dazed tears making pools on her round young face, John Steever's head pillowed in her lap. "You'd best tell her," Daniel said to Rebecca, "that we've got to bury him now."

Rebecca went to her, spoke gently, lifted her up and held her while the men carried off the man who had said so surely the land was worth fighting for. Someone else would get the worth of it, for John Steever would never see it now.

When the men returned Rebecca went up to Daniel. "Can we have a fire, Dan'l? These need something hot to eat and drink. They will calm down quicker with hot vittles inside of them."

He nodded. "No harm. There's ne'er an Indian within miles of us, nor won't be again."

While the women cooked, the men rounded up what was left of the livestock and tethered the animals. More than half of them were gone. Many of the pack horses, including four of Daniel's, were missing. The provisions and packs were scattered and burst and no one could yet tell how much was lost. The people were bewildered by the attack. It was not to be expected so near the settlements. They were frightened and their courage had drained away. As they ate they muttered among themselves. They wanted to start back at once. No use waiting till another day. "We want to turn back now, Daniel. This is the Lord's hand pointing the way."

"Yes, God knows, it was not meant to be."

"We want to go home, and we aim to leave out ere night falls."

Daniel raised his hand and they quieted. "We knew," he said, "when we left the settlements there would be Indians to contend with. It wasn't likely they'd start pestering so soon and it was bad luck that a war party of Shawnees should be crossing just now. But they have cleared out. They've took what they wanted of the stock and have made tracks for the Ohio. Likely we can finish the journey without more trouble. We are a strong party. We can send back for more provisions and we can go on."

"No!"

"Don't listen to him!"

"I'm turning back, now!"

"It's not you," a woman's voice cried, "that lost your man today . . ." Then, remembering, John Steever's widow put her hand over her mouth and shrank back into the crowd.

"We'll decide in order," Daniel said. "We'll take a vote." He pointed to a tall man up front. "How do you vote, Jonathan Derwent?"

"I say go back!"

"Benjamin Graham?"

"Go back!"

"Abraham Lyne?"

"I'm turning back."

The voting went on. Not a voice was lifted in favor of going on. Rebecca sat by the fire and waited, her least ones about her knees. Maybe Daniel would go back, too. Maybe now that he knew no one would go on, he would turn back his own head. Maybe now that his whole party favored turning back, he would forget that other land and take her home again and they would live peaceably in the settlements and raise up these least ones decent and God-fearing as young ones were meant to be raised up. It was too late for James, but these others . . .

She looked about her strange surroundings. Back home the late sun would be shining softly on the shingleboards of the cabin roof. The rail fence would be warm from its heat, and the apple tree at the corner of the house would be throwing a long shadow across the steppingstones. Back home it was almost time to cut the corn and gather the pumpkins and pick off the gourds from the vine on the woodshed. Back home these least ones would be safe.

She lifted her eyes and looked at the craggy mountains that barred the road to the west. The rock cliffs were already shadowed and they looked broody and dark and forbidding. That way lay the wilderness road — a weary and blood-stained road. She shivered slightly and wished she might not have to travel it.

At last the voting ended and the question she had been waiting for was put. "What do you aim to do, Daniel? What are your intentions?"

She saw the sandy head go up, saw the thin mouth firm, saw the faded, squint-wrinkled eyes turn toward the mountains. Before he spoke she knew what he was going to say. His face had been turned westward too long. "I aim to go on. My intentions are just what they was in the beginning. They've not changed."

90

There was a clamor of voices. "Alone? You'll never make it!"
"By yourself?"

"On your own hook? Man, you're crazy!"

Stubbornly, he insisted. "The danger is over, I tell you. There
will not be another Indian betwixt here and the forts."

They shook their heads, not willing to believe, and then they
crowded around Rebecca. "Come back with us, Rebecca."

"You can stay with us till Dan'l makes a place for you."

"Bring your least ones and go with us."

"He can come for you next year."

She looked at Daniel and saw that he was watching her. Her
hand touched the soft hair of the child leaning against her
knees. Daniel nodded at her. "I can come for you next season, Rebecca."

Quietly she stroked the child's hair. James's had been just as
soft. Then she looked slowly around at the people clustered
about. "I thank you," she said, relinquishing the home, the
Yadkin, the peace, the safety, "but I reckon I'd best go with
Daniel."

In goodness of heart the people shared with them, then.
"Take my big bay, Dan'l. He'll carry a right smart load."

"Take this flour. We can get more in the settlements."

"You can have this bar of lead, Dan'l. I'll not be needing it
now."

"Here, Rebecca, is my Rose of Sharon quilt."

They accepted the things offered, setting them quietly aside;
then they helped the people make up their dwindled packs. At
the last there were a few tears, a few shamed looks among the
men and then they were gone, back down the trail over which,
only yesterday, they had come.

Daniel slid wearily to a log. Rebecca handed him a bowl of
food and he looked up at her, his eyes unseeing what it was
she was handing him. They had a burned look, as if they had

been turned in on themselves and glazed by what they had seen. Her heart lunged and tightened within her. A man set such a heap of store by his sons. In all their days together she had never seen Daniel look like this. He was hurting fearfully inside. He had been hurting like this all the time, but now he could let it show. "Here," she told him, "eat now."

Methodically, he obeyed her, eating all that was in the bowl. When he had finished he put the bowl down beside the log and went to catch up one of the horses. "Before it's dark," he said, "I'm going back to bury him."

"Yes," she said. "Wait."

She went to one of the packs. Her roughened hands fumbled with the knots. He had tied them so good . . . James. For all his scorn of her woman's ways he had made sure that nothing would happen to it. Patiently she raveled each knot to its end and pulled loose the feather bolster. She carried it to Daniel. "Here. I'd like him to lay easy, Dan'l."

His tormented eyes met hers. "Rebecca, they . . . Rebecca!"

She did not fail him. Never in her life had she failed him and she did not now. She would have time to grieve later. She would have all her life to grieve. Now she must comfort this man who had lost his son, who was tormented because it was through him he had been lost, but who even yet could not give up the dream that had driven him to the loss. "There, Dan'l. There. It's all over for him and he is at peace."

"Yes. I'll be back."

He settled the feather bolster in front of the saddle and rode off down the trail. Rebecca watched him out of sight. Then she turned and laid down the Rose of Sharon quilt for a bed for her least ones.

ACCORDING TO HIS LIGHTS

"A ridgerunner is a man who does the best he can, with what
he's got, according to his lights."

Old Appalachian Proverb

"To the Appalachian the outsider is ignorant of all the simplest, most basic things."

40 Acres and No Mule

JOHN F. KENNEDY turned the spotlight of national attention
upon Appalachia in the 1960 presidential campaign. For fifty
years before it had been a provocative subject for study but
since 1960 the region has been surveyed, studied, researched,
measured, charted, polled, tabulated, photographed and televised
intensely and almost continuously.

The cause of all this study, the Appalachian, is always found
to be irritating, frustrating, stubborn, inflexible and poverty-
stricken almost beyond hope. After all the measuring, charting
and surveying, he is still the cause of uneasy bafflement. He still
remains almost totally incomprehensible to the average American
mind.

In this plethora of material, I have hoped it would be possible
for someone to explore in depth the most informing thing about
the Appalachian, his religious concepts. I have hoped it would
be recognized that he is who, why and what he is because he
is a member of one of the most legalistic, primitively biblical
societies ever formed. But as more and more material has been
published, it is impossible not to realize that even in this modern
day the Appalachian has not opened more than a chink the

93

closed wall of distrust, resentment and dislike that stands between him and all "outsiders." Someone from the "inside" must
therefore speak up.

The latest of the Appalachian studies to be written is by the
Reverend Mr. Jack Weller, a Presbyterian minister who has lived
and worked among the mountain people for the past twelve years.
He has summed up their structure and habits, their dependence
upon socially approved patterns of behavior and the pervasiveness
of their religious concepts. Both the Indian tribal society and the
Appalachian family society have many characteristics common to
all primitive societies.

Primitive societies are markedly similar in being closed and
tribal, the members (by western standards) inarticulate, naive
and childlike, emotionally immature, impulsive, easily bored,
lacking in self-discipline, unable to maintain interest over long
spans of time. They are characterized by family and group orien-
tation and loyalties. Harmony within the group or tribe is essential and any singularity or individuality is frowned upon. Leadership within the tribe is achieved in accepted ways within the
framework of tribal approval. The members of the tribe are
apprehensive of change, suspicious of strangers; they have their
own codes of honor; they devotedly love small children, are per-
missive with them, but they expect youth, at puberty, to enter
the adult life. Their religion is personal and central to life,
highly emotional and characterized by noise and action. Death is
marked by loud weeping and ritual mourning.

These things have been accepted for years in other primitive
societies. Because it is not understood that Appalachia is also
tribal and primitive they cause anger, irritation, frustration and
contempt in those who come in contact with the Appalachians,
or try to work with them. The fact that the Appalachian is who,
why, what, when and where he is rightfully and inevitably as a

result of his place in his own society has largely escaped study and reflection.

Without understanding this, the approach to a study of Appalachia has several built-in factors that lead to error. First, the researcher is as inevitably a product of his own culture as the Appalachian is of his. He brings to his study the inbred assumption that the molds that turned him out are the right molds and his own culture the right culture, and the Appalachian is a part of that same culture and can be measured by the approved measuring instruments. He comes into the area from the outside and he observes, views, questions, interviews, surveys, analyzes, and he assumes that the results he gets are accurate. They may be and they may not be.

Let me use just one illustration to show how unrealistic some kinds of statistics can be for the Appalachian. Suppose an opinion poll is taken to determine how many Appalachians value education. Now, an opinion poll is about the most meaningless kind of survey that can be taken in Appalachia, but the surveyor is not aware of it. From long training in the importance of tribal harmony and approval, the Appalachian has developed an immense respect for all social approval. He has an extremely sensitive antenna for sensing what the approved attitude and reply will be.

He has also been exposed to civilization long enough now to understand that outside values are placed upon many things that have been relatively valueless to him. So the very fact that an opinion poll is being taken gives him his first clue to the kind of replies he should give. The questions in this survey are important or they would not be asked. The way the interviewer looks, his tone of voice, what he unconsciously stresses or does not stress, all give the Appalachian further directions. He is now asked if he values education. Many Appalachians do, but the man who does not knows he is expected to, so he gives the expected reply.

When the researcher has finished, he tabulates his results and he arrives at a figure. Out of so many people questioned, 80 percent, say, replied that they valued education. Seeing the figure, the sociologist concludes that interest in education in Appalachia is rising. Actually, the figure means nothing of the sort. It means only that 80 percent of the people interviewed *said* they valued education. Nobody knows how many truly value it. Nobody knows how many, sensing the approved reply, gave it. You have a meaningless statistic — *if* you know Appalachia.

The researcher can compile thousands of tables of statistics. They are easily obtained. But an interpretation of them is something different altogether. When all the statistics are in and tabulated there is a picture of the Appalachian. But it is like a still photograph. The life is missing.

Second, the only valid measuring sticks, the Appalachian's religious concepts and his family life, are very difficult to obtain because of the Appalachian's inherent dislike, distrust and resentment of the outsider. Nearly every Indian speaks of his tribe as "the People." His ways are the "right" ways; his mores, norms, standards are the "right" ones. No Indian wants, either, to be a white man. So with the Appalachian. It would amaze the outsider, probably, to learn that the Appalachian feels superior to him, considers him inept, more than a little ridiculous and foolish. The outsider, to the Appalachian, is ignorant to the point of ridiculousness of the simplest, most basic things. He comes breezing in, too hearty, too familiar too soon. He is ill mannered. He is "talky" and "pushy" and "nosey." He is "braggy" and always showing off. He rushes around and makes a complete idiot of himself. With the outsider, the Appalachian is courteous. He opens his doors and is hospitable. But not for one minute, so long as an outsider is present, is he himself. All the time the outsider is present the Appalachian is sensing, feeling, reacting as he thinks the outsider expects him to. He approves or disapproves according to the leading he obtains from the look, the voice, the mannerisms of the guest. When the guest has left, the family commune together laughingly. "Ain't he got the foolishest notions? But I reckon we done all right. Told him what he wanted to know." They have done precisely that. As best they could sense it, they have told him not what they truly believed, but what he wanted to hear.

Appalachia is made up of many parts, regions and subdivisions. It is not one amorphous mass. Much of it is coal-mining region, much of it marginal farm areas, much of it ridge-and-saddle, much "up the holler," much spur and fringe. Each subregion may have a few individual characteristics because of its own peculiar conditions, but anyone who has traveled through the whole vast network, worked in it, visited, studied it, as I have done, with the entrée of an Appalachian husband who is at home with any other Appalachian, is impressed with the consistency of certain traits, characteristics, mores and norms that run through all the counties and the various states like a common cord. Indeed, it is the very consistency of these traits in *all* of Appalachia that enables anyone to speak at all of "Appalachia."

I am not an Appalachian by birth, but I have been married to one for twenty-eight years and have lived as a member of this primitive society within the family, the religion, the economics and the politics of the society. I have had an excellent workshop in which to study and what I have learned has been learned in the intimacy of acceptance within the society. I have not, however, limited my study to the immediate environment. What I have learned has been checked against all the other regions of Appalachia, West Virginia, North Carolina, upper Georgia and our own Cumberland plateau counties. I have found everywhere the same religious concepts and the same close family loyalties and traditions.

In the north end of Adair County in Kentucky, we are not the deep mountains or the coal-mining regions. We are hill-and-holler farm and timber people. We live in the intricately tangled hills and hollows of a broad, long, fingering mass of spurs and foothills of the Cumberlands. Here there is a pocket of pure Appalachianism, without the admixture of foreign blood prevalent in some of the mining areas. We have had slight influxes of West Virginia and North Carolina Appalachians since the 1920s. These people are perfectly at home among us, with religious beliefs and family ways entirely like ours. My husband's father used to go into West Virginia to work in the mines in the winters. He was perfectly at home there. My husband's people have lived in this community for seven generations. We live within two miles of the spot the first of his people settled in 1803.

It was almost totally inaccessible country when my husband first brought me here. It had no road system, no electricity, no telephones. One graveled road led in. Dirt roads, creek beds and logging slides were used to get about up the ridges and down the hollows. The mail was carried by jeep, and when a creek that had to be forded three times was up, it did not arrive. I remember one snowbound time when there was no mail for a week. Supplies were brought in by a "huckster" — a sort of traveling grocery store. His schedule was once a week but in the winter we were lucky if he got through once a month. And in winter the only way we could reach the county town was by a logging slide down the back side of the ridge, on down a creek bed, then around devious dirt roads. A jeep could do it but a mule would have been better.

Less than five miles from us was even more rugged country in which one big family-clan lived, intermarried and bred for generations. To drive down their ridge, when you could, was to see with only a few exceptions the same last name on every mailbox for ten miles. The last killing in a fifty-year-long intrafamily feud had occurred as late as 1930.

I groped and fumbled in this new environment and the first few years caused my husband and his people much embarrassment. But slowly, within the family, with much patient, gentle, courteous guidance, I was instructed in the right ways, the right language, the right behavior. I was told not to talk so much, not to ask questions, never to dispute, argue or correct. I was taught never to offer advice. I was told if I did not agree with someone to keep quiet. I was told I must never act as if I took pride in anything I had done or owned. I was taught that it was all right to tell news but that gossip was frowned on. The difference between news and gossip, I learned, was in the expression of personal opinion or judgment. To my chagrin I learned that allowances were made for my ignorance because I had not been properly "raised up." I could not be expected to know much.

I could behave discreetly enough, but my "ways" caused considerable consternation. I had brought with me the furnishings of a four-room apartment in the city, which included a piano, rugs, walls of books, my desk and typewriter. The way I cooked, the way my home was furnished, the way I kept my house, the way I occupied myself within it could not be hidden and all were conclusive evidence that I was "proud" and that I "put myself above other people." The entire family-clan rallied loyally to apologize. Admittedly I was "quare," but it was to be remembered I was from "off." I had had these things in the city. I could not be expected to discard them. An apology also had to be made for the fact that I "wrote books" and did not tend chickens, cows, pigs or even the "garden patch." A good neighbor, a woman I came to love dearly, could not believe that any woman could be happy without "something to tend." She furnished me with a dozen baby chickens shortly after we had got settled in.

Slowly, very slowly, I realized that nearly everything the Appalachian is proceeds from his religious concepts. The Bible was quoted to me so constantly as the basis for all behavior that it was impossible not to understand eventually that in everything that matters the Appalachian actually lives in Thessalonica, Philippi, Corinth and especially in Ephesus and Galatia. The apostle Paul writes letters to him. He tells the Appalachians what they should believe and down to the minutest detail how they shall behave. No aspect, no intimacy, of their life escapes his instruction. He admonishes them, chides them; he grows impatient with them; he warns and encourages them; he guides and directs; and he promises them the kingdom of heaven if they are faithful. They strive to understand him and to obey him, and they wait for the chariot to swing low and carry them home. In the whole pattern of his life the Appalachian is an early Christian.

This did not tally at all with what I had always read, that the Appalachian is irreligious. There were even statistics to prove it. Only 10 percent to 15 percent of all Appalachians belonged to churches. But no society is entirely irreligious. In the whole recorded history of man no society has ever been found in which there were not religious concepts of some sort that bound it together, informed and furnished its habits and customs. Why, then, was the Appalachian, so biblically religious that his entire society was based on it, considered irreligious? *Because he did not join churches!* And the facts were incontrovertible.

In almost a hundred years of effort, the established and organized churches have made so little impression on him that the percentage of those belonging to churches in Appalachia has risen only a meager amount — from around 5 percent to 10 to 15 percent. And if that final figure were broken down it would undoubtedly show that fully half of it is concentrated in the towns — that 5 percent would be a truer figure for rural and village Appalachians. Why? There had to be a reason. He was religious, rigidly religious, but he *would not join churches.*

The truth was slow to unfold as I pursued this study, but it finally became clear. The Appalachian is a Pauline Christian, a biblical Christian, but he is not only nondenominational, he is violently antidenominational. He will have nothing to do with organized churches, that is, the established churches with a central organization, church membership rolls, a literature and an educated ministry, because the organized churches are "denominations."

Many Appalachians believe the denominations had their origins at the tower of Babel and have been scattering confusion over the face of the earth ever since. To him, the denominations not only have no scriptural authority, but far, far worse, they have "added to" the Bible and thus are actually guilty of "going against the Bible." To many Appalachians *it is a sin to belong to a denomination.*

The only "denominations" he will have anything to do with are those that claim *not* to be denominations — such as the splinter groups that have broken away from the established churches, the many Baptist splinter groups, the various primitive groups that have also arisen from rigid Bible interpretations. These groups rarely have a central organization, do not insist upon church membership rolls, do not have an educated ministry.

Every census year, therefore, for generations the Appalachian has replied to the question concerning his church affiliation, the denomination to which he belongs, "I don't belong to none." This was my mother-in-law's reply in the census year of 1950, which she made in my presence and set me to thinking and studying. She had added, "I don't hold with the denominations." There is no more deeply, devoutly, truly religious person in the world than my mother-in-law. She is the purest example of the

Appalachian Christian I know, yet all her long life she has replied to any question concerning her church affiliation, "I don't belong to *no* church." Multiply this by hundreds of thousands of Appalachians, over the generations, and there is the statistical assumption that, because so few belong to churches, the Appalachian is irreligious.

The early Appalachian brought at least some vague denominational concepts and theology with him into Appalachia. Because he was largely Scotch-English in origin, they were mostly Calvinist. But separated from society he slowly developed his own Bible-based religion and he largely based it on the remembered scriptural basis for the doctrines of Calvinism.

Harry Caudill in *Night Comes to the Cumberlands* tells how for so long the doctrine of infant damnation anguished the souls of the Appalachians. But slowly this denominational concept, too, was abandoned. Using the Pauline epistles mostly for guidance, interpreting them as best he could for himself, the Appalachian became wholly nondenominational.

There was no ministry. Paul enjoined him that any man led of the Spirit should be heard, so he raised up his own lay ministry. Paul had taken no pay except hospitality in his ministry; he had earned his living in other ways as other men did. Therefore a preacher should not be paid for preaching. He should be given hospitality, a collection might be taken up to pay his expenses, but he should never make his living by preaching. To this day the Appalachian has an in-built dislike for the educated minister who has made of the ministry a paid profession. Preaching is a grace, added to man by the Spirit, and he should not cash in on it. The educated, denominational minister has a harder row to hoe in Appalachia than almost any outsider because he violates so many of the Appalachian's long-held, traditional religious concepts.

The Appalachian's religious concepts dictate the social patterns for him. Much of his social behavior is grounded specifically in the apostle Paul's letter to the Galatians. He is told here not to indulge in backbiting, and that all works of the flesh are to be avoided. They are spelled out in detail. He is to avoid adultery, fornication, uncleanness, lasciviousness, idolatry, witchcraft, hatred, variance, emulations, wrath, strife, seditions, heresies, envyings, murders, drunkenness, revelings, and such like. He is told not to be desirous of vainglory, provoking one another, and that if a man thinks himself to be something when he is nothing, he is deceived. The Appalachian strives to avoid all these things.

He is also reminded here to love his neighbor as himself, to honor his father and mother, to do good. He is told that the fruit of the Spirit is love, joy, peace, long-suffering, gentleness, goodness, faith, and that if he lives in the Spirit, he must walk in the Spirit. He is promised a place in the kingdom of heaven if he is faithful. He believes these things and he strives to abide by them.

The outsider coming in thus finds a society in which a man does not seek leadership, in which individuality is sunk and any singularity is frowned upon. These things would be desiring vainglory. The Appalachian would be thinking he is something. He would be putting himself forward; he would be elevating himself above others; he would be acting as if he were better than others. He would be walking proud.

The outsider finds men who will not engage in free debate. It is argument and variance. It is provoking one another. It generates wrath, hatred, strife. It is troublemaking. Feelings get stirred up. People are hurt and there is general unpleasantness. Except in matters of religious and biblical interpretation, so important to the Appalachian because it concerns his immortal soul, he is not disputatious. He strives in all ways to be pleasant, agreeable, to give no offense.

The outsider finds a people who are remarkably honorable,

good and decent personally and in their dealings with each other. In a day when all the corruption and evil of which mankind is capable seems to be coming like pus out of its pores, it is healing to find an entire people, still, who so honor the commandments that they do not, generally, lie or cheat or steal. Even a white lie comes hard to an Appalachian, and stealing is held in such abhorrence that it is not necessary to lock one's doors.

In Appalachia a man's word, in personal dealings, is as good as his bond, quite literally. Thou shalt not bear false witness is taken seriously. From the sale of a cow or a car, to the sale of a tract of timber or house and land, the Appalachian does not knowingly misrepresent anything about it. Every trade or sale is concluded with, "Now, if it ain't just like I've told you, let me know and I'll make it right." He does make it right if some error has crept in.

The outsider will find a society where men and women honor their marriage vows and the divorce rate is very low. He will find a people who honor their parents. Not even an adult Appalachian will argue with, quarrel with or speak disrespectfully to his parents, and in their old age parents are cherished and cared for in the home of a married son or daughter.

Not organization-minded, the Appalachian does not channel his good works through the church or the community. He is personally committed to being a good neighbor. With his own kind he is generous to a fault, his hospitality is boundless, and no call for help goes unheeded. The opposite of more sophisticated people who do not like to be personally involved, the Appalachian feels he *must* be personally involved.

The outsider coming in will find a people so courteous, in whom courtesy is so practiced and ingrained, that it has become almost the gentle Oriental custom of saving face. Never do you expose a man to ridicule or humiliation and embarrassment.

The Reverend Mr. Jack Weller in his book, *Yesterday's Peo-*

ple, cites one of the most beautiful examples of this type of face-saving I have come across. It went awry because Mr. Weller did not know his role. He tried to get the opinion and decision of a church committee to repair the church driveway with mine slate, which could be had free. No one would venture an opinion. Thinking the men were shy of speaking up, Mr. Weller went ahead with the project and the inevitable happened. The first hard rain turned the mine slate into mush and mire and he had to have it bulldozed off.

Every man on that committee knew what would happen, but not one spoke up. Mr. Weller says he was later told they did not want to oppose him. True. But the rest of the story they could not tell him. They were embarrassed by Mr. Weller's ignorance, made extremely uncomfortable by it. But to tell him he was wrong would have been to show up his ignorance and make him look ridiculous. This they were too courteous to do.

Unbelievably sensitive to any loss of face himself, the Appalachian could never have comprehended that Mr. Weller would not have felt ridiculous, that he would have laughed at his own ignorance, that he would have been grateful for their advice.

I wish Mr. Weller had known his Appalachian a little better, for he would have known that by the lack of comment the project was unworkable and he would have dropped the whole matter. For if the Appalachian cannot agree with you, he will in no way explain further. He will simply keep silent. Had Mr. Weller known this he could have saved his *committee's* face. As it was, he did the worst thing he could have done. He persisted and in his failure he not only made a ridiculous figure of himself before the entire community, he made a ridiculous figure of all his church people. *Their* preacher had been foolish.

But this is the kind of intimate, intricate interweaving of thought and action that is so mystifying to the outsider and so wholly understood by the Appalachian that he could not, if he would, explain it. It would require an explanation of the entire social structure. It has been the pattern of his behavior for generations; it is the only pattern of behavior he knows, and he can only assume it will be understood.

As a woman, I have often wished the apostle Paul had not been a bachelor and, I strongly suspect, a dyspeptic one at that. He might not have made a wife's place so lowly had he been a husband. But the place assigned to wives, accepted and practiced by generations of Appalachians, is found in Paul's letter to the Ephesians, in particular the fifth chapter:

> Wives, submit yourselves unto your own husbands, as unto the Lord.
> For the husband is the head of the wife, even as Christ is the head of the church: and he is the saviour of the body.
> Therefore as the church is subject unto Christ, so let the wives be to their own husbands in every thing.

In all ways a husband is the head of the house. He makes every decision; he does not share his opinions with his wife or ask hers. His will is the only will. A wife is silent, obeys her husband and serves him. She does not ever in public dispute him, cross his wishes or in any way cause him embarrassment or humiliation, with her tongue or with her actions. She does not eat at table with him, not, at least, until recently. This habit has changed. She and her daughters used to serve the husband and sons. When the men had finished, the women ate. In church she sat apart from him, with other women. In walking together, a wife walked behind her husband.

I have vivid memories of my first years on "the ridge," when I watched my husband's old uncle — the patriarch of his family-clan, walk down the dirt road to "meetin'" every Saturday evening. It would be "first dark" — dusk. In one hand he carried an unlit lantern to be used going home. In the other was his Bible.

He walked exactly in the middle of the road. Behind him, six paces perhaps, dutifully followed his tough little knot of a wife.

He was the only one left on the ridge, the last of a long, long line to adhere so rigidly to the tradition. But to the day he died, four or five years ago, he and his wife followed the old way.

Slowly the Pauline conception of husband-wife relationships has been ameliorated, but there are still holdovers of it. Appalachian wives still wait on their husbands more than most wives, still defer to them publicly, still teach their children to honor their father as the head of the family.

In the early days, struggling to interpret the Bible, to determine the right ways and the right behavior, the recognized most purely religious man, through his long study of the Bible, its portents, prophecies and admonitions, and through his own conduct, became the most respected man. To this day the man most respected, most honored, most admired in Appalachia is not the man who acquires the most education, riches, possessions. He is the man who, according to Appalachian concepts, is the most religious man — the best Christian. There are no upper, middle and lower classes in Appalachia. There are only two classes — sinners and Christians. A man is a sinner until he has the mystical experience of being "saved." He is then a Christian.

We have one evangelist in the state, one voice crying in the wilderness, one conscience crying shame. If Harry Caudill's Southern Mountain Authority could have become a reality, a federal project as was the Tennessee Valley Authority, a long step would have been taken toward solving the Appalachian problem. Since Appalachia is being supported largely out of the public purse already, it is difficult to understand why an enlightened government did not move in this direction until one remembers that it is Bethlehem Steel, U.S. Steel, Ford Motor Company, International Harvester and others who are so entrenched in the area. Perhaps the federal government flinches, as do the state governments, from antagonizing these industrial giants. One also remembers that through the enlargement of T.V.A. the federal government, ironically, has a vested interest in Appalachian coal.

President Kennedy enjoined us, "Ask not what your country can do for you . . ." But the Appalachian *must* ask, and he deserves a better reply than he is getting.

WHEN THE 'LECTRIC COME
TO THE RIDGE

"As the Appalachian child grows older he begins to shape
and form in the mold of his society."
                                        40 Acres and No Mule

THE BOY held his dog to heel while the butterfly, speared by a
shaft of sunlight through the woods that bordered the river,
teetered over a trumpet flower. "Hit's goin' to light," he whispered to the dog. "Hit's goin' to light an' then we kin see its
wings."

The butterfly hovered uncertainly, warmed by the sun, beating
its wings ecstatically in the drenching sweetness that poured from
the flower. This flower, or that. It was undecided. This deep,
unpierced bell of bloom, or that dark, amber tear of honey. Rap-
turously it circled and dipped over the vine, tipping a wing at a
trumpet and then, unable to bear such sweetness, spiraling dizzily
upward. Here, there, it flitted, wavering, fluttering, darting. A
quiver threaded the ribs of its wings and they spread and dropped
over the bell of the trumpet.

A sigh slipped from the boy's throat and his hand touched the
dog warningly. He slid one foot noiselessly forward and bent to
look. The sun laid a bright bar across his slight shoulders and
touched his straw-thatched head with gold. His face tensed and
stilled as he looked, and he whispered, "Hit's blue." His mouth
quivered and a tremble of excitement shook him. "Hit's blue,
with yaller spots. Oh, hit's the purtiest one we've ever seed!
Look, Jupe, hit's got red around the aidges!"

The dog had been still as long as he could. He yawned and settled back on his haunches to scratch at a flea. Frightened, the butterfly bent its wings rigidly and then lifted them into startled flight.

"Now see what you done," the boy scolded. "You done skeered it away. Cain't you never be still when yer 'sposed to? Hit was arestin', an' you skeered it away."

The dog whimpered and slid to its belly, inching toward the boy, thumping its tail and licking pleadingly at the boy's feet. It fawned and begged and held its shamed eyes from the beloved face.

The boy relented. "Well, I reckon you never knowed no better. An' if a flea's bitin', I reckon you gotta scratch. But it looks like they're allus bitin' jist when you'd ort to be still. Lost me that squirrel down in the holler other day. An' you done skeered the fishes plumb outen the Beaver Hole chasin' that rabbit jist now. I'd ort to wup you one, that's what I ort to do. But I'll not today. Next time, though, you jist let them thar fleas ketch you."

The dog went wild with joy, knowing he was forgiven, and leaped and plunged and circled and pawed. His tail beat a fast tattoo in the air and he pranced jubilantly. Then he dashed to a fallen tree and dug madly at a groundhog hole. He barked importantly and eyed the boy anxiously. Just see, he said, just see what I've found. "Humph," the boy snorted, "you needn't to be showin' off thataway. That ole den's so old the groundhog's been dead a year. C'mon now. You done ruint the fishin'. Let's go dig some sang." He hauled in his fishing line and took it off the pole. He cast the green cane aside. "C'mon, boy."

They followed a path though the woodsy bottoms, across a field, and began to climb the ridge. The boy's eyes took in the gum and sassafras, the sumach, the heavy veins of dogwood seedlings. Morning dew hung sparkly and brilliant on every leaf and blade, showering a small rain across the path when the dog brushed against the bushes. The boy stopped at a hickory tree and looked closely at the hulls scattered under it. "They's been a squirrel here," he told the dog. "Yestiddy, likely. Them nuts is still fresh. We'll bring the gun an' git him tomorrer."

The dog's ears stood up and his tail went stiff. "Now now, Jupe," the boy said. "We ain't got the gun this time. Tomorrer we'll come back an' git him." The dog let down and trotted back to the path.

When the path cleared the woods and penciled off through a pasture the boy and the dog angled on down the ridge. "Ain't no use lookin' fer sang hereabouts," the boy said. "Wait'll we git down in the holler."

The north face of the ridge swelled gently, easily, shouldering itself toward the deep ravine that gashed it midway. Suddenly the easy slope sheered off abruptly and plunged downward. Steep and sharp it fell straight down into the holler, its sides patched with thick rugs of moss under the trees. The boy dug in his heels and slid from one bed of moss to another, sinking his feet deep in the soft mat, letting its plush brake him against the downhill pull. The dog scampered ahead, waiting in the easy places.

The floor of the holler was narrow, boxing in a shallow stream that raced rapidly between its walls. White water foamed around the rocks and chattered noisily. The boy and the dog drank deeply and then followed the stream up the holler, branching off into a deeper ravine on the right. Here the floor widened and was bedded with a heavy leaf mold through which a rank growth of small sprouts and plants pushed themselves.

"Now, this is it," the boy said. "Here's whur the sang grows best. I takened notice o' this place last year."

He cut a slender sapling and sharpened it with his big barlow knife. "Right thar by that down tree" — he pointed the stick —

"they'll be a patch." The dog laughed and wagged his tail. "You'll see," said the boy. "Jist you wait an' see." They came up to the log. "See thar! I told you hit'd be thar."

Across the log a bed of ginseng lay dark and green, slender stems spiking upward, pronging at the top to bear the soft ivy green leaves. "All of 'em three-prongs," the boy exulted. "No! That's one of 'em a four-prong. See that thar big un next the log, Jupe? See, hit's got four prongs! Oh, hit's untellin' whenever we've found a four-prong un."

Jupiter sniffed the log and hoisted his leg. "You, Jupe!" the boy yelled and the dog fled ignominiously.

Gently the boy dug the plants from their bed and, breaking off the tops, slid the roots into his overalls pocket. "Hit won't take many like them thar to weigh heavy," he said. "We'll have us three-four ounces 'fore you know it. Bet ole John Barry's eyes bug out when we take 'em in the store. Bet he'll be s'prised we got so much. Bet hit'll bring anyways three-four dollars."

When they had cleaned the bed he and the dog wandered on, up the big holler and down it, up the little un and across, always looking for the dark-veined sang whose roots, when dried, were good medicine for so many ailments, and which brought seventy cents an ounce when sold to the country storekeeper at the Gap.

The boy's pockets filled until they bulged and the dark hollers grew bright with the noon-riding sun. A steamy, airless heat rose from the walled ravine. The dog no longer raced ahead. He lay in the shade waiting, his tongue lolling and his sides heaving. The boy's shirt turned dark with sweat. He squinted up into the sun. "Reckon it's about time to go home," he decided. "Dinner'll be ready time we git thar."

He whistled to the dog and they started the steep climb out. The boy was reaching for a root to pull up by when he stopped abruptly. His nose wiggled and he sniffed. A faint, sour smell lay on the air. He turned and sniffed again. It was stronger now.

He stiffened. "Jupe," he called. "You, Jupe! Here! Copperheads! Here, Jupe, copperheads! Git 'em, boy!"

The dog circled the boy, nosing carefully, a deep growl rumbling in his throat. His ruff was stiff on his neck and his mouth snarled, leaving his teeth bare and white. Carefully he moved, circling, tightening the circle every round. The boy stood motionless, only his eyes following the dog. "Git him, Jupe," he whispered. "Git him!"

Suddenly the dog pounced and then jerked his head high, his front paws stiff against the ground. The boy saw the white teeth bury themselves in the snake's neck and watched while the dog flung the snake from side to side. "Good, Jupe," he said. "Good dog."

He leaned against the tree and felt a little sick. A copperhead allus did skeer him. The dog finished off the snake and came trotting over, tail high. There you are, he said to the boy. Not a thing to it. Just part of the day's work. If he could, he'd have dusted off his paws. The boy bent and hugged him. "Good dog. Good dog."

They came clear of the woods on the rutted, dusty road that saddled the hogback of the ridge. The boy plopped his feet in the dust, squeezing it up between his toes, squirming over its heat. The dog lagged behind, his tail drooping. The road was noon-hot, heavy and long. The boy switched idly with his stick at the weeds, spraying the thick powder of dust that lay on them into the air. He sneezed and threw the stick away. Wish it wasn't so fur home, he thought.

Dinner smokes were tailing out of the cabin chimneys when they came around the bend upon a crew of men working by the side of the road. There were tall poles lying in the field and a great roll of wire was heaped to one side. The boy's eyes widened and he edged toward the men.

They were digging a deep hole in the ground and one of the

men was painting the end of a pole with something that smelled sharp and tangy. It turned the pole black. Nearer and nearer the boy inched. Another man had some queer-looking thing strapped on his legs. It had spikes on it.

"Hi, sonny," the man painting the pole called.

The boy ducked his head in an agony of shyness and wiggled his toes. He noticed the patches on the knees of his overalls and felt shame for them.

"Cat's got his tongue, I reckon," the man said to the one beside him.

"Hit's not!" The boy spoke sharply.

"Well, now, that's more like it. You live on this ridge road?"

The boy nodded. " 'Bout a mile on down the road." His curiosity conquered his shyness. "Whatcha doin', mister? With them poles an' that thar wire an' stuff? Whatcha gonna do with 'em?"

The man laughed. "Why, we're laying the electric line. You're going to have electricity back here in these hills. You know what electricity is?"

Again the boy nodded and a startled, eager look swept over his face. "I seen the 'lectric lights in the store over at the Gap oncet. Air we gonna have lights like them thar?"

"You sure are. In about two weeks we'll be ready to turn 'em on for you. You go to school?"

"Yes. Down at Spout Springs."

"Well, you can do your studying by a good light in just about two more weeks. No more coal-oil lamps here on Hickory Ridge. How'll you like that?"

But the boy was making tracks down the road, spinning a dusty cloud from his heels.

All the way home he ran, and raced through his own front yard. He flung the screen door wide and tore through the house to the kitchen. "Ma," he called. "Hey, Ma! The 'lectric's comin' to the ridge! Ma, the 'lectric's comin'."

His mother was dishing up dinner, and the fire from the wood stove in the corner of the cook room had laid a steamy blanket over the house. The woman wiped sweat from her face with the tail of her apron and pushed at a straggling lock of hair with the back of her hand. The boy pulled at her dress. "Ma? Didja hear me? Ma, the 'lectric's comin'. I seen the men aputtin' up the poles down the road apiece. An' they said hit'd be ready in about two weeks."

"Go shet the screen, Jeff. Hit's hung up an' the flies'll be aswarmin' in."

Impatiently the boy ran back and pulled the door to. "Won't it be somethin' now, to have lights like them over at the Gap, Ma? Jist think. Nice an' brightlike. An' I seen John Barry light 'em oncet an' all he done was turn somethin' an' they come on. Just a little ole thing he turned an' they was bright light like daytime."

The boy whirled and flicked an imaginary switch. "Snick," he said, and ran through the three rooms of the house, flicking switches in every room. "Snick," he said. "Jist like that. See, Ma, the lights is on."

The woman laid a hand to the small of her back and straightened. "Wash up, Jeff. Yer pa's comin' in now an' dinner's ready."

The boy hopped around the room, three steps on one foot, three steps on the other. "Oh, hippety-hip, skippety-skip. Oh, snickety-snick an' spickety-spick. Snick, lights on. Snick, lights off. Snick, lights on." He whirled and danced around the room.

The man came in and hung his shattered straw hat on a nail by the wash shelf. He eyed the boy as he poured water in the tin basin. "What ails him?"

The woman poured clabber-milk in thick, white cups. "The 'lectric's comin'."

The man ran a snaggle-toothed comb through his sparse hair. "So?" He put the comb back in its rack. "Set down, Jeff, an' quit that prancin' 'round. We ain't got the 'lectric yit."

"But we *will* have, Pa. I seen the men aworkin' down the road. They was puttin' up the poles, an' they had wire an' little glass cups an' ever'thing ready. An' they said hit wouldn't be but two weeks till they could turn it on." The boy slid along the bench back of the table.

The man heaped his plate and fell to eating. The woman waved a sassafras branch at the flies and heaped the boy's plate. "Eat yer dinner," she said.

On Monday when the boy went to school the talk was all of the electric. "I seen 'em," he boasted to the other boys. "Me an' Jupe was sang diggin' a Sattidy, an' we seen 'em acomin' home. They was puttin' up the poles."

"I seen 'em, too."

"Me too."

"I bet I seen 'em first," Jeff insisted.

"Naw, you never. I seen 'em when they was crossin' the holler over by Crooked Creek. We're a-aimin' to have the lights, an' Ma says she's agonna have her a washin' machine an' a 'lectric iron." This was Willie Price, a tall, freckled, gangly boy. "You all aimin' to have the 'lectric, Jeff?"

"Why, shore," the boy said. "Hit's acomin' right by our house."

Each day after school the boy went to watch the men. They crept down the road a few poles each day. The boy watched them string the wires into the houses along the way and waited impatiently for them to reach his house. He counted the days.

"You'll soon be to my house," he told the men one day. "Hit's the next un 'round the bend."

"The next one?" one of the men asked.

The boy nodded. "Next un jist 'round the bend."

The men looked at each other and went on working. One man dug his shovel into the ground fast and hard. "You'll break that thar shovel," the boy cautioned. "You hadn't ort to gouge it so hard." The man grunted and swung the dirt in a wide arc.

That night the boy told his mother, "Tomorrer they'll be to our house. They're jist around the bend. They'll git here tomorrer."

Tomorrow was another Saturday and the boy stayed all day with the men, Jupe hanging around on the edge. About noon the men set the pole directly in front of the house. But when the pole was set the men went on down the road. Jeff was puzzled. At all the other houses they had strung wire to the side of the house. They didn't do that at his house. Well, maybe they was goin' to eat an' was comin' back later.

He went in to dinner. "They got our pole up now," he told his mother. "But they ain't strung our wire yit. Likely they'll git to 'fore night, though." He dried his hands carefully on the feed sack they used for a towel and slid behind the table.

His mother waved at the flies. "We ain't gonna have the 'lectric, Jeff. Hit costes money to git yer house fixed fer it an' it costes three dollars ever' month to the light company. We cain't be spendin' for sich."

The boy's eyes were unbelieving. "But hit's right thar on the pole," he said. "Hit's jist right outside. They said we'd have lights in two weeks. They *said* it, Ma."

"They ain't the ones going to pay fer havin' the house fixed fer it, an' they ain't the ones to pay the three dollars ever' month, neither. We ain't gonna have the 'lectric, Jeff, an' that's all they is to it. You'll jist have to make up yer mind to it. We ain't got the money."

The boy pushed his plate back. His stomach fluttered like it had little butterflies in it, and he couldn't touch his food. They wasn't goin' to have the 'lectric. Why, they jist had to have it! Why, thar it was! Right outside the front yard! Snick, lights on. Snick, lights off. Oh, they jist had to have the 'lectric. Ever'-body else would be havin' it an' they'd be onliest ones 'thout it. Hit wasn't to be borne they shouldn't have it.

A knot stuck in his throat and hurt him all through and his chest felt heavy so that he couldn't get a good breath. Oh, hit wasn't to be thought of. Why, he'd been the first to see 'em puttin' in the poles. He jist knowed Willie Price had lied when he said he seen 'em over on Crooked Creek. Hit was him seen 'em first. An' they was goin' to turn it on, come Tuesday. All up and down the ridge the lights would go on. All at one bright, beautiful moment they'd go on. Jist Jeff Tabor's house would be dark. Jist his'n of 'em all. The lights'd be asparklin' like candles on a Christmas tree, so purty an' daytime-like. Ever' house'd be lit up, come Tuesday. Ever' house but his'n. One small tear ran down his nose. He shook it off and blinked into his cup of milk. He couldn't swallow a drop. Hit jist wouldn't go down.

Suddenly he brightened, eager and hopeful. "You could have my sang money, Ma," he said. "I've got nearabouts ten dollars, an' likely three dollars more of them roots I got last time." Maybe they could have the 'lectric for a few months anyway.

"Hit costes clost to fifty dollars jist to wire the house, Jeff," the woman said. "Yore sang money'd jist be a drap in the bucket."

The boy's heart chunked down to his stomach again. He shoved the bench back against the wall and wandered through the house to the front porch. He wrapped his arm around a post and leaned his head against it. Hit wasn't right. Why was it, on the whole endurin' ridge they was the onliest ones couldn't have the 'lectric? Why was it they was allus the ones had to do without? Make do with a ole blind mule when ever'body else had a good team? Made do with a ole rusty step-stove to cook

on, when ever'body else had a good black range with warmin'
ovens? Make do with homemade overalls when ever'body else
had boughton ones? Hit jist wasn't right, somehow. The lump
came up in his throat again and came out in a sob. He turned
his head against the post and let the salt tears flow unheeded.

Monday came and went. The boy was quiet at school, saying
no more about the 'lectric. The excitement ran high. "Tomorrer's the day," the others shouted. "Tomorrer's when they
turn the 'lectric on. Hey, Jeff, we got a light in ever' room.
Even in the loft room. You all git lights fer all yer rooms?"

Jeff turned away. Tomorrer they'd know the Tabors didn't
git the 'lectric. Tomorrer when all the lights went on they'd
know. He wished he hadn't come to school today. He wished
he could go 'way off in the woods an' stay till after tomorrer. Jist
him an' Jupe. So they wouldn't have to see the lights, an' see
ever'body aknowin' the Tabors didn't have the 'lectric. He
couldn't bear today and tomorrer.

But he did, drooping quietly through the hours. Mebbe the
sun wouldn't come up on Tuesday. Mebbe he'd sleep all day
an' not have to go to school. Mebbe, if he waked up and went
outside there'd be the wires arunnin' to their house after all.
Mebbe somethin' could happen yit.

But the sun came up and Jeff waked early and when he went
outside the pole stood there, lonely and bare. No wires stretching to the house. A thin, bilious saliva flooded the boy's mouth
and he swallowed hard. Hit was jist goin' to hafta be, then.
They wasn't nothin' goin' to change it. The Tabors jist wasn't
going to have the 'lectric. An' the kids at school would snicker
an' whisper behind their backs an' say again what they'd said
before about Poke Tabor bein' a do-less man an' how his hands
fit a fishin' pole better'n they fit a plow handle. Hit was jist
goin' to hafta be.

He left his breakfast untouched, but he took his lunch bucket when his mother handed it to him and he set out doggedly for school. Jupe trailed behind, perplexed and saddened by the boy's quietness.

"Hit'll be at seven tonight," the boys said. "Seven on the dot the men said. Jist at first dark they'll turn it on."

"We done got ever' light turned on an' ready," Willie Price said. "When they turn it on, they'll all be lit up at oncet."

Jeff doubled up his fist. He'd like to hit that thar Willie Price right on the nose. Allus abraggin', he was.

The day moved on and the teacher finally called, "Books away." Jeff lingered behind so as not to have to listen to the talk goin' up the ridge. Jupe was waiting for him outside and the boy rubbed his nose against the dog's thick fur. "Jupe," the boy whispered. "Oh, Jupe!" The dog licked his tongue over the boy's nose and whimpered. This trouble the boy was bearing, maybe he could lick it away.

The sun slid down behind the ridge and the first whippoorwills began to call. The cow belled her way across the pasture and the boy and the dog went to drive her to the barn. Hit would be soon, now. Soon. Dark was alayin' over the trees, an' the night dew was risin' fast. The boy wet his feet in the grass as he went toward the house. If I jist didn't hafta see 'em, he thought. If I could jist go to bed an' things'd be like allus. If I jist didn't hafta know about it.

His mother called him to supper. As they sat down she lit the lamp. Dimly it glowed over the table, flickering small shadows around the room. The boy choked and bent his head. Now was the time. Now, hit was here. Hit wasn't to be borne.

"Reckon the other lamp'd give more light," the woman said, "but I'm too tard to git it."

The boy looked at the small flame; then suddenly his young face set in determination. He jumped up and took the lamp into the other room, setting it on the table near the window.

Quickly he took the lamp on the mantelpiece and lit it, and he set it on the table, too. He went into the back room and brought the biggest lamp they hardly ever used because it took so much oil, and he lit it and set it beside the other lamps. Now. Now, they was all lit and they made a bright, soft light. They glowed all through the room and they showed through the window onto the porch outside. They showed plumb down to the road, bright and gleaming. They was almost like the 'lectric.

He went out and sat in the grass of the yard and pulled his knees up to his chin and looked at the light. The dog nuzzled him and rested his head on the boy's shoulder. Absently the boy pulled the dog's ears. He felt sad and a little lonesome, as if he'd gone someplace and left something good and sweet behind. He'd like to have it back. He felt a little lost without it, but he sensed dimly it was gone forever.

"O' course, Jupe," he told the dog, a small sigh slipping out, "o' course Ma ain't goin' to let us burn the lamps ever' night. Hit would be a pure waste of oil. But someday, Jupe." He hugged the dog fiercely. "Someday the lights is goin' to be on ever' night at the Tabors'. Don't you grieve, Jupe, an' don't you fret. Jist wait an' 'fore you know it . . ."

He buried his face in the dog's neck. "I cain't take you fishin' no more, Jupe, for I cain't take the chance of gittin' my hands to fit a fishin' pole. Fish don't git you no money. An' I cain't take you sang diggin' no more, fer sang don't git you enough money. You got to plow to git money. You got to plow terbaccer an' corn to git money. You've not ever thought about gittin' money, Jupe, but you got to git used to it. You've jist gone to school an' gone fishin' an' dug sang an' hunted squirrels. But they ain't gonna be no more o' that, Jupe. Commencin' tomorrer we got to plow. Gittin' money is the biggest thing they is an' commencin' tomorrer we're aimin' to git it."

He stretched out on the grass, pillowing his head on the dog's flanks. His fingers snapped and he laughed. "Won't be no time . . . won't be no time till all we got to do is, snick, lights on — snick, lights off. Won't be no time."

The dog whispered in his throat and curled and rested his muzzle against the boy's face.

Then the lights went out and the boy and the dog slept in the dark.

TETCH 'N TAKE

"I had written the short story 'Tetch 'n Take' for *Kentucky Writing*. It was based on a true incident in the enormous Giles clan."

Around Our House

"TROUBLE WITH YOU, JED," says Grampa Clark, propping his foot on the lowest fence rail and laying a puddle of tobacco juice in the dust of the road, "trouble with you is yer too pa'tickler. Ary woman' better'n none at all. If she kin bake a biscuit she'll do to tie to. Yer too choosey, an' a man yore age cain't be so picky. You jist got to tetch 'n take."

Jedediah hitched at his overalls and, taking careful aim, laid another puddle of tobacco juice right alongside of Grampa Clark's. "Well do I know it," he says, "but I jist cain't get up my narve to ast the Widder Shanks. Ever' time I go over thar I aim to, but they's a thing jist ties my tongue, like. She's as fat as a meat hawg, her jaws is allus aflappin' an' besides she won't have no truck with them hound dawgs of mine."

"Aw, shoo," says Grampa, "a leetle weight never hurt no woman. I like 'em on the chunky side myself. Good as a stove to snuggle up to of a cold night. An' you kin allus close yer ears to her jawin'. As fer the dawgs, ain't you the master of yer own house? Jist set yer foot down, man! Jist tell her to take me, take my dawgs. I've heard the Widder dishes up the tastiest vittles in Bear Holler. If hit was me, now, I'd consider it a right smart trade to git to eat good an' have a handy woman to do fer me.

Ain't no two ways about it, a lone man makes a pore job out of doin' fer hisself."

Jed laid his bony shanks against the fence and pulled a deep sigh out of his chest. "He does that. I know fer shore. I stir soon of a mornin', never layin' no longer than cock-crow, an' I try masterfully to dish up tasty vittles. But hit's allus the same. My cornpone's soggy, my side-meat's greasy, my gravy's lumpy and not even the dawgs'll swill my cawfee. I've nigh ruint my stummick, to say nothing of the dawgses'."

"I know jist what you mean," says Grampa. "I was a widder man fer ten long year myself. Jist too pa'tickler. 'Lowed I could hold out. But when my stummick give out on me I was powerful glad to wed up with Agnes. An' that's jist what you better do with the Widder Shanks, whilst they's time. You ain't likely to find none that'll suit you better. Besides," he says, slipping it in kind of slylike, "I've heard the bachelor man from over at Yaller Dawg Holler has been acastin' eyes at her of late. In my opinion, you'd best git yerself over to the Widder's come Sunday an' take the day with her. You'd best waste no time gittin' into motionment. That bachelor man is liable to sneak her right into matrimony on that black mule of his'n."

Jed unglued his bones from the fence. His hackles rose like a dawg getting ready to fight. "The bachelor man!" he says, nigh strangling on the words. "Why that ornery low-life! Ever'body in these parts knows I've been courtin' the Widder these past six years. They ain't a soul but knows I've staked out my claim. Why, I'll skin that polecat an' stretch his hide to my smoke-house door! I'll roll him like a barr'l! I'll . . ."

Grampa Clark laid a hand on his arm. "I'd not mix nor mingle none with the bachelor man if I was you, Jed," he says. "He's a right smart stack of man. I'd jist take the day with the Widder come Sunday, an' leave him wake up a Monday with the Widder snuck clean outen his way. That's what I'd do, was I you."

Jed fisted his hands and pondered. Then he pointed his chin whiskers at the sky and nodded his agreement. "I'm beholden to you, Grampa," he says, "fer handin' me yer advice. I'll foller it. Come Sunday I'll take the day with the Widder, and I'll lead her to the halter come Monday. That'll fix that there bachelor man!"

"Hit will that," Grampa says. "Hit will fer shore. Now don't go losin' yer narve. Jist stiffen up yer backbone, an' remember the worst is jist gittin' it said. Oncet that's done, the rest is easy. Iffen you don't now, Jed, folks all up and down the holler is goin' to be p'intin at you an' sayin', 'Look how the proud has fell. Look to what Jedediah Spears has come. Alettin' the bachelor man from Yaller Dawg Holler sneak his woman away from him.' "

Jed shook his head at the idea. It wouldn't bear thinking on. "My narve," he says, "has stiffened. An' hit'll not weaken."

Grampa Clark slapped him on the back. "Good. Now, don't fergit yer store teeth. The Widder sets a heap of prize by appearances. You want to look yer best. Well, I'd best be gittin' on. Jist go with me."

"Cain't," Jed says. "Jist stay on."

"Got to be moseyin', I reckon. Wish ye luck, Jed." And Grampa Clark laid one foot in front of the other down the road, raising a dust behind him. Jed kept his eye on him to the curve, then, mournfully, he laid one foot in front of the other down the road, raising a dust behind him, up the holler to his cabin. He had a unknown sight of things to do to get ready for Sunday.

Come first light easing the sun up over the ridge Sunday morning, Jed stirred. His stomach was all of aquiver with excitement. It could likely be this was the next day but one he'd have to dish up his own vittles. He ate his breakfast, and then he scoured himself with hard soap. His clothes were laid handy on a chair nearby. He'd washed his overalls and patched the hole in the knee. He'd got out the white shirt he'd not worn since Idy was laid in the ground over in the Lo and Behold churchyard. He'd scraped the mud off his Sunday slippers, and he'd turned the band on his blue felt hat. On top of his clothes, so as not to forget, he'd laid his store teeth. Plague-taked things wasn't worth a nickel for chewing, but they was mighty white and shiny. Pretty as pearls, even if they did fill up a body's mouth a heap. He reckoned he'd have to remember to laugh some this day, so's the Widder would take note he was wearing his teeth.

The mist was riding high in the trees when he whistled up the dawgs and sloped off down the holler toward the Widder's. Solomon and old King David were the two best fox hounds in these parts. Never missed a track or a trail. Never lost a fox. Jed ruminated on his dawgs. Hit did beat all, he thought, how quare wimminfolks was about dawgs. Allus ajawin' about 'em trackin' in an' smellin' up a place. Idy'd been the same in the beginnin', but ere long she'd give over the idee. Said she reckoned they was her cross to bear. But he misdoubted the Widder would give over as easy as Idy. They was a sight more of her to hold out. But be they ever so good, he remembered, dawgs couldn't dish up vittles. No matter how many foxes they could trail and track, they was still just dawgs. An' hit wasn't to be borne no longer, this doin' fer hisself. He was diggin' a early grave with his own teeth. He clapped a hand to his hip pocket. By grannies, he'd like to fergot them store teeth. He slid them into his mouth and eased them into place.

Up hill and down holler he followed the trail. Solomon and old King David slanting low on the ground ahead, sniffing and panting like they hoped to come up on a fresh scent any minute. It fair made Jed's heart bleed in his bosom to think what all unbeknownst to them he was doing. It made him feel like a Judas, when he looked at those two pore innocent dawgs. But he stiffened his nerve and kept to the trail.

When he came out on top of the ridge in sight of the Widder's cabin, he pulled up short. For there, in plain sight, hitched to the fence post right spang in front of the Widder's house, was a long-eared black mule. A long-eared black mule with red tassels on his bridle and a saddle on his back. And who could such a mule belong to but the bachelor man from Yaller Dawg Holler!

A fast-burning anger wheezed through Jedediah. By grannies, he says to himself, the bachelor man is taking the day with the Widder. Adippin' from a man's own spring. Athievin' from a man's own chicken yard. Atrailin' a man's own fox. Jed was so wrathful he chomped down hard on his store teeth and blew his cud of tobacco right out onto the ground. He sharpened his feet against the dirt, and he tightened his belt a couple of notches. He sizzled and he fried. He wiggled his ears forward and backward. By grannies, he says, I'll pick the pin feathers outen that bachelor man! I'll grind him up an' make mincemeat outen him! I'll chaw him up and spit him out! And then he balled himself up and took off down the hillside, his arms windmilling the air and his breath puffing steam before him.

The Widder opened to him, but there was no joy in her greeting. "Leave them dawgs of yore'n outdoors, Jed," she says, and she never so much as told him to fetch a chair. "Me an' Bruh," she says, "is jist aimin' to leave fer the all-day singin' over at Tabernacle. Ain't got time to more'n wish you good day."

The air whistled through Jed's nose. So! Her an' the bachelor man was going to the singin', was they? He laid his eyes on the bachelor man. He was a heap of man, that bachelor man from Yaller Dawg Holler. Grampa Clark was right. He was a right smart stack of man. Jed took him in and decided maybe he'd better smooch talk him a little before making mincemeat out of him. So, slick as butter, he says, "How you all aimin' on goin'?"

The Widder tossed her head. "On Bruh's mule. How else?"

"Single or double?"

"Double."

Jed slewed a look at the bachelor man who hadn't so much as spoke a word yet. Not even a mannerly howdy. "I misdoubt that mule'll carry double," Jed says.

"He'll carry," says the bachelor man, and he stood up six foot tall and went past Jed out the door like he wasn't even there.

The Widder tied her bonnet on. "Hit's a pity," she says in passing, "hit's a pity you've not got you no mule, Jed. Jist them two wuthless old hound dawgs."

Jedediah was struck all of a heap. Wuthless! Wuthless! Solomon and old King David? The two best fox hounds in Bear Holler? Well, by grannies! He could feel his wrath foaming inside of him. Wuthless! He choked on his lower plate and all but swallowed the whole set of teeth, he was that mad. He coughed them around a minute and then slid them clean out of his mouth into his hand. Much good they was doing, anyhow. Then he followed the Widder and the bachelor man out to the gate.

The bachelor man crawled onto his mule and gave the Widder a hand to hoist her up behindst him. She lunged, but she never even left the ground. There must of been a good two hundred pounds of the Widder, and it took a right smart hoist to budge her. Jed snickered. The Widder withered him with a look. He wiped the grin off his face. "Leave me holp," he says politely, and he commenced to go around the south side of the mule toward the Widder.

It was then the idea come to him, and he never resisted long. Like a flash his hand snuck out and lifted the saddle blanket, and he slid his store teeth under, teeth side down. Quicklike, he done it, patting the blanket into place, and then he bent to hold a hand for the Widder's foot. He heaved and the bachelor man hove. The Widder puffed and panted. Finally they got her off the ground and swung in a wide curve over the back of the mule. She settled like a pan of yeasty dough.

But not for long. When she landed the mule laid back his ears and rolled his eyes, and he brayed a mighty trumpet to the skies. He leaned his nose to the ground and then he stood on it, his hind legs splitting the air so clean they whistled. When he landed, stiff-legged, the Widder bounced like a flapjack being turned in the skillet. When she went up her bonnet lit on a rose bush and when she come down her side-combs grated themselves on the fence paling. All two hundred pounds of her was jolted plumb to her hairpins. When she landed, those store teeth of Jed's must of sunk to the helve in the mule's hide. With a blast like thunder, and a couple of wicked side kicks, the mule took off down the holler, the bachelor man sawing at the bit and cussing a blue streak, the Widder screeching and clawing like a wildcat around his neck. "Lawdy, lawdy," says Jedediah, thunderstruck and awed. "Look at what them store teeth has went an' done. I do hope the Widder don't pulverize 'em. Man, man, look at that mule go!" Then he greased his heels in a hard run after them. Solomon and old King David was belling that mule like it was a fox. "Stay with 'em, boys," Jed whooped, and he fanned the breeze right behind them.

When he rounded the curve and come in sight again he skidded his heels in the dirt. What he saw was a sight to behold. The Widder was leaving the south end of the mule, aflyin' just like she'd took to wings, right through the middle of the air. Jed didn't allow there'd been another good bite in them teeth, but he must of been wrong. His mouth flew open and he swallowed his Adam's apple. Then he hid his eyes in his shirt sleeve. He never wanted to see the finish. Likely, he thought, I have committed murder this day. Likely hit's a ball an' chain fer me the rest of my days.

Then he heard such a screeching and abellowing and agoing on as never had he heard in all his born days. Such a yelping and howling! He peeped through his fingers with one eye, expecting to see the Widder smashed six ways to thunder all over the holler. But what he saw froze him right in his tracks, and plumb filled him with anguish. For the Widder had landed plunk in the midst of Solomon and old King David! There they were all in a heap, the two best fox hounds in Bear Holler, with the Widder lying sprawled on top. Oh, woe! Oh, misery! A groan come up from Jedediah's toes. Likely, he says to himself, I have committed several murders today.

Like the west wind he blew down the path to his dawgs. He couldn't even take any pleasure in the sight of the bachelor man high-tailing it on down the holler, raising such a dust as hardly to be seen. For his heart was chunking in his throat, and the salt tears were flowing down his cheeks and his stomach was heaving like jelly.

"Git me up from here, Jed," the Widder begged. "Git me up. Oh, rue the day I ever paid heed to that there bachelor man! My bones is melted an' broke! My chest is caved in! My hide is skun an' roe! I'm all of aquiver. Git me up from here!"

But Jed had no thoughts for the Widder. "You ain't kilt," he says. "But hit may well be my dawgs is ruint. Git over an' leave me see." And he shoved the Widder to one side.

Solomon moaned and old King David groaned, but they staggered up to their feet when Jed called them. Their sides were heaving and their tongues were hanging out, but they wasn't split asunder. Jed felt all over them and satisfied himself they weren't spavined or disjointed in any way. He patted Solomon and petted old King David and he hugged them both a hundred times, he was that glad. It was like a miracle they hadn't been stove clean in and their insides mashed to glue.

The Widder hoisted herself up. She shook down her skirts and hitched up her stockings. "I'll never agin say a harm's word about them dawgs of yore'n, Jedediah," she says. "They're all that's kept me from gittin' a broke neck this day. I'll feed 'em an' tend 'em like they was younguns. They shall eat my meat hawg an' my fryin' chickens, too. An' I'll give 'em the run of the heartfire if you want. When we're wed, I will, Jed."

Jed blinked at her. He had plumb forgot he had aimed to ask her to wed with him. She went on talking. "Now, the way I see it, Jed," she says, "when we're wed you kin jist move yore things over to my place. That shack of yore'n fitten fer nothin' but kindlin' wood noways. But I'll come over an' see if they's ary thing of Idy's I kin use. I allus had a fancy fer that brass bed of her'n. You got a Rastus plow you better bring along, too, fer come spring you kin use it in the corn patch . . ." She went on and on, barely pausing for breath.

Jed watched her tongue flicking the words against her teeth, disposing of him and his house and property, and he watched her jaw keeping time with her tongue. He blinked again and swallowed hard. All at once he felt like there was a noose around his neck. He opened his mouth when she stopped long enough for him to get a word in edgewise, but the words of agreement wouldn't come. He swallowed again and loosened his collar, took a deep breath and tried once more. Some words came out, but they wasn't what he intended. He'd aimed to say, "Yes, ma'am," and get it done and over with. What he said was, "You had best git the bachelor man to bring his Rastus plow over, ma'am, and you had best l'arn to ride his black mule, fer I allow me an' Solomon an' old King David won't be movin' over amongst you. Thank you kindly, though, fer the offer." Then he tipped his blue felt hat mannerly and he parted the bushes and stepped lightly onto the trail. On second thought, he turned back and spoke again. "When the bachelor man gits through pickin' them teeth outen that mule's hide," he says, "you kin tell him I make him a gift of 'em. I misdoubt I'll ever need 'em agin." And he left the Widder standing with her hair knot hung like a doughnut over one ear, and her jaw loose like it had come unhinged.

My, but he felt fine and fancy free. He fair pranced when he walked, like the ground under his feet was clouds. He stretched his neck and breathed easy. Glory, but that had been a close call! He could feel that rope around his neck yet.

Next day he made his apologies to Grampa Clark. "Hit wasn't," he told him, "that I lost my narve, Grampa, fer I never. Hit was just that of a sudden I lost my notion. Thar she was as willin' as the risin' sun, but I had got unwillin'. She had me roped, throwed and hog-tied, Grampa, an' all I could think of was gittin' loose. Of a sudden I knowed I'd ruther die of my own cookin' as to be listenin' to that Widder tellin' me come hither, come yon, fer the rest of my life."

Grampa squinted at him judiciously, and then he laid a puddle of tobacco juice in the dust of the road. "In my opinion," he says, kind of slowlike, "you jist ain't the tetch 'n take kind of man. They's some is, some ain't. Likely you ain't."

"Likely I ain't," Jed says agreeable. "But anyways," he says, brightening up, "I'm a-improvin' with my vittles. They was right tasty fer supper last night. Even the dawgs et with relish."

"Well," Grampa says, "seein' as how you'll be doin' for yer-self a right smart time now, I believe if I was you I'd send off an' git me one of them cookbooks tells you how."

Jed pondered. "I might," he says. "I might do that. I'm beholden fer yer advice, Grampa." He whistled up his dawgs. "Jist go with me."

"Cain't. Jist stay on."

"I got to be moseyin'. Solomon an' old King David'll be wantin' to run tonight, I reckon. Might raise the old red one."

"Might," Grampa says.

Jed laid one foot in front of the other up the holler, and a dancey little cloud of dust, as free and easy as the air, followed along behind him.

(This story, published in *Kentucky Writing*, July 1954, was the nucleus of a book written many years later, called *Shady Grove*.)

DEAR SIR

"Appalachia was not a subculture of American society, a folk class, but an island long isolated in the middle of America, a primitive society with its own mores and norms."

40 Acres and No Mule

Etna, Kentucky
February 2, 1961

District Director of Internal Revenue
Louisville
Kentucky

Dear Sir:

This leaves me fine and hoping you are the same.

Well, no, it doesn't to say leave me real fine, for I've got an awful cold and am afraid I'm coming down with the virus. But then I always say you've got to expect a few sniffles in the wintertime. I just rub my chest good with goosegrease and turpentine and hope for the best. Depends on the way you look at it whether what I get is what I hope for. But it's as good a remedy as anything else. Goosegrease and turpentine.

I got a letter from your office last December with one of those income tax forms in it. Form 1040-F it had printed on it and the instructions said fill it out and send it back by January 31st, on account of I farm.

What with one thing and another I didn't get around to it and Jodie said I'd better write and tell you why. He says you're awful strict about the income tax and will likely sue me if I don't let you know. I told him I misdoubted that. He says he saw by the papers where you put people in jail even. I told him I could read the papers same as he could and it was mostly gamblers and horse-betting folks and crooked politicians and not honest, hard-working women trying to get along.

Just in case, though, I'm writing to you about it.

The reason I didn't get around to it was, and if you ask me it was awful short notice to write in December and expect folks to write back to you by the end of January, especially when the tobacco hadn't been sold yet and me not knowing how I stood on the hay and corn, what with the drought last summer, to say nothing of the hogs and Christmas turkeys. But the main reason I couldn't finish filling out that form was on account of the guineas. I've settled about the tobacco now. It sold on January the sixth and brought a tolerable good price. I've got the hay and corn and fertilizer figured now and we killed the hogs on Christmas Day. They weren't as fat as some I've had but I told Jodie we'd best kill while the freeze was on and take what we could get. The turkeys dressed out fair to middling, though I near froze my hands off.

If you'll tell me about the guineas I can finish filling out this form now and send it to you.

So please hurry and answer.

Your friend,
Minnie Seebrun

* * *

Etna, Kentucky
February 10, 1961

Mister C. F. Smith
Office of the Director of Internal Revenue
Louisville, Kentucky

Dear Mr. Smith:

This leaves me feeling pearter and hoping you are the same.

The last time I wrote I had a real bad cold but am glad to say it's some better now. Goosegrease and turpentine did it. For a spell I wheezed like an old-pump-organ, but am just a mite tizicky now. I'd be glad to send you a jar if you stand in need of some.

I'm real pleased to know your name. I don't write a letter once in ten years but when I do I like to know who I'm writing to.

Mister Smith, I have already got one of those Form 1040-F things. Don't you remember you sent me one in December? So enclosed herewith I am returning the one you sent. Mister Smith, I don't want to appear fault-finding but it is little things like this that have given us Democrats the bad name of being wasteful with the government's property and of running the country into debt. It is just such things as sending folks income tax forms that have already got one that has given the Republicans the inch they've tried to stretch into a mile. You are not a Republican are you, Mister Smith? There must be a hundred other folks in Kentucky that don't yet have a form 1040-F and need one. Please send this one to somebody that needs it and don't be extravagant with the government's postage and printing money.

I don't know about this thirty-day extension you tell about, but Jodie says I'd better take it. So I'll take it. If it's free, that is. I am not able to pay for it, though, for while I got a tolerable price for my tobacco there wasn't as much of it as common, and what with the drought last summer the hay and corn didn't do so good either. So if you charge for it, just leave it lay.

136

You didn't say yet what to do about the guineas.

We're having a right smart spell of snow and wet weather lately, but I always say the wetter the winter the better the plowing, come spring.

There is a scarcity of news so I'll stop now and fix Jodie's supper.

Your friend,
Minnie Seebrun

*   *   *

Mister C. F. Smith
Director of Internal Revenue
Louisville, Kentucky

Dear Mister Smith:

This leaves me fine, but Jodie is puny now. Too much fresh sausage, I told him. But he says he didn't hardly touch the sausage. Stuck strictly to ribs and backbones.

I'd feel sorrier for him if I hadn't been having trouble with him and Ella Stonecypher again. Jodie is a good man. The best hired hand I ever had and we're aiming to get married as soon as he gets his divorce papers from his first wife. But he's easy led and that widow, Ella Stonecypher, has been casting sheep's eyes at him all winter.

Mister Smith, she is the most uppity woman ever I saw. She is a widow that just moved into the settlement last year and a born troublemaker if ever I saw one. Says she's not but forty years old. Now, when I tell my age as forty I'm telling the truth, but that woman will never see fifty again or I'm a muley-faced cow. Built exactly like a bed slat. What a man can see to admire in her is more than I can tell. I run a little to fat, I'll admit, but I'd think a man would rather have a woman with some heft to her than one that was skinned down like a pin-picked chicken.

Ever since that woman moved into the settlement there's been nothing but trouble with all the widowers and bachelors swarming around her like bees after honey. It must be her money for she's got a little, I hear. Her farm is nothing to speak of. Mostly rocks and woods. A man would be hard put to it to make a living off of it.

I've kept Jodie in hand pretty fair, for a burned child dreads the fire and he got burned good and plenty with his first woman that spent all his money and ran him into debt and then went off with another man. Lately, though, he's been pulling at the leash a mite, cornering up with her at the church socials and hauling wood for her in his spare time, and promising to burn off her tobacco bed for her in the spring. I've held my tongue, though, and said naught. Just kept my eyes open.

The other night was too much for me. It was at the pie-supper at the church, for the benefit of buying new hymn books. I made a banana cream pie, which is Jodie's favorite, and many's the time I've seen him eat half a one without stopping to come up for breath. I fixed it up in a real pretty box with a patriotic design. Red, white and blue. I might as well have put it in a plain shoe box for all the good it did. Do you know what happened? When my pie went up for sale I made a sign to Jodie who was on the other side of the room with the rest of the men-folks that it was mine and he was to bid on it and buy it. He never even looked my way. Just sat there and let it sell to Silas Tate, and he knows good and well I can't abide Silas Tate. He's lame in one leg and can't say his name without stuttering. Drives a body crazy.

But that wasn't the worst, Mister Smith. Jodie bought Ella Stonecypher's pie. I had to sit there the rest of the evening with Silas Tate sputtering in my ear and eating my good banana cream pie with Jodie off in the corner with that widow, eating hers, and snickering and laughing with her the whole time. And she had just a plain, double-crusted mincemeat, which Jodie has never cared for. I know, for I walked around in back of them to see. But there he sat, eating mincemeat pie like he relished it the best in the world. Oh, it was a miserable night, I can tell you. I couldn't help but speak my mind on the way home. "Jodie," I says, "how come you didn't buy my pie?"

"Never knew," he said, "which one it was."

"If you'd of looked my way," I said, "you could of told. I was making you a sign."

"Never saw you," he said.

"I know you never," I said. "You was too busy making sheep's eyes at Ella Stonecypher."

"No such of a thing," he said. "Wasn't making sheep's eyes. Man's got be civil, don't he?"

"I saw you laughing and talking to her all evening," I said, "so don't try to deny it, Jodie Jones."

"After I bought her pie, I did," he said. "Some."

"How come it was her pie you bought?" I said.

"Just bought a pie. How was I to know it was Ella's?"

"That's what I'd like to know," I said.

Well, Mister Smith, one word led to another and by the time we got home I was so mad I was shaking all over and there is a considerable amount of me to shake. When Jodie pulled the truck up at the back door I just flounced myself out of it and I said to him, "Jodie Jones, you can't have your cake and eat it too. Just don't ever speak to me again. You just do your work and go your own way and I'll go mine."

Commonly Jodie is a mild-mannered man but he has got a temper when he is riled. And he was riled. He says, "If that's the way you want it that's the way it'll be." And he raced the motor up so it would drown me out and he drove off to the barn and left me standing there.

Mister Smith, that was three days ago and he's not spoke a word to me yet. This world is indeed a vale of tears and sorrows, like it says in the hymn. I'm afraid Jodie and me are through forever.

I appreciate you giving me the thirty-day extension but I'd not of been in need of it if it hadn't been for the guineas and you've not yet told me what to do about them.

So I'll stop now and put this in the mailbox.

Your friend in trouble,
Minnie Seebrun

*   *   *

Etna, Kentucky
February 25, 1961

Mister C. F. Smith
Director of Internal Revenue
Louisville, Kentucky

Dear Mr. Smith:

You've not answered my last letter but I thought you'd want to know that I'm still in good health but in low spirits.

Jodie is still holding out and I'm afraid he is going to see Ella Stonecypher of an evening. Used to, when we got through with the night work and had eat our supper he would come in and sit and listen to the radio with me till bedtime. Now he just does up the work and eats and goes off someplace. My neighbor, Sallie Brown, told me she'd heard he was over at the widow's nearly every night. He's someplace besides here, for sure.

Every night I lay here after I go to bed waiting to hear him step up on the porch and to hear his door slam. Last night it was past ten o'clock when he came home. I don't know as he can keep up his work if he goes on losing sleep this way. I'm awful worried, Mister Smith. Maybe I was hasty with him. I'd like the best in the world to be on speaking terms with him again, but a body has got to take a stand sometimes. I've took mine and I don't see how I can back down now.

You better give me another thirty-day extension, Mister Smith.
If you've got an extra one, that is. I wouldn't want to misput
you. But you've not ever told me about the guineas and I can't
finish filling out this form until you do, and time's passing. I've
been looking to hear from you any day, but doubtless this is your
busy time of the year.

So I'll stop and eat dinner now. It's a funny thing that food
don't taste very good when you've got to eat it by yourself.

Your grieving friend,
Minnie Seebrun

* * *

Etna, Kentucky
March 3, 1961

Mister C. F. Smith
Director of Internal Revenue
Louisville, Kentucky

Dear Mister Smith:

Well, of course Jodie's worth it, Mister Smith. He's the best
hand I ever had. He can stack twelve shocks of corn in a fore-
noon all by himself and he can cut and stick half an acre of
tobacco any day in the week. He's just easy led and if Ella
Stonecypher would leave him alone we'd never have a minute's
trouble.

Besides, Mister Smith, and I wouldn't say this to just anybody
but you've been real friendly, when a woman gets my age she
can't be too picky and choosey. She's kind of got to touch and
take. Don't you worry a minute about Jodie not being worth the
trouble. If I could just put blinders on him and get him past
Ella Stonecypher we'd make out just fine.

Speaking of guineas, Mister Smith. I'm obliged to you for
sending me another of those thirty-day extensions but if you'd
just tell me what to do about the guineas you could save your-

self the bother of mailing me any more. I could settle up right shortly with you.

Your worried friend,
Minnie Seebrun

* * *

Etna, Kentucky
March 7, 1961

Mister C. F. Smith
Director of Internal Revenue
Louisville, Kentucky

Dear Mister Smith:

This leaves me in good health but still in low spirits and I would not wish the same on my worst enemy, which you are not.

It may be that things are a little better but I'm not sure. Jodie is still holding out although he's taken to eating with me again and he kind of grunted at me this morning.

It's hard for me to hold my tongue for I'm naturally a friendly person. I have vowed not to speak first but I forgot when he came in for breakfast today and asked him if he'd rather have pancakes or biscuits. Commonly Jodie wants biscuits for breakfast but there's times when he relishes a good, light pancake with real sorghum molasses. I didn't know but what this was one of the times. Like I said, he kind of grunted at me and it sounded more like pancakes than biscuits, so I made him up a stack. He ate every bite so I must of guessed right and maybe it was a good sign he's weakening. I'd be glad if he was for I'm getting in the way of going around talking to myself, not having anybody better to speak to.

I don't know what can be taking you so long to decide about the guineas, Mister Smith. There is five dozen of them.

So I'll stop and work a little on my quilt. It's the Double Wedding Ring pattern. It makes me sad to look at it right now, though, for I intended to use it on mine and Jodie's bed when we got married. The way things are now it looks like I'd better of picked the Lone Star pattern. It might suit better.

Your lonely friend,
Minnie Seebrun

* * *

Etna, Kentucky
March 15, 1961

Mister C. F. Smith
Director of Internal Revenue
Louisville, Kentucky

Dear Mister Smith:

This leaves me fine and hoping you are the same, and Mister Smith, as I always say, right is bound to triumph over wrong in the end and that's exactly what it's done. I thought you'd like to know. Jodie is done with the widow and we are speaking again and everything is just fine. It come about this way.

There has been a new supermarket built over in the county seat and they were going to have their grand opening last Friday night. I like to go to things like that for they have free drinks and ice-cream and cake and they usually always have a drawing and give away a lot of prizes. This one was giving away a bedroom suite. Walnut with a waterfall front. I didn't want to miss having a chance on it for I knew it would come in handy when me and Jodie got married. Of course I've got a house full of furniture that was my mother's but I always say a young couple just starting out ought to have a few things of their own brand-new. Especially a bed. It makes a good start. I didn't know whether we'd ever need a bedroom suite or not, with us not speaking and all, but I'd not given up hope so I made out like I didn't know Jodie was in the room and commenced talking to myself about how much I wanted to go to the opening and if somebody would just get the truck started and take me maybe I'd be lucky and win the bedroom suite and some groceries, too.

After a while Jodie got up and went out and I listened, and the next thing I heard was the truck starting and I flew around and got ready and we went and got there in plenty of time. There was an awful crowd but I like folks and it never gets too crowded for me. I just push and shove right through the midst of them and have as big a time as the next one. Looked like everybody in the county was there and I was enjoying myself. In a heavyhearted kind of way. I had a good hold on Jodie, too.

I saw Ella Stonecypher over by the meat counter where they were serving out free drinks. She had on a brown dress that made her look as sallow as a dish of sauerkraut and she had a new permanent that made that red hair of hers, which I have no doubt is dyed, stand up like every hair had declared its independence. My hair is naturally curly so it never frizzes up all over my head. Oh, there is points in my favor even if I do wear a size forty-two dress.

Well, Mister Smith, I don't know just how it was that Jodie got loose from me but it must of been when they had the drawing for the groceries. Jodie was right behind me but I had to turn loose of his coat for a minute while I got my ticket out of my purse. I thought I had a hold of it again as soon as I found the ticket. Anyway, I wasn't lucky on the groceries, and there was twenty-five dollars' worth, which I could of put to good use. But when I turned around I got the shock of my life. I had hold of the coat of a man I never saw before in my life. Jodie had got away as slick as rain off a duck's back.

My heart just sunk clear to my heels, Mister Smith, for when I looked right quick to see if Ella Stonecypher was still there, she was gone too and I knew straight off they'd sneaked out together.

144

I made my way as fast as I could through the crowd, elbowing folks right and left and doubtless making lifelong enemies of some of them, but I had to find Jodie. I got out finally and I looked behind the store and over at the filling station and up the alley and in all the cars parked on the lot. Where do you think I found them, Mister Smith? In my own truck! I could hardly believe my eyes when I came up on them, snuggled up in the back so close you couldn't have got a straw between them, kissing and carrying on in the shamefulest kind of way.

Now, I'm a lady, Mister Smith, and I always say a lady ought not ever to forget she's a lady, but that was just more than I could stand. In my own truck, mind you. Jodie and that widow.

I just reached out and got Jodie by the collar and gave him a quick yank and set him on his own two feet on the ground beside me. Jodie is built a little on the spare side and I can easy pick him up with one hand. "What," I says to him, "do you think you're doing, Jodie Jones?"

He mumbled something I couldn't hear but Ella Stonecypher spoke up loud enough. She came crawling out of the back end of the truck with hay and straw stuck in her hair and clothes all over. "What," she said, snickering, "did it look like he was doing, Minnie Seebrun?"

"I'll thank you," I says, "to hold your tongue and keep out of this."

"You'd best be careful of your own tongue," she says.

"If you don't mind," I said, "I'll give you more than a tongue-lashing, Ella Stonecypher."

"You wouldn't dare," she says.

"Oh, I wouldn't," I says.

"No, you wouldn't," she says.

Mister Smith, I was so mad I just hauled off and gave her a good slap, and it was a good one if I do say so myself, for it cracked like a buggy whip and almost knocked her down. I weigh close to two hundred pounds and when I lay the flat of my hand to somebody they can feel it, I tell you.

Well, to give her credit, she came back fighting and we had it round and round there for a time. But she wasn't any match for me, claw and scratch and kick as she would, and I soon had her running squalling and yelping toward the store.

Jodie had been dancing around us like a grasshopper on a hot stove, yelling at first me and then her, begging and pleading with us to stop. Neither of us paid any mind to him but when Ella went tearing off I was still so mad and upset I turned and commenced on Jodie. "I'll teach you," I said, "to go flirting around with Ella Stonecypher behind my back. You're my man," I told him, "and I'll not have any more of these goings on." And I just bopped him over the head with my purse.

Mister Smith, I got the fright of my life for when I hit him Jodie went down like a pole-axed steer. He never even moved. Just fell down and lay there like he was dead. "Oh, my goodness," I said, "I've done killed him."

I bent over him and started begging him to speak to me. Then I thought to listen to his heart and it was still thumping so I knew he wasn't dead. I commenced working on him, rubbing his hands and the back of his neck and slapping his face. It was several minutes before he came to.

He sat up and held his head and moaned. Then he looked at me. "Minnie," he says, as solemn as a judge, "when a woman fights for her man it's bound to be a sign her love is true. Minnie, you have fought for me and I believe in your love." He held up his hand and swore. "I am never going around Ella Stonecypher again as long as I live. Nor any other woman. I will be faithful to you until death do us part. But Minnie," he says, "what in God's name did you hit me with?"

I looked in my purse, and so help me, Mister Smith, I'd clean forgot about the pipe wrench I'd put in there to take to the hardware next time I was in town. It was too big for my purpose and I meant to trade it. Little wonder he was knocked out.

I didn't own it, though. I just sniffed and said to him, "A good breath would knock you over, Jodie Jones."

Well, all's well that ends well. Jodie and me are at peace again and all we have to do now is wait for his divorce papers. Then we can get married.

I lost out on the drawing for the walnut bedroom suite. They had it while I was trying to bring Jodie to, I guess. It was too bad, for a woman from the next county won it and I do like to see things like that stay in the home county. If I have good luck with the tobacco this season I mean to buy one just like it. Waterfall front and walnut. Doubtless Jodie and me will be needing it next year.

I thought, since we have been corresponding so regular, you would like to know the happy ending of Jodie and me.

Your glad-hearted friend,
Minnie Seebrun

P. S.   What about the guineas?

*   *   *

Etna, Kentucky
March 29, 1961

Mister C. F. Smith
Director of Internal Revenue
Louisville, Kentucky

Dear Sir:

Enclosed herewith is Form 1040-F and you could of saved us both a lot of trouble if you had wrote frank and open in the beginning.

Mister Smith, I am surprised at you and I am bound to believe you are a Republican after all. Everybody knows I won those guineas at a drawing last May. It was in the Louisville *Courier Journal*. With my picture. But I don't expect you read the Louisville *Courier Journal*, seeing as it's a Democrat paper.

They had a drawing at a poultry house up on Market Street. Gave away five dozen guineas to the one that could come the closest to guessing the weight of the lot. I've handled chickens and turkeys and guineas all my life so I just got Jodie to drive me up there in the truck and I looked at them and sized them up and wrote down my guess. Hit it right on the nose. We loaded those five dozen guineas onto the truck and brought them home the same day.

All I ever wanted to know, Mister Smith, was whether I had to count those guineas as capital gains or excess profits. Seeing as I didn't pay anything for them. Any Democrat could of told me right off.

But I don't hold a grudge and even if you are a Republican I wish you well in the future, though I must say things don't look too bright for you Republicans right now. It's been real nice knowing you.

So I'll stop and fix Jodie's supper. Baked guinea and dressing, since you don't give a profane word in a hot place about my guineas.

Yours truly,
Minnie Seebrun

Spout Springs

ADIOS, MISS EM

"It may have been that summer, or perhaps it was the next,
we had the elegant funeral."

A Little Better Than Plumb

INTO THE SILENCE of the sunny morning, into the peace of the
petunia bed, bedlam suddenly broke. From the orchard there
came the variously pitched yells, screams, shrieks and whoops of
several children, the deep ragged howling of a dog and the ear-
splitting, yowling squalls of an enraged cat.

Miss Em's reflexes were good. They caused her to yank so
vigorously at the weed she was pulling that it was suddenly uprooted and she was sent reeling back into the thorny embrace
of the rambler rose. "Drat!" she said vehemently. Then, pluck-
ing herself loose from the rose's prickly clutches, she marched to
the orchard.

Three round-eyed little boys watched her coming. They were
lined up like stair steps, their faces apprehensive. "Seth —
Paul — Jimmy," she said, calling the roll down the line from the
tallest to the shortest, "I've told you about teasing Augustine."

It was a ridiculous name for a cat, but she had had no choice
in the matter. It had been given her by the German yard man,
who when in his cups had a sentimental fondness for singing
"Ach, du lieber Augustin." She had no great love for the animal, but she was afraid it would come to harm if she turned it
out.

"Yes ma'am, Miss Em, but we weren't teasing him. Ring was

chasing him and we were trying to make him stop," the oldest boy explained.

Miss Em reflected that their efforts would have been confusing to a dog of more intelligence than Ring. With him, she was certain they had been an encouragement. "Can't you keep your dog tied up?"

Reproachfully the three stared at her. "He likes to play with us," the smallest boy offered.

Of course he did. Miss Em sighed. When you took in little boys you invariably took in a dog, though nothing had been said about a dog when she had rented the orchard to the pipeliner and his family.

It had been a mistake, she thought, to let him put his trailer in the orchard. But money was so short, and the orchard was so shady and quiet, and people had to live somewhere. Her conscience would have disturbed her if she had refused the man.

"We won't bother a thing," he had promised, looking longingly at the big, tree-shaded space. "It's so far from the house you'll never know we're there. It would be such a fine place for the boys."

"All right," she had agreed reluctantly. It *was* a fine place for boys and the Chamber of Commerce said the townspeople must all be hospitable to the pipeline crew. After all, they were bringing thousands of dollars' worth of business to the town, as well as a natural-gas line. "But it's just for the summer," she reminded him. "Three months is all we want, ma'am. We'll be moving on then." They had arrived only a week ago. She remembered how all three of the boys lined up behind the fence the day they had moved in, solemn, curious and watchful as she trimmed the grass edges of the walk. Forty years of teaching school had given her a considerable knowledge of children. She worked on quietly, ignoring them, giving them time to absorb her and the white house and the big lawn. Suddenly, solemnly and in order they proffered their names.

"I'm Seth."

"I'm Paul."

"I'm Jimmy."

"How do you do?" she had said, turning to look at them. "I'm Miss Em."

"I'm seven."

"I'm six."

Five pudgy brown fingers went up from Jimmy. "I'm five."

They waited, two pairs of blue eyes, one of brown, fixed on her expectantly. Miss Em cleared her throat.

Jimmy, whose thumb was hovering near his mouth, asked, "How old are you?"

Paul, the middle one, nudged him and hissed, "Sh-h-h! You not s'posed to ask ladies how old they are."

Jimmy's eyes had widened. "Why?"

"They don't like to tell."

The big brown eyes had come round to rest fearfully on her, conscious of having sinned.

She had relieved him by sensibly explaining to them that they could play in the orchard but not in the yard. They must not tease the cat. They must not bother the garden tools in the shed. They could hang a swing from one of the apple trees but not the peach. They could sail their boats in the little pond at the foot of the orchard, but they must not wade in it because it grew deep at one end. Then she had given them cookies, and after thanking her gravely and meticulously they had marched off home.

Their mother was a harried, tense young woman — harried and tense not only from the constant coping with their boundless energy but from the necessity of moving every few months.

She had sighed her dislike of it to Miss Em the first day. "It's no way for children to live, and I know it. But Harry's always been a pipeliner and I guess he always will be. I just have to make the best of it."

Miss Em supposed she did try, and it was not really her fault that in one week the boys had broken a limb from an apple tree, smashed the window of the tool shed, torn three palings from the fence and reduced Augustine to a quivering mass of nerves. Three times in three days she had rescued him. The boys must learn there were consequences.

She faced the stair steps. Seth and Paul were very blond and their eyes brilliantly blue. Jimmy had brown eyes and a wide smile that made dimples under his ears. His thumb sought his mouth in his uncertainty now, and his brown eyes were almost liquid with anxiety.

She must seem an ogre to him, she thought, an old-maid ogre who measured out nothing but scolding words. She knew their mother must have threatened them with, "If you don't be good Miss Em will make us move."

She wanted to reassure him; she could never bear to see a child frightened. But the schoolroom had taught her that discipline, to be effective, must be stern. Smiles were for rewards. She kept her face sober. "You'll have to get Augustine down from that tree," she said.

Three pairs of eyes turned to look at the tree. The lowest limb was far from the ground. Three pairs of eyes, full of misgiving, turned then to look at her. "Gosh, Miss Em," said Seth, "it's too big a tree to climb."

Paul, who had freckles and big ears, eyed the tree measuringly. "I can shinny up it if you'll give me a boost."

She shook her head. "You're too heavy for me to lift."

Jimmy's eyes rested on her swimmingly. "Am I too heavy?"

He's afraid to climb, she thought, but he will, if necessary. "You're too heavy, too. You'll have to think."

"Daddy can get him down when he comes home tonight."

"No, you must get him down yourselves. It's only fair. Your dog chased him up the tree. I expect you to bring him home by lunchtime." She walked away, leaving them with their problem. Was it too big? she wondered.

It was very quiet in the orchard for perhaps fifteen minutes; then there was a great banging and clattering, a few shouted orders, excitement in uplifted voices, a yell or two, a squeak of some kind, then quiet again. After a few moments it started all over, and it continued, off and on, for perhaps an hour. Miss Em went on with her weeding. They're building a ladder, she told herself, and a very sensible thing it was of them to do, too. Give a child a task and leave him alone with it. It had been a maxim of hers.

She dug out dandelions, uprooted crabgrass, stung her hands on thistle and dock, conscious of the noises in the orchard but not at all apprehensive about them. The sun was almost directly overhead when she heard them coming. She could not have missed hearing, for they were chattering loudly in their excitement. They rounded the corner and broke into a run. "Hey, Miss Em! We got him!"

She straightened to look. They were grimy, their shirttails were out, there was a big rent in Seth's pants, but they did indeed have Augustine. Jimmy was carrying him, cradling him gently as if he were a baby. Proudly he handed him over.

"Fine," she said calmly, stroking the cat. "How did you manage?"

"Oh, we built a ladder. Come see, Miss Em. We built a dandy tree ladder."

She put the cat in the house and followed the boys to the

orchard. She stared in amazed dismay. Marching rakishly up the trunk of the tree, no two slanted alike, were four palings from the fence. The fence, she saw, was now gap-toothed on both sides of the gate. She might as well, she thought bitterly, take the gate down, too. Nothing could be more unnecessary. Dear Lord, she thought, just let me get through this summer! Just give me patience for the next three months!

The boys were looking at her expectantly, waiting for her praise. "Isn't it a dandy ladder, Miss Em? Look, you can go up in a zip! Watch me, Miss Em!" Paul's legs twinkled up the slats and he straddled the lowest limb.

"Move over. I'm coming up too!" Seth scrambled up the slats and joined him. "It's easy, Miss Em. You could do it, too."

"I doubt it," she said dryly. Jimmy stood, his thumb in his mouth, watching. "Did you get Augustine down for me, Jimmy?"

The thumb popped out. "Didn't any of us. He jumped down by hisself when Seth went up after him. But I caught him when he tried to run away."

"That was very thoughtful of you." She measured him a wan smile and was rewarded with an ear-dimpling grin. Well, she was hoist with her own petard. And they *had* used initiative, even if at the expense of her fence. She must be fair. "It's a fine ladder, boys," she called up the tree. "Come down now and I'll give you some lemonade and cookies."

They drank a gallon of lemonade and ate a whole batch of cookies, then wandered aimlessly over the house. In a school-room Miss Em knew what to do with children. In her own home she was at a loss. She let them wander. They ended up in the living room, gazing around curiously. "You've got a guitar," Seth pointed out.

"Yes."

"Do you know how to play it?"

It was her one musical accomplishment, though it had been years since she had touched the instrument. She picked it up. As a girl she had played, and the feel of the instrument in her hands now brought back memories of summer picnics on the river; of boys and girls long since grown, married, many of them dead; of the one man she might herself have married, given a few more moonlit nights — but there had been a death in his family and he had had to go away. She thought of the skating in the winter and hay rides and the taffy pulls. The guitar had accompanied them all. "Play something for us," Jimmy urged.

Self-consciously, she tried to think of a song and came up with a ballad, a very slow and sad one. She sang all its verses, gathering courage as she went along, while the boys stood in front of her, watching her hands, listening respectfully. "Gee," they said when she had finished, "that was pretty, Miss Em."

"We know a song," Seth volunteered.

"Do you? If you'll sing it, I'll try to accompany you."

"It's 'The Chisholm Trail.'"

She had never heard of it. "Start singing and I'll pick it up."

They lined up and cleared their throats. A little shyly they looked at one another, then Paul nudged Seth. "You start off."

Seth stared at his feet a moment, then lifted his head and began singing. The other boys chimed in. "Come along, boys, and I'll tell you my tale; I'll tell you my troubles on the old Chisholm Trail. Come a ki-yi-yippee, yippee-ay, come a ki-yi-yippee, yippee-ay!"

My goodness, Miss Em thought, a cowboy song! Valiantly she struggled to find the key and keep the rhythm. It was difficult, because as verse followed verse and the boys gained confidence they increased the speed of the song, until at the end they were racing madly and her fingers were having to fly.

"Well," she said, feeling out of breath, "that was fine, wasn't it?"

In a way it had been fine. Their voices were small, but sweet and very true, and they had swung along very gallantly. She put the guitar away. "I think you'd better run along now. Your mother probably has your lunch ready."

Without question they accepted the suggestion, flung themselves out of the house, banging the screen door behind them, calling back over their shoulders, "*Adios,* Miss Em. *Adios.* We'll come to see you again sometime."

Adios? Then she remembered they were from Texas.

She hadn't expected them back so soon, however. At what seemed the crack of dawn the next morning she was roused by a loud knocking at her back door. Who in the world? she wondered, reaching for a robe and trying to wedge her feet into mismatched slippers. Only half awake, she fumbled toward the door. The knocking was very insistent. "I'm coming! I'm coming!" she shouted impatiently.

In sleepy disenchantment she eyed them as they stood lined up on her steps. "What are you boys doing here at this time of day?"

"We aren't boys, ma'am," Seth told her sternly. "We're the men from the zoo. We've come to build a cage for your tiger. I'm Mr. White."

"I'm Mr. Brown."

Jimmy giggled. "I'm Mr. Black."

"We heard your tiger is giving you a lot of trouble and we've come to fix a cage for him."

"For heaven's sake, Seth," she began.

"Miss Em, a tiger is a very dangerous animal," he interrupted her eagerly. "And they shouldn't be allowed to run loose. Besides," he warned her, "it's against the law."

She saw that they had dragged along a wooden orange crate. "Oh, all right," she said. It was probably the quickest way to be rid of them.

"Where do you want to build it?"

"Here on the back porch, where you can watch him." Seth gave her a winsome smile. "You'll have to feed him and it'll be handy."

They dragged in the crate and she wondered what more they could do to it. It looked very substantial as it was. Then she saw they had other tools besides a hammer and some nails. Seth had a can opener and a screwdriver. Jimmy had a burned-out radio tube and a discarded wire sieve. They clustered around the crate, examining it in detail. "We'd better fix the spurlix first," Seth said, nodding his head wisely. "The konker has come un-konked."

Spurlix? Konker? Miss Em sat on a stool, curious now. They went to work, banging, measuring, attaching things, bending, listening, frowning, their hands flying about. "Hand me the bixter," Seth said to Jimmy. "Not the big bixter, the little one."

"We didn't bring the little bixter. Here's the skootak."

Jimmy handed him the wire sieve. There was a silence and then Seth said, "The squamlet won't do, either. What about the sticklebit?"

Paul handed over the screwdriver. Seth shook his head. "The sticklebit is too little. Mr. Black, you'll just have to go back and get the little bixter."

Jimmy hustled out the door, giving her a grin as he passed. He came back with an old toothpaste tube, thrust it at Seth. "Here, Mr. White."

Seth took it, dropped it in the tomato can, tied one end of the electric cord around the can and the other around the can opener, poked the can opener through the wire sieve and attached the whole to a crack in the wooden crate. He buzzed like a saw for a moment, then Paul began buzzing and finally Jimmy started buzzing, too. They buzzed at different speeds and in different keys for several minutes; then Seth nodded his head. "It's okay, men. Miss Em, I think your tiger will be perfectly comfortable in this nice cage."

They gathered up the hammer and nails and filed past her to the door. Dazedly, she watched them. As they reached the door, Jimmy turned around and gave her a seraphic smile. "If you have any trouble, Miss Em, just call us. Our telephone number is eleven-twenty-thirty."

She nodded, speechless.

They were halfway across the lawn before an uncontrollable impulse struck her. "Boys," she called, "just what *did* you do to the cage?"

Over the stretch of lawn, over the rosebushes, over the petunias, came Seth's clear, looping answer. "Why, Miss Em, we put in an air conditioner."

As the summer wore on she became accustomed to their visits at any hour of the day. She became accustomed to all their whimsical pretend games and learned to take her part in them easily and deftly. She was once an admiral when an expedition sailed for the North Pole. Earnestly, Seth explained that the North Pole had come loose and the President wanted them to go find it. "It won't do to have it floating loose in the ocean, Miss Em."

"Of course not," she agreed.

Feeling not the least bit silly, she stood at the helm of a tin washtub while Paul, in the crow's nest on the stepladder, called down sailing directions to her.

Once she was a policeman looking for stolen jewels, flashing a cereal-box-top badge. Handsomely, they let her shoot the robbers when they were tracked down, and, flushed and excited, she pulled the trigger on Jimmy's water pistol too soon and got them all wet.

Once she was a spaceman, a cut-out plastic vegetable bag

over her head for a helmet. Once she died dramatically, hanged as a cattle rustler. That was when she had objected to riding a wooden sawhorse on the range. "You can be the cattle rustler," they had said. She had a rope burn on her neck for a week from the hanging. The boys' mother was aghast.

"Miss Em, *don't* let them bother you so much."

"Oh," she said vaguely, "they don't bother me. I send them along home when they make little nuisances of themselves."

But she didn't fool even herself. She did not know when they had ceased being three little boys who threatened the peace and quiet of her first summer of retirement and became instead three good friends. She did not know when she began to know them as persons, know that Seth was tense, nervous, sensitive and brilliant; that Paul was clever, loyal and determined; that Jimmy was docile, sweet, even-tempered. It just happened very gradually, until she found she was taking care with each, remembering his own personality, his own individuality.

Little by little she got used to them, to their casual "Hi, Miss Em" when they came, and their equally casual "*Adios*, Miss Em" when they left, to their noise and their games, until one day when their mother took them away for the day she had an odd feeling of loneliness in the big house. It was too quiet. The silence itself was very loud, and she realized that she had become so accustomed to their noise that it was like the birds in the trees, the jar flies humming their endless songs all the long, hot days, the tree frogs croaking hoarsely at night. It was strange, she thought, what one could get used to. She was used to children, of course, but not in her home. Her home had always been a cool, lofty retreat for her, her own quiet domain. Now it was the domain of the boys.

Not that they were always noisy. They came quietly sometimes, and she fed them and played the guitar for them. And they played with Augustine.

She had kept him in the house since the adventure with the dog, in the beautifully air-conditioned wooden crate. The boys all adored him, played with him, stroked him, held him, petted him, fed him. "Isn't he soft?" they said, rubbing their hands down his fur.

"Doesn't he make a funny noise inside?" holding him close to their ears.

They felt they owned him since they had rescued him from a tree and made him a cage.

So it was with a guilty feeling Miss Em had to tell them one morning that he had gone away for a little while. "Just on a little adventure," she said reassuringly. "He'll be home tonight."

Fervently, she hoped he would. He had been so restless the night before, mewing uneasily and scratching at the door, refusing his food and pacing from his box to the door. Finally she had let him out. "It's very silly of you," she told him. "You'll just get into a fight. You'd better stay home where you belong."

But he had been off like a shot, leaving her only a wave of his tail in gratitude.

He did not come home that night, however, though she called and the boys called. Nor the next day, nor the next night. They went to look for him. They looked in every tree in the orchard, in the long grass beside the pond, in the woods and meadows beyond the orchard.

"He's just gone, Miss Em," Jimmy said tearfully. "He's been kilt, I betcha."

"Oh, I don't think so," she said, trying to comfort him. "He'll come home by and by."

Each day they looked, the boys mournful and disconsolate, Miss Em increasingly anxious. He had never stayed away so long before. She grew to dread the mornings when the boys appeared, hope on their faces that she had to watch fade as she shook her head.

"Drat the animal," she said to herself. "Where can he have got to?"

It was a week to the day that she found him in the back yard, alive, but only barely. One ear was almost torn off; he was tattered and torn, bloody and clawed. Her first thought was, the boys mustn't see him like this.

She took him in the house, cleaned him up, bandaged the worst places and had him in his box on a bed of clean rags by the time they came. They were overjoyed that he had come home, hung over his box and crooned to him, but they were horrified at the sight of his condition.

"Was he in a fight, Miss Em?"

Grimly she said he must have been. The nature of tomcats was best left unexplained, she thought.

"Will he get well?"

"I hope so, but he's very sick."

They suggested remedies. "Maybe he needs a shot of penicillin."

"Maybe he needs a tetanus shot."

"Maybe if you gave him a vitamin pill?"

"We'll call the vet," she promised.

They hovered when the man came, watching his face for a clue. "He's injured internally, Miss Em," he said finally. "He's slowly bleeding to death. Shall I put him away easily?"

Her heart thumped. Death, she thought. Do they know about it?

"What does he mean, Miss Em?" It was Jimmy tugging at her skirt.

Well, it had to be faced. "He means perhaps he should put Augustine to sleep quietly, since he can't live."

"Kill him?" Seth asked quickly.

"Well, yes . . ."

Like an explosion it came from all three. "No! He can't kill him, Miss Em. He might live."

The man looked at her and she shook her head. The boys had decided.

They were tireless in their efforts to help the cat, lifting him, turning him, trying to get him to eat. They all were beside him when the end came on a hot, sultry afternoon. It was Paul who said quietly, "I think he's died, Miss Em."

"How do you know?"

"He's stopped breathing."

Strangely enough, there were no tears now. They had agonized over his illness, hung over him, wept over him, but quite calmly they accepted his death. Even Jimmy only stroked the silky fur and said, "Poor Augustine, poor Augustine. You're dead now, Augustine."

She had expected tears and tantrums. Instead, Seth said gently, "We have to have the funeral now."

"What do you know about funerals?"

"Oh, on TV they have them. We can put him in a box and dig a grave, Miss Em."

Well, he had to be buried. She rummaged around and found a box, lined it with tissue paper, lifted Augustine into it. Gravely the boys took it outside and she showed them where to dig. "Back of the tool shed," she said. She left them then, thinking perhaps they would rather have their funeral alone.

It was Jimmy who appeared at the door. "You'd better come now. We're ready."

She followed him. They had dug a deep hole, which they had lined with grass. The box was covered with flowers. It lay beside the open hole. The three boys stood solemnly at one side. They had gone home, she saw, and put on their best clothes, washed their hands and faces, wet down their hair.

Seth was officiating. When she joined them, he said, "Bow your heads. We've got to pray. You want to say the blessing, Jimmy?"

Three crew-cut heads and Miss Em's own iron-gray were soberly bent while Jimmy's sweetest, most innocent voice chanted, "Come, Lord Jesus, be our guest; let this food by Thee be blessed. Amen."

Miss Em gulped. But a table grace wasn't the worst graveside prayer that could be said, she supposed.

Seth took charge again authoritatively. "Now we got to sing. All join hands."

Obediently they made a circle around the grave. Seth cleared his throat and hummed a note or two. Then he started the song, "Come along, boys, and I'll tell you my tale . . ." The others chimed in generously. "I'll tell you my troubles on the old Chisholm Trail. Come a ki-yi-yippee, yippee-ay, yippee-ay, come a ki-yi-yippee, yippee-ay."

"You're not singing, Miss Em," Jimmy accused her at the end of the first chorus. "Everybody's got to sing, don't they, Seth?"

Solemnly, Seth nodded.

Miss Em sang, "Come a ki-yi-yippee, yippee-ay."

Augustine was being gathered to the last corral, where no doubt he would join Old Paint. She might as well help herd him on his way.

For some reason they didn't want to go home that evening. She fed them and then they all sat on the wide front porch and watched the first stars come out, listened to the whippoorwills, looked at the fireflies lighting the early dark. Jimmy crawled into Miss Em's lap, put his thumb in his mouth and sleepily snuggled against her. They wanted to talk, and they talked about death and God and day and night and fairy princesses and airplanes and diesel locomotives. Then they wanted stories and Miss Em told them until her throat ached.

Jimmy was asleep when their father came for them, and he lifted the little boy gently from Miss Em's lap. It felt empty and cold where he had been.

"Come on, boys. It's nearly bedtime."

Drowsily, the other two boys clambered down from the swing where they had been flanking Miss Em, began to say good night.

"We'll be pulling out tomorrow, Miss Em," their father said. "The job's finished here."

"So soon?" she said, startled.

"The summer's over, Miss Em. I expect you'll be glad to see us go, at that. These boys have been a bother to you, I know."

Oh, no, she cried silently, one hand reaching out to touch a bristly young head. Bothered me? Not ever. Why, what would she do without them? How would the days ever be filled again?

"Good night."

They were swallowed up in the dark.

She didn't sleep that night. He had taken her by surprise. Of course, it was the first of September. He had said three months when he rented the orchard. It had been three months, but she was still unprepared for it. It had seemed no time at all. She had almost lost count of the days, so busy the summer had been, so full, so very full. She counted over the days and the memories. Yes, the three months were gone. Ruefully she remembered asking the Lord to give her patience to get through the time. She wished she could ask him now to give her just one more golden day.

She was up before the sun, made her coffee and sat and watched out the window. She wanted to see the boys once more, but she didn't know whether she should or not. She hadn't said goodbye. She had been too stunned. Perhaps it was better this way. Just let them slip out of her life. It would do no good to tell them goodbye. This summer would fade from their memories — they were so young. They would not long remember Miss Em. Seth might, and maybe Paul, but Jimmy? She remembered how soft and snuggly he had been in her lap last night. In forty years of teaching she had often comforted a hurt child, a sick child, a bewildered child; but never, not once, had one crawled into her lap and gone to sleep there, as if she had been his mother. Jimmy was too little — he would not remember her.

Unhappily, she stared out the window, and then she saw them coming, as they had so often come early in the morning, Seth leading, Paul following, Jimmy bringing up the rear. She met them at the door.

"We brought you some presents." Seth offered his.

"We made 'em." Paul offered his.

"But you're not s'posed to open 'em till we're gone." It was Jimmy offering his.

They were flat, thin little packages, wrapped in grocery paper, tied with dirty twine. Gravely she accepted them. "Thank you very much."

In a quick, smothering flurry of wiry arms, she was hugged and wetly kissed; their heels flashed over the grass and they were gone. From the orchard their voices floated back. "*Adios*, Miss Em. We'll come back and see you sometime." Oh, do, her heart wept, do! But she knew they never would.

Inside, she waited until her eyes had stopped blurring before opening their gifts. On a shirt cardboard each had drawn a picture and colored it with crayons. Seth's was a flowery wreath, with "To Miss Em from Seth" lettered in red inside. Paul's was a heart, thrust through with an arrow, also inscribed, "To Miss Em." Jimmy's was a very stark and realistic picture of a cat, stiff and dead. "Augustine," he had labeled it simply.

She heard a motor start and went to the door. The trailer

was swinging around, battened down now, empty, headed home to Texas. The boys were on the back seat of the car that was pulling the trailer. Catching a glimpse of her, they waved hysterically, kept waving until they disappeared at last down the drive.

Miss Em waved, too, as long as she could see them, and just as the car turned onto the highway called, although they could not hear, "Goodbye! Goodbye!" Then fiercely, lovingly, she whispered, "*Adios . . . Oh, adios, amigos.*"

(This story was published originally in *McCall's*, February 1959.)

STEP BY STEP

"He was their stepgrandfather but they didn't know anything
about that at the time."
                                        A Little Better Than Plumb

HIMMIE, they called him.

There were three of the boys, two with silvery blond hair
and bright blue eyes, and the youngest an oak-leaf brown with
soft, chocolatey eyes. They usually stood in a stair-step line.
"Because," they said, "that's the way we were born."

Inevitably, they were asked, "Who is Himmie?"

Inevitably, they answered, "Himmie is our favoritest grandfather in the whole, wide world."

"That," their grandmother said, "is the most inclusive state-
ment I ever heard. One gets the idea there are thousands of
grandfathers scattered from here to China to choose from, and
Henry has been handpicked from among them."

Her daughter, who had mothered the three boys, laughed.
"It certainly leaves no room for doubt."

They were on their annual summer visit, Jeanie and her sons.
The first time they had come the boys had been one, two
and three. Carrie had been appalled when, the big airliner having unloaded all its other passengers, there had then emerged
the pilot carrying Seth, the copilot carrying Paul and the stew-
ardess carrying Jimmy, who was not yet walking well. Jeanie
had come last, burdened with various and sundry diaper and
bottle bags. Carrie had watched her wilted daughter come down

the steps and had felt both love and admiration for her. It had taken courage to bring three babies all that long way from west Texas, and she did not think she would have attempted it. But Jeanie was determined that her boys should know their grandparents and faithfully every summer since they had come for this visit on the farm.

From outside the window, now, there came the soft drone of Henry's voice. "He was very angry because I ran the tractor over his house. He told me, and his whiskers were bristling, 'It was extremely thoughtless of you.' I apologized and explained to him that I had no idea he was living in the cornfield. I told him that I would not do it again, but he was afraid I would forget. He put his hands in his pockets and he paced up and down the furrow, his brow wrinkled with thinking. 'I have it,' he shouted finally. 'I'll paint a sign to hang over my door. You can't possibly run over my house if there is a sign.' I agreed that it might be a good idea."

"Himmie," a small voice interrupted, "what color were his pants?"

There was a pause. "Red, I think."

"Aren't you sure?"

"Well, I'm *nearly* sure. It was growing late, you see, and they *may* have been a dark orange."

"I expect they were red."

"I really think they were."

"Did he have a jacket, too?"

"Oh, yes, he had a jacket. A very fancy one, with gold braid on the cuffs. And he had an admiral's cap."

"Why?"

"Because he was in the navy once."

"Oh. What color was the jacket?"

"Blue. It was *navy* blue."

Inside, Jeanie glanced at her mother and giggled.

"Go on, Himmie. Did he paint the sign?"

"Yes, he painted the sign. There were several cans of paint in the woodshed left over from when your grandmother painted the living room, and Freddie Fieldmouse mixed and he mixed and he mixed until he had just the color he wanted."

"What color was it?"

"Sky blue."

"Then what?"

"Then he found a clean board for his sign and he was ready to paint. But right there he ran into trouble."

"What kind of trouble?" The young voice was anxious.

"Well, you see, Freddie was so small he couldn't hold a paint brush. He tried and he tried — he tried every paint brush he could find, but they were all too big. So, do you know what he did?"

"What?" It was the barest whisper of a question.

"He just dipped his whiskers in the paint and used them!"

There was a long silence. "Didn't that get his whiskers all messed up?"

"Oh, yes. And of course he couldn't get the paint off. That's why, if you happen to see a very small, very tiny little field mouse running about the place with sky-blue whiskers, you'll know it's Freddie. To this day the paint has never come off his whiskers, and to the best of my knowledge he is the only blue-whiskered field mouse in the world."

"Golly! Gee!" There was another long pause, and then, inevitably, one more question. "What did the sign say, Himmie?"

"The sign said, 'This is the house of Freddie Fieldmouse. No admittance without the password!'"

"What was the password?"

There was the sound of whispering, and then came the spiraling, gleeful shout of Jimmy, rising and falling as he flew, triumphantly, to find his brothers, chanting in a singsong voice,

"I know the password, I know the password, I know the password."

Carrie laid her sewing down. "That was quite a masterpiece, and if it hasn't made the master hungry enough to eat Freddie Fieldmouse and all his brothers, I'll be surprised. Food will be the next object of his attention."

Her voice had a tender tone, however. She was a small, plump woman with graying reddish hair. She had been a widow with a married daughter, supporting herself by teaching, when the heavy, balding, ruddy-faced bachelor farmer had come courting. She never thought of his kindly and loyal affection for her daughter and the boys without a feeling of gratitude to him. He might so easily have created difficulties. Instead he had accepted her family and made them his own, and the little grandsons adored him.

When the meal was over and the boys had gone to bed, Himmie said decisively, "There is no reason why you shouldn't go to New York with your mother, Jeanie. I can ride herd on these boys for a couple of days."

"Oh, no," Jeanie protested. "They would wear you out. You have no idea . . ."

"If only it hadn't come up now," Carrie lamented, "just when you're here for your visit. I'd put it off but they said it was important."

Carrie had continued to teach after marrying and she had been asked to write a textbook. The publishers wanted her to come to New York for a conference on some of the details.

"Take Jeanie with you," Henry insisted firmly. "It will do her good to get away from the boys for a while, and the two of you will enjoy a little vacation."

"Henry," Jeanie said, "don't tempt me if you don't mean it."

"I mean it. Go on and have some fun. The boys and I will manage fine. I'll take them to the county fair and we'll go fishing and swimming. You'll find us menfolks all in one piece when you get back."

So it was decided, and a week later the women of the family boarded the plane for New York. There had been many last-minute instructions. "They have plenty of clean clothes, Henry . . . Just T-shirts and jeans for everyday, remember . . ."

"Henry, there's a ham in the refrigerator, and a baked chicken. There's a store of canned things in the pantry. There are cookies and two pies . . . and be sure and have Thelma come in tomorrow to wash the dishes. You'll have everything in a mess . . ."

Henry grinned. "You'd think you were going to be gone a month instead of two days. Get on the plane and be on your way. We'll manage."

"Yes," Seth shouted happily. "We're going to the fair and see the horse show and eat hot dogs and cotton candy and . . ."

Henry saw another warning on Jeanie's face, so he waved her off. "Have a good time!"

As the gate closed and he turned to herd the boys back to the car, only Jimmy, who was clutching his hand, a little tearful over his mother's leaving, was present. Two seconds ago they had all been beside him, waving and shouting, hanging on to the fence, swinging on the gate. An official had had to warn them off. Now they were out of sight and gone. He hurried into the waiting room. Seth, who was the oldest, with ash blond hair and brilliantly blue eyes, was making the drinking fountain spout to the ceiling. Henry got him by the shirttail. "Where's Paul?"

"I dunno."

"We've got to find him." He clutched Seth with one hand, held on to Jimmy with the other and went searching. Up and down the long corridors of the terminal he went, peering into offices, into the men's room, into the dining room. No Paul, and no one had seen him, either. He was beginning to think, with a sinking heart, that he might have to send the girl behind the newsstand counter into the women's rest room, when she said, "There's a snack bar down at the other end of the hall. Have you looked there?"

"No."

He and the other boys traipsed the long length of the corridor again. Paul was sitting at the counter, swinging carefree legs, swiveling the stool, consuming the last of a chocolate soda.

"Hi!" he yelled cheerfully, seeing them. "They make good chocklit sodas here, Himmie. Want one?"

"No. How did you intend to pay for that, young man?"

The round little freckled face looked serious. "Golly, do you have to pay for 'em? I just told her I wanted one and she gave it to me."

Himmie hauled a quarter out of his pocket, wedging Jimmy between his knees while he turned loose of him. "Come on, now. Let's get started home."

He had only two hands and perforce one boy must be left on his own. Deciding that Seth was the most likely candidate for responsibility, Himmie enjoined him solemnly, "Now, stay right with us. We have to cross the street outside and there's a lot of traffic. You might get run over."

Absently Seth nodded and followed at his own pace as the little cavalcade started off. At the door Himmie turned. Seth was still halfway down the hall, fiddling with the gum machine. He bellowed at him, "Seth! Come on!"

The boy's run was something between a skip and a hop. "Can I have a penny for the gum machine, Himmie? Can I? Please."

The other two boys began to plead also. "Please, Himmie. Please."

"All right." He gave in, largely because Jimmy's liquid brown eyes were still a little sad. He searched for pennies. "Now, don't take all day. Put your pennies in and come straight back."

They whooped and sailed off, using the slick, waxed floor as a rink for skating and sliding. "Look, fellows, no hands!" shouted Seth, and Himmie groaned as he saw him narrowly miss upsetting a fat matron and bounce back to collide with a porter, scattering his load of luggage. "Boy," the porter roared, recovering the bags, "you better watch out where you is goin'."

"Yes, sir," Seth said, politely helping him collect the luggage. "Here's your cap, too, sir."

Himmie hurried over. "Come on now, Seth. Get your gum and let's go."

"I can work it, Himmie. Don't help me. I know how to work it."

"Well, work it, then!"

A scarlet red ball of gum bounced out of the chute, Seth grabbed for it and missed and it went rolling across the floor. "Let it go," Himmie yelled, but Seth had already pounced on it and had it in his mouth. Himmie stared at him. Jeanie would have been horrified. Well, it was too late now.

"Put your penny in, Paul."

Paul's ball of gum was a sickly green, but learning from Seth he had covered the chute with both hands and got it safe in his mouth without difficulty.

"Now, Jimmy."

The little golden brown boy slid his penny in the slot and pulled the lever. A white ball came rolling down the chute and hastily Himmie reached for it. "There."

But Jimmy put his hands behind his back. "I don't want a white one."

"Why not? They're all alike inside."

Stubbornly, Jimmy shook his head. "I want a red one, like Seth's."

"But Jimmy, there's no telling when another red one will come out. Here, take this white one now, and be happy with it."

"I want a red one," Jimmy wailed. "I want a red one just like Seth's!" The tears were very close. The small chin was dogged but the sweet, wide young mouth was quivering. It's mostly because of his mother, Himmie thought, and he couldn't bear for the child to feel so forsaken. "All right, Jimmy. Let me get some more pennies. We'll get you a red one."

Bystanders were grinning and watching as the man stood by the machine, poking pennies in the slot. The balls of gum came rolling down, black, white, yellow, blue, until there was a handful of them distributed between the boys. Sweating, the ruddy-faced man, his face considerably redder now, wondered if another red one ever *would* be released. When the boys' hands were full, he told them to put the sticky balls in their pockets.

"Whatcha trying to do, mister?" a clerk at one of the counters asked, leaning far over to see.

"I'm trying," said Himmie, between his teeth, "to get a red ball for this boy."

The clerk laughed. "For heaven's sake, mister, it might take all day. Here, I'll unlock the thing and you can get him one."

"I want it to come down the slide," Jimmy said, threateningly.

"He wants it to come down the slide," Himmie repeated, and the clerk laid the key aside.

To an audience of all the passengers, most of the porters and a scattering of clerks, they kept poking pennies in the slot and kept working the lever that released the gum. There was a lot of advice. "Tilt it a little."

"Shake it."

"Turn it upside down."

Finally, a red ball came bounding down the chute and Jimmy

clutched it happily. "There, you see, Himmie? It's just like Seth's."

"I see," the man said grimly. "Now, come on."

He got them home, a distance of some twenty-five miles from the airport, and as they trooped into the house a cry for lunch went up. "I want scrambled eggs," Seth said.

"I want a hamburger," Paul said.

"I'd rather have soup," Jimmy piped up.

"You will each," Henry said firmly, "have a ham sandwich and a glass of milk, and then you are going to lie down and take a nap."

"But, Himmie." The three voices were in unison, and horrified. "We don't take naps anymore."

"Since when? You took naps last summer."

"Since this winter," Seth assured him. "We're too big."

Uncertainly, Henry eyed them. They did look pretty big to be going to bed in the afternoon, but Jeanie hadn't told him and she had used to be very stern about their naps. "I don't know . . ." he began.

"Aren't we going to the fair?" Paul asked. "You *promised* we'd go to the fair, Himmie."

"I want to ride the merry-go-round," Jimmy chanted.

"Ah, that's for little kids," Seth jeered. "I'm going to ride the ferris wheel."

"I want to see the horse show," Paul said, stoutly.

"All right." Henry gave in. It wouldn't matter this once. "Change your shirts and we'll be off."

It was ten miles to the fairgrounds and for ten miles they sang, lustily, variations on the theme of "The Streets of Laredo." It was easy, Henry thought, deafened, to tell they came from Texas.

They ate hot dogs and cotton candy. They rode the merry-go-round and the ferris wheel. They threw darts, shot popguns, drank lemonade and they watched, starry-eyed and fascinated, the horse show. In each ring they picked their favorites, watched them walk, slow walk, trot, canter, but they especially loved it when the announcer called, "Let your horses rack, ladies and gentlemen, let 'em rack on off!" Then the horses went thundering by in the beautiful, fast, muscle-rippling, disciplined gait that looked so effortless and had to be taught so patiently. "Aren't they beautiful?" the boys breathed worshipfully. "Can't they rack the *best?*"

Watching their radiant faces Henry thought affectionately they might live in west Texas but they were beginning, pretty early, to be good little Kentuckians.

Going home when it was all over they were quiet, stuffed with food, tired and a little sleepy. Finally Seth sighed, wistfully. "Well, Charlie can't rack, but he's prettier than any of those horses."

Charlie was an old horse, a little lame in his left hind leg, that Henry had kept when he mechanized the farm. He had been a good, faithful animal for twelve years and Henry could not bring himself to trade him off now, in his old age, into the hands of strangers who might misuse him. A little ashamed of his sentiment he had told Carrie, "He'll be a good horse for the boys when they're old enough to ride."

He was a sorrel, with a flax mane and tail, and the boys loved him devotedly and loyally. They compared every horse they saw with him, judiciously concluding each time, "He's all right. He's a good horse, but he isn't as nice a horse as Charlie."

The past summer the boys had been allowed to begin riding him, just around the barn lot and always with Henry or their mother present. With some reason they now felt he had become their personal property.

The horse show fresh in their minds, they wanted to ride immediately on getting up the next morning. "Not this morning," Henry told them. "I have to mend the pasture fence. The cows got out last night. You can ride this afternoon."

"Does somebody *have* to be with us, Himmie? We're getting pretty good."

"I know you are. But you're not good enough yet to ride alone. Help me with the fence this morning; then we'll ride."

But they soon grew weary of handing him staples and they grew restless with the slowness of the work, with the heat and with the weeds along the fence rows, which made their ankles and arms itch. "I *wish*," Jimmy said finally, leaning against a post, disconsolate with boredom, "we could ride Charlie *right* now."

Henry, who was beginning to be bored with the heat and the job, too, snapped at him, "Well, you can't. You may as well forget it until after lunch."

He saw the slow tears well up in the liquid brown eyes and his heart smote him. Here they were, motherless for another day, and he was growing sharp with them. He was suddenly inspired. "I tell you. Go down to Mr. Lee's and see if Pete is doing anything. Maybe he can ride you."

Pete was the son of the tenant on the farm. He was an older boy, twelve perhaps, and had been farm-reared; Henry thought he could be depended on to oversee the riding. Actually, the boys could probably have managed alone and come to no harm, with Charlie so old and gentle, but he didn't like to risk it. "If Pete isn't busy you can ride now."

Joyously, the three small boys trooped off, turning cartwheels, shouting, running, raising a dust in the dry, weedy lane. Henry watched them go, fondly. It took so little to make them happy.

He saw them come back to the barn with Pete, saw Pete catch up and saddle the old horse, saw each boy taking his turn at riding slowly and sedately round and round the lot. He finished his chore and then went to the house to set out lunch.

When he called them, they came, but they came slowly, dispiritedly.

They washed up, seated themselves around the table quietly. Too quietly, Henry thought. They had not said a word since they came in the house. "Did you have a good ride?" he asked.

Still not speaking, they nodded.

"Fine. Now, we've got chicken and dressing today. Pass your plates."

Seth obediently passed his, but he eyed Henry strangely — as if he had never seen him before, Henry thought.

Paul passed his plate with the same big-eyed look, and a queer, sidelong glance at Seth.

Jimmy just shook his head. "I'm not hungry."

"Oh, you must be, after all that riding. Come on, fellow, let me have your plate."

The little boy's chin quivered and his thumb sought his mouth, but obediently he handed over his plate.

None of the three ate heartily, however. They watched him, with odd, almost frightened, hidden glances. They wiggled on their chairs; they looked meaningfully at each other; but they only picked at their food. "What's the matter with you boys?" Henry asked finally. "Don't you feel well? What are you so quiet about?"

The two younger boys looked at Seth, who often was the spokesman for the three, and Seth's eyes dropped first to his plate, then lifted courageously to Henry. "Pete said . . ." he began. "Pete told us . . ."

He stopped and Henry saw with amazement that the blue eyes were deeply troubled.

"Well. What did Pete say? What did he tell you?"

It was Jimmy who burst into sobs and wailed loudly, "He said you weren't really our grandfather. He said you were just our stepgrandfather!"

"Well, my goodness, what's wrong with that? What's there to cry about, Jimmy?"

"I don't like steps," Jimmy hiccuped. "I don't want you to be my stepgrandfather!"

"Look, fellow . . ."

"Are you *really* our stepgrandfather, Himmie?" Paul asked, and Henry saw that his chin was none too firm.

"Well, yes . . . but . . ."

They eyed him truculently and accusingly. Good Lord, he thought, a little wildly, this *would* happen now, without Carrie's good, sensible head to see him through, or Jeanie's warm, sweet arms to comfort the boys. "See here," he said, "what difference does it make?"

"Steps," Seth said grudgingly, "are mean."

"What do you mean?"

"Well, they *are* mean, Himmie. Don't you remember Cinderella had a stepmother and she made her eat scraps and wear old clothes . . ."

"I don't want to eat scraps," Jimmy wailed. "I don't like old clothes!"

Paul picked up the story. "And Pete said he knew a boy that had a stepmother and she beat him every day with a big stick and made him sleep in the barn. Pete said steps were awful mean."

"I won't sleep in the barn, Himmie," Jimmy cried. "I don't like barns . . . there's mice in the corncribs."

Aghast, Henry stared at them. Sweet Jumping Jupiter! Angrily he thought he would like to get his hands on Pete. And he would like to get his hands on every storyteller who had woven an anguished tale making villains of stepmothers. They should have anticipated it, he thought, he and Carrie and Jeanie, but . . . who could have foreseen it would become an issue like this!

Jimmy's little golden head was bowed on the table and his

shoulders were shaking with sobs. "I don't want you to be my stepgrandfather. I don't like steps. Steps are the *worst*! I don't *like* 'em, Himmie!"

Henry gathered him up and strode to the couch with him. "Come on, boys," he called, "and we'll talk about it."

It was not enough now that he had always been devoted to them. It was not enough that they had always trusted him. That trust had been undermined, and in the same way that the damage had been done, it must be undone. A little doubtfully, giving him plenty of room, Seth and Paul took places on either side of him. In his arms, Jimmy was stiff. He held him firmly, however. He took a long, deep breath. He was conscious of a devout wish — a prayer. Let me make this good. Let me make it good enough to convince them. He began. "Now, all of you know that Cinderella is a fairy story, don't you? You know that it didn't really happen."

They nodded. Their mother had always been careful with such stories, because of the giants and ogres and witches. It was understandable that she had never thought about the stepmother.

"Well, I am going to tell you a story about steps. This one is *not* a fairy story. It really happened. You understand that?"

Again they nodded. "All right. Once upon a time . . .'

"That's a fairy story," Jimmy interrupted. "They always begin that way."

"Very well. There was once a little boy . . . Is that all right?"

Jimmy's head moved on his chest.

"There was once a little boy who was very unhappy because he had no mother."

"Why didn't he have a mother?"

"She went away. She died." He hurried on. "This little boy had five brothers and sisters, all younger than he, and he had to do all the cooking for them, wash their clothes and iron them, give them their baths, wash all the dishes, sweep the floors, and besides he had to go to school, too, and he had to study at night after his brothers and sisters were in bed."

"Didn't he have a father?"

Henry gave thanks for the questions. It meant they were listening and becoming interested.

"Yes, he had a father, but the father had to work all day in the fields. He didn't have time to help in the house. And when he came in at night he was too tired. The little boy had to manage as best he could."

Jimmy, he thought, was a little more relaxed. The boy's body felt heavier and softer.

"It was very difficult for the little boy and sometimes at night when he tried to study he would be so tired that he would fall asleep before he had finished his lessons. So he began to fail in his school work, and he tried to study harder, but he was so tired all the time that he couldn't. When the end of the year came, he didn't pass, like all the other boys and girls. He had to stay back in the same grade."

"Gee," Seth said, from the wisdom of two years in school, "I wouldn't like that."

"He didn't either. But it couldn't be helped."

"Didn't the teacher *know* how hard he had to work at home?" Paul asked.

"Yes, she knew, and she tried to help him. But boys and girls have to learn to pass, and the little boy just hadn't learned enough."

Jimmy bounced in his lap, sat up straighter. "Poor little boy."

"What happened?" Paul asked.

"Well, one day the little boy's father went away for a few days . . ."

"Did he leave them by theirselves?" Jimmy was incredulous.

"Ye-e-es," Henry said, adding hastily, "He was a pretty big boy, you see."

"How big?"

"As big as Seth. Seth could manage by himself, I expect."

Seth nodded. "But I wouldn't like it."

"No. The little boy didn't like it either, but when his father went away he did the best he could."

"Where did the father go?"

"I'm coming to that. He went to the village."

"Did he ever come back?" Jimmy's eyes were enormous.

"Yes. He came back the next day. And when he came back, do you know what he brought them?"

"Candy?"

"Ice cream?"

"A new puppy?"

"No. He brought the little boy a new mother."

"A new mother!"

"Gee, Himmie, wasn't that swell of him?" Seth's eyes were blazing. "Gee, that was the best thing he could have brought him, wasn't it?"

"Oh, good!" Paul bounced. "And the new mother could do all the cooking and the dishes and the floors and everything, couldn't she?"

"She could. And she did. She was a nice mother and she cooked the best bread and cookies and pies. And she kept the floors so clean, and she kept the little boy's clothes washed and ironed, and she helped him with his homework and he never failed at school again."

Jimmy's eyes, raised to Henry's, were softly untroubled again. "Gee, she sure was a nice mother, wasn't she? I'll bet they liked her a lot."

"They did. They loved her, and she loved them. She taught them to say their prayers, and she tucked them in every night when they went to bed."

184

"What was the prayer she taught them?"

Quietly the big man recited it:

> "Matthew, Mark, Luke, and John
> Bless the bed that I lie on.
> Four angels to my bed,
> Four angels round my head;
> One to watch, and one to pray,
> Two to care for me till day."

In wonder, three pairs of astonished eyes looked at him. "Why, that's our prayer," Jimmy said.

"I know. Your mother heard me say it one time and liked it so much she decided to teach it to you."

"Gee. Did the little boy say it every night? We do."

Henry nodded. "Every night, all his life. He still says it, and he's a big man now."

There was a long silence. Then Seth, nuzzling Henry's shoulder with his chin, said, "Who was the little boy, Himmie?"

"Me."

"You?"

"Me. I was that little boy."

"It was you that got the nice new mother?" Paul asked, his dimples crinkling.

"It was I who got the nice new *step*mother."

Paul blinked. "Stepmother?"

"Yes. My new mother was really a stepmother."

"But she wasn't mean at all! She didn't make you eat scraps and sleep in the barn, did she?"

"She was a *good* stepmother, wasn't she?" Seth said.

"She was a good stepmother."

"All steps aren't bad, are they?"

"Certainly not. Most of them are very good. Most of them are better than any other people."

Seth looked quizzically at him. "Himmie, what *is* a step?"

"It's when your real mother or father, or grandfather, has gone away, or died, and someone takes his place and loves you just as much."

They pondered his answer. Then Jimmy's thumb left his mouth with a plop. "Oh, I see. It's a really someone, and they're a step because they *step* in and love you. Isn't it, Himmie?"

Henry hugged the little boy tightly. "That's exactly right, Jimmy. Now . . ." He heaved himself up off the couch, the clinging boys making it difficult. He felt very tired, too, suddenly. "Now, get your swimming trunks. We're going to the river."

They might be, he thought, all in one piece when their mother returned, but a few more crises like this and he was going to be pretty fractured.

He heard their Matthew, Mark, Luke and John that night and tucked each boy in. When he came to Jimmy the thin, strong young arms strangled him, and the soft, still babyish mouth brushed his chin. "Himmie," he whispered, "you're my favoritest stepgrandfather in the whole, wide world."

WE BUILT A LOG HOUSE

"There are still those who would tell you our house got built by guess and by God."

A Little Better Than Plumb

IT MAY HAVE BEEN because we already owned a log fishing camp, or it may have been because in the last three novels I had written the people had built log cabins and, like drugs, we were addicted to them.

Whatever the reason, when we went crazy with spring fever in 1957 and decided to build a home in the country, we perpetrated the further folly of building it of logs.

We thought for once we were being logical. The history of our married years has been one of valiant but futile efforts to overcome a native tendency in each of us, disastrous when pooled, to be as naive as babes in the wood about all practical matters. No matter how sensible we think we are being, it never turns out that way.

Triumphantly, however, we pointed to the already owned fishing camp, whose purchase had been one of our most foolish acts, and said we would start from that.

Living in town after several years on a farm we had been overcome with nostalgia and in a moment of madness had succumbed to our longing to walk on the earth again and we had bought the dreary thing. Then we were stuck with it.

We could neither sell it nor give it away because it was on a stretch of Green River that the fish avoided as if the waters were polluted, and it was down under a dreadful hill that towered over it so darkly and gloomily that the cabin was like the tunnel of love — without the love. It was also as cold as charity, which should have warned us. Blithely, however, we attributed its refrigerating tendencies to the fact that the sun never shone on it.

"Wait," we told each other, "until we get it moved to some high, dry, sunny place. It will be lovely. It will be our living room." Then, we said further, we can buy two or three more old log houses (of which there are a great plenty in Kentucky) and with a little ingenuity we shall have a nice log house. We did not doubt that we had the ingenuity.

The fact that we had paid twenty-three hundred dollars for the cabin, one room with lean-to and loft, and would pay three hundred and fifty dollars more to have it moved, making the raw materials of the living room cost twenty-six hundred dollars disassembled, wholly escaped us. We were being practical. Saddled with a white elephant, we were turning it to good use.

We busied ourselves to find an acre or two of land to move it to. One acre, we said, would be fine. It is typical of us that what we finally bought was seventy-six acres, of which sixty-two are in woods so steeply ridged and hollowed that not even the fireplace wood can be cut off it. Nothing on wheels can get back up those hollows to haul it out. It is sixty-two acres of pawpaw thickets, rocks and inaccessible trees. The other fourteen, immediately surrounding the house, are flat, level valley land.

We had always loved this place. We had driven past it every time we had gone to town for years and it was always beautiful, with its shady grove of trees, its clear little creek running through the front yard, its ancient apple orchard and picturesque old ruin of a barn entirely covered with a huge wistaria vine. The fourteen acres of lush meadow surrounding the tiny farmhouse made a lovely green frame for it. So we bought it, and it was typical of us, also, that we paid twice what it was worth, simply because of its beauty.

Neither of us gave a thought to the fact that the water table of the valley *had* to be the water level of the creek — to be precise, two feet below the surface of the ground! When we tore down the old farmhouse and began digging the foundations for the log house we hit water, a trickle of it, at sixteen inches. We hit geysers at twenty inches and had to borrow an irrigation pump to keep the trenches dry enough to pour the concrete footings. We daily expect the massive stone fireplace we built to sink out of sight of its own sheer weight. Oddly enough, it has not yet done so. Perhaps a drowned mountain peak supports it. It would be the only thing solid enough.

But I loved the creek and I loved the ancient apple orchard and I loved the picturesque old ruin of a barn and I loved the flat green meadow cupped by the hills in the background. Of course the creek floods the yard now and then, but it has been courteous enough to stay out of the house — up to now. The apple orchard remains lovely, but my husband promptly had the old barn, wistaria vine and all, torn down. He does not admire picturesqueness. Not, he says, at the probable expense of human lives. The barn was ready to fall and he was afraid it would collapse when someone was inside.

We spent that summer driving all over the country looking at and buying old log houses. They were always located in the worst and most remote places. We trudged over cornfields, across blackberry patches, through briar thickets, up snaky ravines, down hill, up hill, to look at each one we were told about.

To match the logs of the fishing camp we had to have poplar, so many of the ones we looked at wouldn't do. Some of the best, built of oak, wouldn't do. Others, eminently suitable, suddenly soared in price and wouldn't do. It was very strange how an old log house, abandoned to field mice, wasps and snakes for fifty years, should so unexpectedly become such a valuable hold-ing. The tears of sentiment and emotion we witnessed! Mother was born in that house. She would have been one hundred years old last Decoration Day. We never saw a log house under a hundred years old, naturally. Every year over that added fifty dollars to the price, so we quit looking at old homesteads. In-stead, we looked at and bought barns, about which people seemed not to be so sentimental.

Eventually, enough logs accumulated, three stone chimneys bought, a poplar frame house acquired somewhere along the line (for its hand-hewn beams and excellent boarding), everything was moved to the building site.

It was more than a little overwhelming. You have no idea how many logs are in four log houses. Or how many poplar boards are in one frame house. Or how many buckeye boards are in one ramshackle old farmhouse torn down to make room for the new house. Or how many stones are in three fireplaces. All fourteen acres of meadow were littered with the stuff and I had an uneasy feeling they were never going to be the same again. How right I was! Two years later we are still trying to clear the clutter away!

But, we told ourselves, and all our well-meaning friends told us also, there is always a mess when you build the do-it-yourself way. We still had faith. We still believed we could do-it-our-selves. Chin up, we said. Think how inspiring it is. Think how original it will be. Think how beautiful it will be. Think what satisfaction it will be when we have done-it-ourselves. Everyone knows, we said, how creative it is to do things with your hands. Thirty days later we hired four men to do-it-themselves!

It was a big house we planned, not in the number of rooms, but in the size of the rooms. We could hardly avoid a big house when each log room had been a home for an entire family. The living room, which was the former fishing camp, was eighteen by thirty feet. Ceiling nine feet. Hand-hewn beams showing, naturally. The master bedroom was eighteen by twenty. Same ceiling. Same beams. The kitchen was eighteen by twenty. Ditto, ceiling and beams. Over each of these log rooms was to be a dormer bedroom. Only the connecting rooms, which were not log, the dining room, study, bath and entrance hall, were of normal size. "How are you going to heat those big rooms?" we were asked by doubtful neighbors.

Airily, we replied, "Butane gas, of course. Simple."

Alas, it proved far from simple.

We began building in September and we got the foundations poured, the sills and subflooring laid and the log walls raised before cold weather overtook us. Further building proceeded by fits and starts.

It blew and rained and snowed and iced and sleeted and blew and rained again, all winter. The roof of the house was to be made of hand-riven shingles. We had crawled over hundreds of acres of timber to find "board" trees, and had bought eight huge oak trees. We had had them cut and hauled to the mill, had had them sawed into two-foot lengths and delivered to the home of the man who was going to rive them out. He had made ten thousand beautiful, old-fashioned, rough-looking shingles for us.

They are exactly what the house had to have, and they are lovely since they have weathered and turned silver, but I suspect they are highly impractical. They double our insurance costs, for one thing, and for another, every time we build a fire we go outside and peer anxiously at the roof to make certain it isn't burning, too. We talk seriously of putting some kind of water system, a sprinkler or something, on the roof, but we haven't yet been able to figure out a way to hand-syphon the creek water up to the roof, so I expect we'll just continue to be anxious.

The roof also caused us a lengthy delay. Because of the moon.

A shingle roof must be put on in the dark of the moon. "Why?" we asked. "Why must the roof be put on in the dark of the moon?"

"The boards will curl if you don't," we were told. "And your roof will leak."

Panicky over the thought of a leaky roof we waited for the waning moon. We watched the almanac like hawks. "The moon changes at nine-oh-five tonight," we reported to our building superintendent. "Get a big crew of men ready and work like fury for the next two weeks."

A crew of men reported to work the next morning. They swarmed all over the scaffolding and we figured that in two days the roof would be on. Two hours later — rain. Or snow. Or sleet. Crew of men goes home. Every day for two weeks it happened. Light of the moon? Weather fine. Dark of the moon? Dismal.

The building had reached the stage where the next step *had* to be the roof. Not one thing could be done until the roof was on. So we waited out those beastly dark-of-the-moon times. From Thanksgiving to the Ides of March, we waited. Then, growing desperate, we said, "It's just superstition. Put the roof on anyhow. The dark of the moon be hanged."

The crew of men reported and three rows of roofing, the long way of the house, went on. Same thing. Rain. In the *light* of the moon now. We began to suspect that someone up there did *not* like us. We were not meant to have a roof over our heads. "All right," we said, defeated, "go home. We will wait till spring."

A week later we sadly went to view the temporarily abandoned structure. We felt a fateful fondness for it and could not stay away from it very long. There was some sort of masochistic comfort in simply looking at its gaping, roofless skeleton. The labor bill had now come to almost as much as we had meant originally to spend on the entire house, but we were committed. You don't turn your back once you have put your hand to the plow. You don't tear down houses and move them and clutter up a peaceful valley and then walk off and leave it. It was like a great battle that, once set in motion, could not be stopped. With fine bravery we encouraged each other. "This time next year," we said, "it will be finished, and think how comfortable it is going to be. Think how pleasant and cheerful the log fires in that stone chimney are going to be. Think . . . think . . . think . . ." We didn't dare think, for at the moment there was no promise that it would ever be pleasant or cheerful or anything but an unfinished, gaping, roofless skeleton.

When we went to look at our puny little three rows of shingles that day, to our horror every miserable hand-riven board had turned up its toes and curled them in contempt of our lack of faith. So much for superstition. The moon is something besides a target for rockets. It is a power and a pull on tides and shingleboards and he who refuses to believe is promptly put in his place. Wiser, and infinitely sadder, we ripped the shingles off and laid them aside for kindling wood.

Finally, in April, the roof went on and building speeded up. The chinking between the logs was finished. The walls of the connecting section were put up. Window openings were measured and windows ordered. Flooring was bought.

We wanted an old, wide flooring and we thought we had it. It came from the poplar frame house. But the planing mill told us that it was so worn that, by the time they dressed it, it would be too thin. As a substitute we chose knotty pine. Knotty pine, we were told, was considered second-grade flooring. First-grade had no knots. But we wanted knots. Very well, knots we got. "Oh, yes," we were told, "all our flooring is kiln-dried. There will be no shrinkage." Happily, we ordered thirty-two hundred feet of it and saw it go down with pleasure.

Now, fate began to hit below the belt.

About the time the flooring was going down the internal revenue departments, state and federal, heartlessly took the rest of the money we had allotted for the house. To add tragedy to catastrophe we learned also that something was radically wrong with some of my insides and I must part with more of them than I liked. And then, in a ridiculous climax, we discovered our fourteen acres of meadow had been turned into a tundra.

About the time we began building, the state highway department decided to rebuild the highway through the valley. Fine. We were all for it. The valley being admittedly low ground, Green River bottoms to be exact, the roadbed was built very high. This was good road engineering, but whoever made the bridge and drain specifications must have been insane because all the drains were placed so high that it took a foot of water to reach them. Our lovely fourteen acres, unable to drain off across the dyke of the road, was left standing in six inches of increasingly stagnant water. The highway department steadfastly refused to do anything about it, so that drainage, if ever achieved, became an individual problem to all of us who owned property in the valley, and another drain on our pocketbooks.

We felt bewildered by this series of untoward events, by the dreadful state and federal income taxes, the dreadfully expensive operation I must have, the dreadful fate of our fourteen acres of meadow. These were things over which we had no control. How could even the most sensible people have foreseen them?

We sat one day on the couch in the small rented cottage in which we were living until the house was finished, and looked at each other despairingly. A little frightened now, we got out paper and pencils and began figuring. We had been very proud of the fact that we were "paying-as-we-went." Free-lance writers do best on that basis, we had learned. With no fixed income, it is best to have no fixed debts, either.

One reason we had determined to build that year was because I had had the unusual, and probably never to be repeated, good luck of having two books in succession chosen by well-paying book clubs. We thought we would be very sensible with the money. This was our chance, our best chance, maybe our only one, to build a home. We had such good intentions. It never occurred to either of us that both those book clubs would pay off in the same year and that Uncle Sam and the commonwealth of Kentucky between them would take the second one almost in its entirety.

And who could foresee a hysterectomy (most aptly named) looming that year? Or idiotic road engineers?

Counting every penny twice and cutting out every beautiful thing we had planned for the house, keeping costs down to the bare bones, it would still take several thousand dollars to finish it. Henry was staunch. "I will do the plumbing myself," he said, never having held a pipe wrench in his hands before.

"Fine," I agreed, "while I am in the hospital having my insides put to rights."

The drainage problem simply had to wait, mosquitoes, malaria and all.

There was nothing to do, of course, but borrow the money to finish the house. Hand to the plow, and so forth. Thank heaven for a banker with a heart, we thought. Some of the borrowed money also had to be used to pay the surgeon and to buy that wing of the hospital in which I was incarcerated for twenty-one days.

When, weak and wan, I came out of the hospital, Henry was fairly well along with the plumbing. He had trouble with the septic tank, naturally, there being no place to put it but in the tundra. He had to borrow the irrigation pump again, but by dint of much sweat and wet feet, well seasoned by an old army sergeant's particular brand of profanity, he got it sunk. That it rises and peers out at us each time there is a frost does not disconcert us. It subsides the next time the sun shines. "It's up," we say today. "It's down," we say tomorrow. We don't need a barometer with a septic tank like a bobbing cork registering every change in the weather.

For some reason Henry did not follow my blueprint in placing the fixtures in the bathroom. Oh, yes, we had a blueprint. I made it on cardboard. Quarter-inch scale. It may have been some aesthetic quality in him that I have overlooked, but he put the "facility" (as it is called in Alaska, and it might as well have been in Alaska — it stayed frozen all winter!) on the outside wall. When you use it, you sit with your head bowed against the wash basin, the gas heater blowing up your legs. But better a gas heater than an icy wind in an outhouse, I always say.

The plumbing works, however. Our one great joy in this whole affair has been our water supply. We have a good, everlasting well of sweet, clean water that runs, with the help of an electric pump, on tap. Gone are the days of the tin washtub on Saturday night, and the eternal waste pails overflowing and the meager little inch of water in the dishpan. We have an unlimited amount of water, even though we have to use a blowtorch to get it to flow when the temperature drops to zero, as it did many times last winter. Still . . . you can't expect perfection in the country. That's what we told ourselves when the blowtorch didn't work and the sergeant had to tear out one wall and thaw out the pipes inch by inch. It could not have been an aesthetic quality that made him put the bathroom pipes in an outside wall, too.

One year from the day the first foundation trench was dug, we moved into our beautiful log house. Kitchen cupboards had still to be built. All woodwork had still to be finished. All tiling in the bathroom had still to be done. A front porch had to be built. A back porch had to be built. They all still have to be done. Moved, we collapsed, mortgage and all.

A constant stream of people come to see our log house. "How beautiful," they say.

"How satisfying it must be to have done-it-yourselves."

"How comfortable it looks."

"How pleasant it must be to sit before that huge fireplace on a cold winter night."

We smile and agree.

We do not mention the fact that we spent a chilly and expensive winter. That the first gas bill was seventy-nine dollars and that it was for November when we had many warm days. The second one reached ninety dollars. The last four soared to astronomical heights. This was our simple solution to heating all those large, airy rooms! Butane gas!

It was partly due to the size of the rooms, which required lots of heat, but it was also because there were so many drafts. Baseboards, we found, won't fit snugly against log walls. And even the tiniest crack lets the wind whistle through like a howling blizzard.

We bought hundreds of boxes of a plastic clay caulking that unreeled in long strips like an endless earthworm, and on hands and knees we poked the stuff into every crack.

But there were still the floors. There will be no shrinkage, we had been told. There has been none except all over the house in cracks so wide that to drop a coin is to lose it forever. There is a treasure of fifty-cent pieces, safety pins, needles, pencils and bobby pins down those cracks, and when we missed the cat once I strongly urged we take up the kitchen flooring. And what the wind does through those cracks is almost unbelievable. On a really blustering day the rugs heave and weave like the deck of a ship and even a mild breeze blows like a mistral through the house. All winter I sat at my desk with arctics on my feet and kept a heating pad going on High wrapped about them. Neither of which prevented chilblains.

So we caulked cracks in the flooring, too, and put down more rugs. We put an end to the gas bills by calling the company to come get their tank. We built a central flue in what had been the dining room and bought two of the ugliest wood stoves ever manufactured, but, praise heaven, they heat!

We closed off our charming living room with its beautiful stone fireplace and our big, airy master bedroom. We dismissed them with a wave of the hand and without a twinge. Come summer, we said, we'll open them up. In winter we will live in the rooms that the two wood stoves will heat. The dining room became a small, snug living room; the study became a small, snug bedroom; and the kitchen, a delight to the heart and soul with its roaring wood fire, became also my study. I took off my arctics and knew warmth and good cheer again.

Also the plumbing was rerouted and no longer freezes up.

Well, so we built an impractical house. The floors in no two rooms are level because the foundations have already sagged a little in the tundra. Doors one day lean in one direction and on another day reverse themselves. None of them will close entirely. There isn't a window in the house that will open. But they don't need to. The house is so cool on the hottest day that it is self-air-conditioned. The floors slope only a little and in the kitchen I can skid from the refrigerator to the stove with a minimum of effort. And as long as the outer doors close, who's going to worry about the inside ones?

On a day when the creek is properly respectful and the sun is warm and bright and the apple orchard is in bloom and the tundra is freshly green, we know that we built well after all. We look at the silvery old logs and the big stone chimney and we know they are beautiful and we know the house speaks for us in a language we understand. We know that some way we'll pay off the mortgage, and we know that somehow we will lick the drainage problem. We know that cold has no terrors for us and that we need not owe our souls to any gas company. We know that faith and hope and courage still can be summoned up, and that they do count for something. We know that though our heads may be bloody sometimes, they certainly need not be bowed. I'm afraid we would do it all over again, chilblains, frozen plumbing, bobbing septic tank and all.

We don't, however, advise anyone else to build a do-it-yourself log house. Not, at least, without examining the intentions of the internal revenue department, your state highway department and your local physician. And not, of course, unless you have a fishing camp to start with and fourteen acres of tundra to build on.

COUNTRY MUSIC

"Whatever their cultivated tastes they are not ashamed of
their native music and retain a fondness for belting it out."

A Little Better Than Plumb

THERE IS a tendency among the falsehearted to look down their
noses at this kind of music. My husband, my friend Pansy
Phillips and I had an experience straight out of a Lichty cartoon
once in one of the smaller cities of Kentucky.

For years Henry and I have crusaded for the Library Extension Division and its network of bookmobiles and regional li-
braries. A new library was in the process of being born in this
small city and I agreed to speak in its behalf. Mrs. Phillips and
Henry were invited to be present.

The city put the big pot in the little one for us and we were
forewarned about a luncheon, the "speaking," then a tea or reception. Pansy and I dusted off our big hats, matched up a pair
of white gloves each, donned out best bibs and tuckers, squinched
our toes into high-heeled shoes, which takes some doing for me
because twenty-two years in the country have made my freedom-
loving toes too antipathetic to tight enclosure! We went hence.

The luncheon was pretty and delicious. Eyeing the peas on
my plate I thought of what Sarah Hutchison, another friend of
mine and the first in Adair County, once whispered to Henry
at a public dinner he was covering for his newspaper, at that
time the Campbellsville *News Journal*. "What," Sarah had

hissed in his ear, "would banquets do without the Great American Pea?"

"Start a fad for brussels sprouts," Henry hissed back.

Sarah shuddered and subsided.

After the luncheon in the small city we made a tour of the proposed library, then wended our way to the club room for the speaking.

The room was full of pretty women, lovely hats, minks and white gloves, the badge of the well-bred Kentucky woman wherever she goes. There was also, however, a perceptible stiffness and chilliness. My goodness, I thought, are they *that* cool to this library project?

Henry dropped into a back pew and Pansy and I followed our guide to the solitary elegance of the front row. These things are usually sponsored by some women's club and there are always minutes to be read, the treasurer's report to be heard, old business to be settled and new business to be taken up. Thirty minutes to an hour pass in this fashion during which time I try to keep an interested expression on my face, a little difficult to do after a good many years of hearing women argue whether to have a bake sale on the courthouse lawn or a country-ham dinner for the volunteer firemen to raise money for their cause. I am sometimes tempted to arrive late and escape this half to full hour of threshing around, but I never have had quite the heart to do it. I imagine it would be unsettling to the program chairman for her guest speaker not to be safely tucked under her wing when the program gets under way.

At the conclusion of business a slight woman, obviously nervous, slid into the seat beside me and whispered that she hoped I wouldn't mind but the music chairman had arranged a short musical program to be given before I spoke. I didn't mind. This, too, is normal. Somebody always plays a violin solo, or a piano solo or sings. It seems to bridge a kind of inevitable hiatus between two kinds of boredom, the boredom of club business and the boredom of the guest speaker's speech.

The music chairman took charge with gusto and expounded, indeed preached, on the great good fortune of the club to be able to hear today two young men from the neighboring town who were between engagements on the nightclub circuit and whom she had been able to persuade to give of their time and talent. She harangued at length on their God-given talent and the astronomical fees they were paid in Newark and Miami and Las Vegas.

The air, which had been stiff with chilliness, now creaked as the ice froze. I nudged Pansy. "Was Elvis born around here?"

She grinned. "I think Memphis claims him."

"Are you beginning to understand the ice?"

She nodded. "They don't dig whoever this dowager has dug up."

With a flourish the dowager finished in true Grand Ole Opry fashion. "Folks, here are the Jones brothers. Let's give 'em a big hand."

As two clean-cut, handsome kids so young they were barely shaving made a running entrance hauling their instruments with them, the hand they got was mighty meager. In fact, you could say it was nonexistent. A few white-kid gloves patted together delicately, and that was all. The boys were rigged out in souped-up cowboy shirts, tight black pants, but they didn't have side-burns or ducktails and they had wide, warm smiles. They also had an electric lead guitar and a steel rhythm guitar.

Light broke on me as they went belting into "The Steel Guitar Rag." The women were almost too embarrassed to bear it, not for their own sakes, but for mine. They had invited as their guest an author who, on the surface, should be cultured, well-bred as they themselves were and appreciative of the fine arts. They had done every lovely thing they could to honor me. It was being ruined by this ill-timed, ghastly performance. Even if I hadn't really liked country music I would have done what I did. It was only courteous. Under the circumstances, however, it was no effort.

I swiveled around and beckoned to Henry who came forward to sit with me. Both his foot and mine patted noticeably to that driving beat and at the end of "The Steel Guitar Rag" we blistered our hands in genuinely warm applause. The kids were good, really good.

They played half a dozen pieces, perhaps, and outside of the hoedowns I must confess they weren't exactly selective. If there is anything more comical, more atrociously ill timed and placed, than two adolescent boys bawling, "You don't love me anymore" to a hundred obvious society matrons, I have yet to witness it. It nears hysteria in its inappropriateness.

There was shocked, horrified, squirmy silence when the drippy ballad ended. I made bold to request one last number, for anything, anything at all would be better than to leave the sickly chords of "You Don't Love Me Anymore" hanging in the air. "Play 'Bile Them Cabbage Down,' boys," I said.

They biled them. They mortally did bile them cabbage down. They biled them down so far they rendered out the fatback and then rendered the renderings! They sizzled and fried that old hoedown until the natural thing would have been to abandon the speaking and form squares and begin swinging partners! .

With the rafters still ringing I was on next and I did a quick shift in my opening and praised the club for recognizing that country music was one of the few music forms native to the United States. "We borrow most of our music forms from Europe," I said, "and whether we personally like it or not, here in Kentucky we should be proud of having nourished an original music."

I wanted so much to ease the embarrassment. It had been

a soul-shriveling experience for these ladies. I guessed that the music chairman had browbeaten the program committee into a pulp of nonresistance. I could see how she could have. I did want them to know their guest was not horrified.

In addition, I wanted them to understand some of the real ingenuity and real creativeness of the two boys. I said how good they were, how better than good, how truly excellent in the country music field with intricacies of arrangement that only true musicians can evolve. I said what the neophyte hears in country music is mostly noise and rhythm. What the connoisseur hears is the melodic line, backed up solidly, with occasionally, in the hands of a genius, some sudden, new, soaring shower of gold stringing. And we had heard it that day in that corny old hoe-down, "Bile Them Cabbage Down." The lead guitar had gone way out into outer space with a rippling, ranging pick that had put some brand-new sounds together.

Well, that's the kind of music we make at our house and once in a while Henry's guitar can go winging off into the blue, too, and give you goosebumps all down your spine.

WE POINT WITH PRIDE

"It has been said that the Appalachian is keenly interested in politics largely because it affords him a respite from boredom. Respite from boredom indeed!"

40 Acres and No Mule

WHEN MARRIED PEOPLE decide to go wading in political waters, it would be well if they made certain their partners are willing to advise and consent. We learned this the hard way.

When it was my time, I had perhaps a 25 percent grudging consent from my husband. When it was his, he had none from me. And each of us consistently refused to advise or consent!

Henry and I had never done more than vote until that fall of 1960 when John Fitzgerald Kennedy became the Democratic candidate for the presidency. We had lived here in the county, first up on what we hereabout call "Giles Ridge"; then we built our log home down in the valley. Conscientiously, we always voted. That was all.

But in 1960 John Kennedy caught my imagination and, though he dolefully shook his head over Kennedy's chances, Henry was a loyal Democrat. When I was approached by Pete Walker, a young Adair County Democrat, and asked to do some writing for the state Democratic Committee, I was excited and willing and Henry was eventually persuaded.

We went to Louisville and checked into the hotel and I met with various and sundry people and I was told the women's organization needed a pamphlet to be used as an organizational guide.

Everybody seemed to have some ideas as to what should go into the pamphlet and they were kicked around considerably while I soaked them up, pooled them, began to sort them out, started choosing and selecting, began to envision a format.

A young commercial artist was assigned to the project the next day to do the illustrations. We secluded ourselves and went to work. She was remarkably quick on the draw and we worked well together. With that alertness of creative people everywhere she met my ideas with instant understanding, her facile pencil limning them in. Within three hours we had drawn up a skeleton of the desired pamphlet. There were cheers from everybody, and Henry and I came home where I could work more leisurely and lengthily on the written material. Inside of a week it was finished, and again we drove to Louisville to deliver it to the artist for complete drawings and to see it go from her to the printer. It was basic, simple and concise and to this day I am quite proud of it. I believe that it was used, with local variations, as a model by the Kennedy people in many other states besides Kentucky.

One thing led swiftly to another. This particular writing job done, Pete thought I should come into the campaign on a more active basis and on the state level. Barkis was willing but Henry felt rather joyless about it. "You don't know," he warned, "how hard they may work you. What about your high blood pressure?"

This is the bane of my existence, this constant battle with that dratted needle on Dr. Todd Jeffries' little gauge. "I'll take care of my high blood pressure," I stated.

"You'll see Todd Jeffries first," Henry retorted. "If he says no, you won't do it."

To my delight, Todd grinned and said it probably wouldn't kill me. Henry had no choice but to let me get into the campaign.

I was made one of three state vice-chairwomen. What it

amounted to was regional chairwoman, for my job was to direct the women's organization and work in the Fourth, Fifth and Sixth Congressional Districts. I was also to continue writing when there was need.

It was one of the most exciting, thrilling, most rewarding experiences of my life. It was tremendously exhilarating to be driving hundreds of miles each week, organizing, writing, exhorting, making speeches, driving on and doing the same thing over and over and over again, watching trends, checking and rechecking, conferring, deciding, the smoke of battle thick all about. The pace was relentless from the beginning but it went beyond that toward the end. The last two weeks of the campaign there was no real sleep, just snatches, no real food, just snacks, and never any real rest at all.

Always timid about making speeches when I or my books were the subject, I thought I might dread them in the campaign. To my delighted surprise I found I was a natural campaign orator, glib, poised, unshakable and intuitive about crowd responses. Never able to remember the name of a solitary person I meet in connection with my own work, I found I could instantly place politicians, that I rarely forgot a face or a name, and to this good day I believe I could travel through the counties I haunted most and recall immediately most of the people I met and worked with. I began to wonder if I wasn't wasted as a writer. Perhaps my real calling was politics. After all, didn't I have an aunt who had served two terms in the Arkansas legislature and hadn't I listened to her tales of her own campaigns interminably and didn't I take to campaigning as naturally as a duck takes to water? Henry paled at the implications and said, "Over my dead body!"

I *think* I was good at organization but it's difficult to know. I had written the blueprint for it but the personnel was chosen higher up. But I *know* I was a good speaker and that I campaigned well. I was so full of enthusiasm, so full of my own honest convictions about this man John F. Kennedy, that I never gave myself any thought at all. Introduced from the platform — and I must admit more people may have come to see and hear the writer than the campaigner, but they sure got the campaigner — I plunged straight into the message that had become all important to me. I passionately wanted Kentucky to go for Kennedy. It didn't, and I was heartsick. Not even the knowledge that we had done our best and some of us had worked far beyond the call of duty, to the point of illness and exhaustion, was any consolation. I wept bitterly and my political mentor, young Pete Walker, seeing my tears that night when Kentucky went for Nixon, grinned and patted my arm and said, "You're a real fighter. You lose hard." I did. I sure did. It took me weeks to get over it.

We met so many wonderful people — all the county and district people, the state people and the national figures. I have so many wonderful memories of those hundreds of unwearying, dedicated women who could from somewhere always call up another spurt of energy, drive another hundred miles, arrange another rally, check their precincts one more time. I don't know anything else that was quite like that sisterhood we formed during that campaign. It was immensely satisfying.

We came to be genuinely fond of Keen Johnson, our own candidate for the Senate that year, and his wonderful sister, Christine, who never seemed to grow tired or weary. If she spread herself as thin over the other two regions as she did in mine I don't know how she survived. For there was never a rally, county or district, that she didn't show up, her beautiful grayed hair in perfect order, her smile warm and friendly, her hand ready for a good grip, saying, "I'm Keen Johnson's sister," and offering her little box of Keen Johnson buttons. Keen Johnson lost because John Sherman Cooper is a magic name with Kentucky farmers. He has gone to bat for the tobacco program too many times.

I have never been able to decide which was the more thrilling for me, the day I met John Kennedy, or the day I sat on a platform beside Franklin D. Roosevelt, Jr. The Kennedys fought hard for Kentucky. We had the candidate himself in the state several times. On one of his visits he was scheduled to speak in my own region at Bowling Green. I was not that day invited to the platform. The candidate was too important for a vice-chairwoman. His prestige demanded the state chairwoman herself. But Joe Covington, one of our inner circle of friends, perched me directly above the platform in a window of the courthouse. Friends in the audience in the square kept waving at me and I waved back blithely. I didn't know until later that I had leaned so far out they had feared for my safety. All their waves had been warnings — get back, get back, don't fall! He was directly under me and if I had spit it would have dampened his auburn thatch.

My moment came backstage when I was introduced to him. The thrill was mine alone. His eyes were glazed with fatigue. He didn't even see me. He said, "Thank you. Thank you very much," and passed on. But I offered touches to my friends for a dollar each for a week and promised to keep my hand unwashed until they had all had a chance!

Franklin D. Roosevelt, Jr., was in closer contact for a longer period, at any rate. It was a district rally and it was held at Glasgow. This time I was on the platform. He was to be the principal speaker, but he was late and we had to begin without him. It was an outdoor rally and the platform was the bed of an outsize truck swathed in bunting. Some minor speaker was exhorting when suddenly there was a stir behind me, then a huge, broad-shouldered man clambered up the ladder and sank into the next chair. I knew him instantly because he looked so like his father. He mopped his brow and straightened his shoulders, checked the crowd for size, settled himself and whispered to me — my presence on the platform meant "official," of course — "How's it going in Kentucky?"

I hissed back at him, "Religious issue."

He was explosive. "Damn!"

That was the extent of my conversation with him and I didn't ever really meet him, but probably for twenty minutes I sat jammed next to him, so close our shoulders touched all the time. He was restless during that twenty minutes. None of us ever really listened to speeches. Among our own state speakers who spoke so often and so valiantly we knew all the variations on the theme. We had heard them so many times we could have given them ourselves word for word. During speeches we watched the crowd responses. We knew instantly when a speaker was missing. Sometimes he could be signaled and if he was one of the more alert ones he could shift and switch and bring the crowd's interest back. But if he was one of the stolid ones, and there were a few, there was nothing to do but sit agonizingly while he plowed stonily on and lost the crowd. We had one of the stolid ones ahead of Franklin, Junior. He should have wound up quickly once young Roosevelt was on the platform. Instead, he continued to the bitter end.

But young Roosevelt certainly didn't miss. Amazed, awed and at one point a little frightened, I watched as the crowd surged forward when he had finished speaking to hold up their children for him to touch, to reach out themselves and shake his hand, to murmur, "God love you, you're just like *him*." They crowded so close and in such numbers that once the old truck bed tilted and I thought God help us all if they turn this thing over! Seeing the danger he clambered down and delivered himself to them, let them maul him, went among them. I remember thinking jubilantly, he's done it. We've got this county sewed up. One of my bitterest memories is looking at the tabulation from that county on election night and seeing the majority Nixon ran up.

Those people who mauled Franklin Roosevelt, Jr., voted for Nixon in November. They couldn't overcome their mortal fear of a Catholic in the White House. It was so easy to misjudge crowd enthusiasm and count it in the credit column. We did it over and over again, I'm afraid.

We had most of the Kennedy sisters in Kentucky at one time or another, and the mother and even the mother-in-law. We had five of the fabulous Kennedy teas. We had Lyndon Johnson and his wife, and it was pleasant to meet them all. But of all the new people I met, among those I enjoyed the most were some very close to home.

It is said that in Kentucky there are not two major political parties, but three . . . the two factions of the Democrats and the Republicans. For thirty years the Democrats have been split, former Senator and Governor Earle C. Clements leading one faction, former Senator and Governor A. B. "Happy" Chandler leading the other. It is said that only each can beat the other and that any political candidate must have the nod of one or the other to win. There are those who say this split goes back much further than thirty or forty years. It goes, they say, clear back to the days of William Jennings Bryan and his cross of gold, the followers of Clements being the natural inheritors of the gold standard and the followers of Chandler being the natural inheritors of the crusade for silver.

I wouldn't know. I only know that Henry and I had usually voted for Clements candidates without knowing they were Clements candidates. We knew almost nothing about factions or in-party fighting. We were the kind of voters who read the newspapers, try honestly to sort the truth from the trash and try intelligently to make a choice between candidates. I have since learned that this is impossible, but since we can't all get into the "smoke-filled" rooms where the decisions are made, it must suffice for many of us.

We did certainly know that Pete Walker was a Chandler man. But he was the Adair County Democratic Chairman. We assumed all good Democrats worked with him.

We certainly learned in a hurry that they didn't and we learned in a hurry that they wouldn't work with me in Adair County because I was sponsored by Pete Walker.

Pete gave me no instructions at all. He didn't mention the factional strife. Either he believed it better for me to learn it for myself or he had no idea how unbelievably ignorant I was. An office was set up for me in Columbia, a telephone was installed and I was in business for Keen Johnson and John Kennedy, ably assisted by Henry and a marvelously capable secretary, Martha Barnes Burris.

Practical politics is really the art of knowing the right people . . . whom to see, who is in control, who can deliver. From the top right down through the precincts it works that way. And a good politician sees not a chaotic, conglomerate mass of individual workers; he sees blocks of votes and he sees the man or men who can control and deliver them. He makes it his business to know those men and to grapple them to him, if possible, with hooks of steel.

The first time I heard those magic words, "See so and so," Pete Walker said them to me.

We were progressing rapidly with county organizations but there was no county campaign chairwoman in my own county. It seemed obvious the state chairman was leaving that appointment to Pete. "What shall I do?" I asked him, which seemed natural enough to me.

"See Cornelia Hughes," he said. "You can trust her."

I knew Cornelia Hughes and her husband ran a motel and restaurant. Henry and I had eaten at their place a few times but I had never met her and to the best of my knowledge had never even seen her. When I went to see her I was met by a small, trim-figured, high-breasted, frowning, rather bristling little forty-ish woman. "Are you Mrs. Hughes?" I asked.

She admitted she was. I told her Pete had suggested I talk with her about the campaign in Adair County.

She sat down and in less than thirty minutes she gave me a blunt, plain, salty lesson in practical politics. I learned from Cornelia Hughes, not Pete Walker, precisely what the situation was in Adair County. The Chandlerites were out and though Pete would continue to be county chairman until December he was in a lame duck situation. The Combs faction were in. There was deep and undying bitterness between the two factions. Pete had not told me to ask her to take any active part in the campaign but I was beginning to pick up a few nuances for myself. I knew he wanted her to play some part and it was probably county campaign chairwoman. I never got a chance to ask her because she told me bluntly before I could that she wouldn't touch the job with a ten-foot pole. "That crowd downtown would cut me up in little pieces," she said. She continued, "If they'll accept her, your best bet would be Nannie Willis."

I was so fantastically ignorant I had to ask her who "that crowd downtown" were! I shall never forget the way she looked at me. She must have thought Pete was out of his mind to be using me on the state level. As I left she called to me, "See Mrs. Bolin. She's one of the cochairwomen in the regular organization. She'll probably help you." Again she grinned. "She's Chandler."

I had determined, however, to see a few men of that crowd on the square. They were businessmen with whom I had had some dealings. Loyal to Adair County, we had always bought as much clothing, shoes, food in Columbia as possible.

So I called on several of the key men and was as frank and honest as I knew how to be with them. I got nowhere. Their distrust of Pete Walker was too great. And I was now tagged

Pete Walker, willy-nilly. When I asked for suggestions for campaign chairwoman, they seemed to have no one to suggest. I mentioned Nannie Willis. She'd be fine, they said. I thanked them and then I invited them to make use of my headquarters in any way they liked. It was, I told them, much too big for me. They could have the entire front for their county headquarters and since the state committee was paying the rent it would cost them nothing. Gravely, they agreed to consider it. For all I know they are still considering it. Somebody moved Pete Walker's desk in, I had the telephone installed and an extension for their use, and they could have been in business. The only drawback was that twice, only twice, one of them darkened my door. I finally used Pete's desk as a display counter for literature and the extension telephone was never lifted off the hook except when I, caught in the front of the building, used it instead of racing to my own desk.

I called on Mrs. Bolin and found her delightfully willing and evidently competent. She had little time to give to campaigning, however, for she was her doctor-husband's receptionist, but she did procure the voting lists for me and she did have a list of precinct committeewomen, essential in our organizational plan.

I did not ignore Adair County because there was so little cooperation and such marked coolness toward me, but I did decide to concentrate most of my efforts and time on the other forty-eight counties in my region. There was no point wasting valuable time butting my head against a stone wall. But I must admit their attitude puzzled me considerably. I wasn't Pete Walker. I was pure and simply John Kennedy. If Pete Walker, whose shrewd mind files away every voting fact and retains it and who knew beyond doubt I had consistently voted against every candidate of his, had the good sense to latch on to me in this campaign, I thought it pretty silly of these people to oppose me. I had voted *with* their candidates and they knew it. And I would have done a good job in their county if they had let me. I take a little credit, also, that I did not allow their enmity to drive me from further dealings with them. I could easily have never bought another nickel's worth from any of them. Instead, even during the campaign when I needed new dresses and shoes, I bought from them just the same. They should have bowed in shame.

Their indifference caused me to turn more and more often to Pete's people for my needs. I would come up needing five cars to take a group of women to a rally, ten cars to take my young collegians to another rally, a committee to do this or that, some funds for newspaper advertising. I had no place to turn for these small favors and gratuities but to Pete's people. They were the only ones willing and they never failed me.

The Rose Kennedy tea, however, was so important that while I didn't have full cooperation from the administration people I had more than I expected — especially from the women.

That tea really hit us smack in the face. It was, of course, Pete Walker's doing. The opportunity at hand, the native son wanted his hometown honored. Mrs. Kennedy was in Kentucky to address the Democratic Women's Club in convention. She agreed to stay over one day and appear in our town. Pete was so wistful about it that I fought even Grover Gilpin, Pete's chief aide, and Cornelia about it. They shook their heads over it. "You can't do it. They'll kill you." Meaning, of course, the administration people.

I got on the phone to Pete. "Grover and Cornelia say we can't handle it."

He hesitated. "Well, all right."

But he sounded so little-boy disappointed my heart smote me and impulsively I said, "You want this pretty bad, don't you?"

"Yes."

Quickly I decided. "All right. I'll ram it through for you. What's the minimum crowd we have to have for it to be a success?"

Over the telephone I could see his grin. "For the newspapers, call it a thousand. If you can string three hundred out I'll be satisfied."

Columbia at the last census listed 2164 souls. It has no bakery. We had to have the usual display of silver and linens, tea and coffee, mints, salted nuts and cookies. The cookies must all be homemade. If I do say so myself I have a flair for this kind of thing. I dug in my toes and began organizing and I just plain organized the willing to death.

There were committees for flowers, for cookies, for silver, for linens, for hostesses, and for myself I reserved the job of working up the crowd. Over the telephone I called twenty county chair-women and I didn't ask, I commanded, that they send five cars full to this tea. I didn't brook any argument and I didn't say please. I said, in effect, this is an order from high command. This is John Kennedy's mother. You be here! And I gave them times to arrive so there wouldn't be any dreadful gaps. I wanted people arriving constantly, no great mob or rush, but no embar-rassing lulls either.

Because I had been so brutally ignored by the administration people, one of whom ran a restaurant also, I calmly decided the tea should be held in Cornelia's private dining room. Cornelia Hughes was such a loyal follower of Pete Walker's that nobody could mistake the move. But my dander was up. I was tired of all this factionalism. We had a president to elect. If the only people who would work with me were Pete Walker's people, then I was jolly well going to work with them.

Pete's loyal aide was Grover Gilpin, a roly-poly, deep-eyed, jolly and genial man I liked very much. In my lowest dumps he could always make me laugh. There was also Ed Janes, a big, hulking bruiser of a man. His wife was Thyra, platinum-haired, ample-hipped, a broad, laughing woman who owned a flower shop and in her spare time worked in ceramics. They were all interesting to me. The administration people wrote to head-quarters: "We might be more active here if the Pete Walker clique weren't so active. They are the roughneck element of the county."

The state campaign director, a man of unimpeachable honor, grinned when the letter came to his desk and tossed it to Pete. Pete grinned and tossed it into the wastebasket. The thrust may not have included me but I was highly intrigued. It was the first time in my life I had ever been called a roughneck!

We put on the Kennedy tea and we put it on in high style. We had the loveliest of the sterling tea and coffee services and the sweetest of our older women to pour. How pretty they were that day, and how gracious, and what unmistakable ladies they were. We had exquisite flowers from home gardens, some of the most beautiful arrangements from the hands of Ilene Jeffries, my doctor's wife. And we had the best homemade cookies in Kentucky. Mrs. Kennedy so liked them she asked for a box to take home with her, which we were so pleased to give her. When her famous son did his spot interviews in north Kentucky later that month and was given coffee and cookies in a Gold Star mother's home he asked if the cookies were homemade. "My mother tells me," he said, "Kentucky women make delicious cookies." We swelled with pride. She could only have meant our cookies.

We had a goodly crowd. It fell short of the thousand I had aimed at but it well exceeded the three hundred Pete had said he would be satisfied with. I have forgotten now the exact figure but it was around seven hundred. The administration boycotted us except for the women who had rallied round and a few brave men. One or two of the state barn boys — highway employees — even showed up though most of them stayed away. Several of the businessmen on the square showed up, too. I felt nothing but contempt for them.

Henry and I were coming to like the Pete Walker people immensely. They played the best bridge in the county and they were witty, clever and interesting. During the campaign, in spare moments, we began playing bridge with them and enjoying them enormously. We did not find them roughnecks at all. On the contrary, Pete Walker had as good a library as my own and was very well read. His library was weighty with political history, naturally, while mine leans to the classics and biography. Cornelia was also a discriminating reader, and Thyra's slim white fingers did wonders with flowers and tubes of paint. We found them blunt, candid, perhaps a little rough, especially on the administration people, but roughnecks, no! We also found them quickly warm and loyal and sympathetic, to each other and to anyone whom they trusted and liked.

About midway through the campaign the Adair County chairwoman, Mrs. Bolin, died. Her death came suddenly and unexpectedly although she had not been well for a week. None of us, however, had thought she was so ill. I was called in the middle of the night. Early the next morning I called Cornelia. "My God," she said, "I've got to get down to Thyra's. There'll be hundreds of flower pieces to make up. She'll need all the help she can get."

The rest of the story is Thyra's. Cornelia didn't wash her face, comb her hair or even dress. Over her nightgown, which was long to her ankles, she threw on a housecoat whose hem was sagging, crawled into the truck and took off. She worked all day and into the night making the floral pieces and then she went with Thyra to the funeral home to help arrange them. "There she was," Thyra told me, "nightgown dragging, duster with its hem loose, every hair on her head declaring its independence, barefooted except for those disreputable mules she wears. People were calling and signing the register and milling around. If she'd had on a Dior original Cornelia couldn't have been more at ease. She stalked around placing pieces and when we got through she flopped in a chair and blew the hair out of her eyes and said, 'God, what a day!' "

That was Cornelia. Eighteen hours by the clock to help a friend in a crisis. That was the woman that the wife of one of the administration men said, "What makes Cornelia go around looking like she does? She could surely comb her hair!"

When the election was over and we had sadly lost Kentucky we continued to see much of these people. I was personally devoted to Pete Walker. I had not been converted to his brand of politics and he knew it but as far as I was concerned his brand of politics made no difference to friendship. I didn't think I would ever be called on to clash with him for Henry and I had decided we would never ever again campaign actively. I had been made ill, we had spent far too much of our own money and I was thrown dreadfully behind in finishing a book I had laid aside. Politics and writing, we told each other, didn't mix. Besides, my blood pressure wouldn't stand any more campaigning. Next time, Todd Jeffries said, he wouldn't answer for the consequences. So, prosit, skoal and goodbye to politicking.

Came 1962 and the in-party fighting over the Senate race in the Democratic primary. The administration had a candidate and Chandler had a candidate. Pete was organizational chairman for the Chandler candidate. It was of only rhetorical interest to us. We had begun the writing of *A Little Better Than Plumb* and were deeply involved in it and had committed ourselves to a June 1 deadline. We were not personally concerned. We meant to, and did, vote for the administration candidate.

Suddenly and before I could blink an eye, we were spang in

the middle of it. Henry came home from Columbia one day and confessed that he had agreed to be campaign chairman in our county for the administration candidate!

I stood on my hind legs and did considerable roaring. "Have you lost your mind?" I shrieked. "Have you any idea what you've let us in for?"

"I haven't let *us* in for anything," he snapped back. "*You* aren't involved in this at all. Nobody has asked *you.*"

He didn't heave any furniture around but the inference was clear. I was to mind my own business. I was, in other words, to shut up. The man of the family was about his own affairs.

I shut up but I did a lot of silent fuming. I thought I knew that nobody wanted one member of the firm without the other. I couldn't have campaigned for Kennedy in 1960 without Henry. I didn't much believe he could campaign now without me. I didn't much think they wanted him without me. What they wanted, I believed, was the team — the Gileses. But if my role was to be the silent little woman, so be it. It was a new role for me but I was loyal. If Henry wanted me to stay home and fry potatoes while he campaigned for the administration candidate, I certainly had a lot of potatoes to fry.

His chairmanship lasted precisely forty-eight hours. The first thing suggested to him, as chairman, was that I be installed in the county headquarters, full-time, to keep it open and run it. That rocked him considerably. At home I was given my orders again. "You are to stay out of this!"

I assured him that was precisely what I meant to do. And I meant it. I wanted no part of this campaign.

This was all on a Thursday. On Friday we were invited to attend the reception for the administration candidate and the Jefferson-Jackson Day dinner in Louisville as guests of a man and his wife who were quite prominent in the campaign. Henry hesitated. I felt some sympathy for him, but not much. In the

1960 campaign he had particularly detested the rat-race pace, the eternal driving, the endless conferences, the pressures and tensions building up. Henry is not geared to smoke-filled rooms nor does his basal metabolism lend itself kindly to rat-racing. Henry wins the race eventually but he does it like the tortoise, not the hare. He must now have had his first uneasy feeling of here-we-go-again.

To save time and space, the administration couple asked us to go to Louisville with them in their car. We accepted and off we went early that Friday morning.

The reception for the administration candidate was actually the opening of his official headquarters. They were in the same old suite we had used in 1960. We had only to walk through those familiar doors again, into the smoke and the hubbub, into the milling groups of the same people we had seen so often in this place, for him to realize sickeningly what he had committed himself to. Worse than that, with old campaign friends and compatriots pulling and tugging at me, gleefully welcoming me into the fray again, he had to face the brutal fact. There was no way under the sun he could keep me out of it short of putting me in a dungeon. His involvement meant my involvement and there was no way out of it.

We hadn't been at the reception thirty minutes, he told me later, before he decided he had been naive and that he must get out and get out before things got cracking. But he had no opportunity to tell me for we were kept on the move all afternoon and had no private moments. I only knew that he didn't seem to be having much fun. His face was white and grim-looking.

I wasn't having much fun, either. The day before I had had a slight sore throat and a low fever. Henry had seized upon it joyously as an excuse not to make the trip. Alas, I had wakened minus the sore throat and minus the fever and his excuse had gone with the wind. Now, both were returning. My throat felt

221

increasingly dry and painful and I knew I had fever again. There were aches and pains all over my body, especially down my back and legs.

Furthermore, on the seventh floor of the old Seelbach Hotel, now the Sheraton, that Louisville hotel that is so old and historical and so associated with Democratic politics, so gracious and comfortable and charming, in which we had stayed so often in 1960, in which we had had so much fun, one figure was missing. Every time we had ever checked into the Seelbach Pete Walker had been there. I kept expecting to see him come lunging out one of the inner doors, his face split with his wide grin, his hand outstretched in his habitual politician's handshake. But he was across the street in another hotel, in another man's headquarters. It wasn't right and I couldn't make it right.

It was a bibulous afternoon. The hospitality room was flowing and Henry imbibed deeply. Stuffed with antihistamines, I had to refrain except for a couple of screwdrivers. I could not anesthetize a single one of my painful memories.

We went to the dinner, couldn't hear a word of the speeches and left early. By this time I was very nearly irrational with fever and so full of aches I could no longer conceal my misery. I went to bed fairly early, praying for morning and my own bed where I could be as sick as I pleased and be no bother to anybody.

Pete and Grover descended upon us in the wee hours not knowing Henry had decided to abdicate. I could have killed them both. They knocked on the door and awakened us. Henry dressed and bade me stay in bed. He joined forces with them in the room of the people we had come with. I have never been able to make heads or tails of what went on in there for two hours. It's certain that Henry was made angry all over again and it's certain that he did not announce his decision to get out of the campaign. For all I know he may even have reversed his decision. Already giddy with bourbon when he left our room, he came back at three o'clock the most totally soused I had ever seen him in all the years of our marriage. When I asked him drowsily what had happened, he snapped at me, "I don't want to talk about it."

Well, fine, I didn't particularly want to talk about it, either.

I composed myself, and Henry went to bed.

What happened next was sheer farce. It was worthy of a playwright. It was bedroom comedy at its best. It belongs on Broadway. Henry suddenly sat bolt upright in his bed. "This room gives me claustrophobia. I can't stand it. I'm going home."

I sat bolt upright, too. Neither of us liked the room assigned to us. It was a little box in the annex. At the Seelbach we had been accustomed to the best. Because we often worked in our room Pete Walker had seen to it that we had the best, space and quiet for comfort and the luxury of a suite. We couldn't help comparing. "How," I asked, "do you think you're going home?"

Henry blinked at me in the dim light of his bed lamp. "In the car, of course."

"We don't have our car with us. Have you forgotten? We came with those people."

He was pulling on his pants. Even in the dim light I could see how stubbornly his jaw was set. "I'll wake them and tell 'em we've got to go home. You're sick."

I yelped. "I'm sick, all right. But you'll do no such thing. I won't let you be so rude."

He was tucking in his shirttail. "*I am going home!*"

I tried to reason with him. All he would say, obstinately and mulishly and repetitively, was, "I am going home."

I crawled out of bed and began struggling into my own clothes. For all I knew he meant us to hitchhike.

Suddenly he had an inspiration. "The bus!"

He called the bus station and learned the first bus to Columbia didn't leave until morning. He banged the receiver down and sat on the side of the bed. Then he had another inspiration. "A taxi!"

This sent me into hysteria as I tried swiftly to calculate what a taxi from Louisville to Spout Springs would cost. Henry was weaving toward the telephone again. Suddenly I had had enough of all this nonsense. There was one person and one person only who could help me get this sweet but sodden and determined husband of mine home. "Call Pete," I said.

In his alcoholic haze and misery Henry made no objections. He rang the Watterson but got no answer from Pete's room. "Try Grover," I commanded.

We had seen Grover at various intervals through the day and vaguely I remembered he had said he meant to drive home after the dinner. As he waited for the connection I reminded Henry of this and I prayed Grover hadn't left yet. Maybe we could hitch a ride with him.

Grover answered immediately. The one-sided and very slurred conversation I overheard seemed to indicate that Grover had changed his mind about going home. He had, in fact, gone to bed though not to sleep. Suddenly Henry faced about, puzzled. "Pete's on the phone, now."

Galvanized, I leaped to the phone and grabbed it. I said just two things. "Pete, come over here. I need you."

Never in my life have I heard anything more reassuring than his calm and unexcited reply, "I'll be right there."

I frankly admit that at that moment I couldn't have cared less what the political implications were of turning to the "opposition." Pete Walker was to me the only stable, staunch, reliable person in the whole situation and I knew that outside of myself he was probably the only sober one. His voice, quiet and calm and full of affection — and nothing or nobody will ever convince me that Pete Walker doesn't have great affection for both Henry and me — quieted me instantly.

He came, big and rumpled and barely dressed, his shirttail hanging out and his big grin beautiful to see. I flew to him and he took me in his arms and patted my shoulder. "We've got to go home," I said.

Grover had come right behind Pete.

Pete asked only one question. "Are you all right?"

"I've got the flu," I said, "but otherwise I'm fine. I'm a little hysterical because Henry wanted to call a taxi."

"Fine," Grover said. "We'll leave as soon as I can have the car brought around."

"Wait," I yelped suddenly as we were about to leave. "Those people! We have to leave a message."

His hat on the side of his head, Henry peered at me. "I've already written a note and stuck it in their door."

I didn't ask what he had said. I was too lightheaded to care but I imagine that, written in a sprawly, barely controlled hand, it was virtually incoherent. Tiptoing past their room I got the giggles. "This is going to be the biggest scandal in the county!"

It was! I went to bed with my fever and flu and saw nobody for nearly a week, but the furor swirled about us. The next day a car full of administration people came out to the house and Henry went out to the car to talk to them. He told them honestly and candidly that he had to get out of the campaign because of my health. That I was sick in bed right then and the doctor had warned me about my blood pressure. That he had not expected me to have to help, so he would have to ask them to let him off the hook.

They had no alternative but to accept his resignation, but it was said all over town we had been kidnapped. It was said we had been tucked back under Pete Walker's wings. It was said that we had sold out. It was even said that Pete Walker had something on us big enough to compel Henry to withdraw and force us to leave Louisville. None of it was true, but Grover would have been less than human if he hadn't boasted around the square that the administration people had taken us up to Louisville but he had brought us home.

We didn't see the last of that little political foray until 1963, when without warning the bookmobile librarian suddenly had to resign. To help out Bob Allender, our good friend, Henry agreed to drive the bookmobile until he could find another driver and librarian. It is to Bob's eternal credit that he never told us of the threatening letters he had from Governor Edward Breathitt. But we finally got one ourselves. It said, in effect, "Get right with the party or get fired!"

The administration people had never believed us and had taken the matter to Frankfort, the state capital, and had told the governor a Pete Walker man was driving the bookmobile. Henry himself had to give it up about that time because he had a small hemorrhage from an irritated esophageal ring, and the constant bouncing around in the big van over the rough country roads to the little one-room schools did it no good. We were afraid it would return.

But I am certain that to this good day the administration people think they got him fired. When Henry resigned, *then,* and not until then, did Bob Allender tell us what pressure had been brought to bear on *him.* He had actually been threatened with his own job, but he had remained loyal.

Thus we have viewed with considerable alarm the confusions politics can involve one in and we point with very little pride to that particular campaign. I might add one more thing. The administration candidate lost!

But you learn a few things and you forget much. This happens and you muddle through. I shall have a hard time, however, forgetting the people who meddled, misinterpreted, wouldn't believe us and in one way or another caused us much vexation. The scars are still there and I do not see or speak to the particular couple who caused us the most trouble. I have long forgiven the others and we think they finally realized their mistakes. But I have felt called upon to ponder a philosophical saying: "This world may one day perish through the evil professional do-gooders wreak upon it."

I don't much like do-gooders. I am like the Appalachian. I do my good in my own personal way, by being a good neighbor, by lending a helping hand, or loaning money to a trusted person in temporary trouble, by not gossiping and above all by not meddling.

WRITE ME A RIVER

"He had the brightest blue eyes I ever saw in an old man and they twinkled with humor as he told me some of his experiences in the old days when steam was in its prime."

Around Our House

(A plan for the first book of a projected three about navigation on Green River)

Overture

(From an interview by the author with Captain Jim Wallace, retired Green River steamboat pilot, August 10, 1962)

"No, MA'AM, I've not ever steamboated on any other river. I was born on the Green, raised on the Green, and it's the only river I ever wanted to steamboat on. The Green's enough river for any man. I spent forty years on the Green and I could run you the river as good today as I ever did though it's been thirty years since I quit.

"No, ma'am, I didn't quit because of my age. I could take a fleet of barges downriver today as good as I ever did, though I misdoubt [with a twinkle] I could run the L and N railroad bridge on a tide as I've done. I quit because steam went and I had no hankering to be nursemaid to a stinking diesel.

"I commenced steamboating when I was sixteen . . . signed on the old *J.C. Kerr* as deckhand, Capt'n Tom Williams, master. Then I got to be roof watchman, then light tender, and when I was nineteen I went on the *Park City* as cub pilot. You got to have three years to take your pilot's license — two on the decks and one in the pilothouse. I passed the first time I taken the examination, all gross tons, all western waters.

"That means, ma'am, I had to write the channel of ever' damned river that empties in the Mississippi, from the Missouri to the Atchalafaya, from the Kanawha to the Cumberland. Taken me three full days. On the Green I never made a mistake. On the Cumberland, I missed a towhead. Clean forgot it. Missed two beacon lights on the Ohio, but I wrote the Mississipi from Saint Paul to New Orleans without error. [Twinkle.] Never steamboated a day on her nor ever even see her. But I could of. I knowed how.

"I commenced on packets but once I'd pushed [towboated] I liked pushing best so I stayed with it. I pushed with the *Peter Hountz* and the *I. N. Hook* and the *Longfellow*, but the *Mary Lacy* was really my boat. I had her for twenty years. Never had an accident. Never had a boat sink under me or burn. Never even stove a hole in one. Had a damn log raft ram me once, but the *Mary Lacy* rode up over it. She was a real fine boat, a good-luck boat. Made money for the Company and was light and easy on the water.

"Write you the river? [Settling back.] All right. You're ready to leave Evansville, say. You got a fleet of five barges to push. First thing you do is gong your engineer three times. That's to let him know you're ready to move. If he ain't too damned hung over, he'll gong you back three times. Then you give him the backing bell — that's two rings, then two more for slow. When you're clear in the channel, you give him the stopping bell and when he's come to, you give him the gong for shipping up. Two bells, then, to come ahead slow. Now, you're going. Your buckets are pulling. You give him another bell to come ahead full steam, and lady, you're moving real nice.

"Well, it's nine miles up the Ohio to the mouth of the Green.

Cross with your markers, head and stern lined up, and favor the Kentucky side. You bend in close when you swing, but you got nothing to worry about. You got Ohio water up the Green to the first lock at Spottsville and it's all good water. You can steamboat any damn place you please, waltz all over it.

"After you lock through at Spottsville, you got a sixty-mile pool of pretty good water to the next lock at Rumsey. Only real tricky place is Mason's Bend in low water. In low water you better hug the left bank till you clip the willows. You ain't got but five foot of water to the right and you can't steamboat in five foot of water . . ."

* * *

Quite frankly, the central character, Bohannon Cartwright, of *Write Me the River,* will look a lot like Captain Wallace and to some extent be based on him. At ninety-one, Captain Wallace looks a young seventy. He is still a giant of a man, tall, big-boned, his shoulders braced back with no stoop. He has no paunch, either. His hair is full and thatchy, though entirely white. He does not wear glasses and his eyes are keenly blue, alive, twinkly or steely according to his mood. His mind is as keen as ever. His memory is fabulous. He quotes dates, precisely. "I went to steamboating on the twenty-third day of January, eighteen ninety." His only concession to age is false teeth. He is slightly hard of hearing, but not hamperingly so. "Never been sick a day in my life," he boasts, and his daughter with whom he lives verifies it. "And you know why? I taken the weather in that pilothouse for forty years. That'll make a man of you!"

* * *

There are two central characters in *Write Me the River* — Bohannon Cartwright, who has the river in his blood, for he, too, was born on the Green, raised on the Green, and will want to steamboat only on the Green; and the river itself.

The story will focus on "Bo" Cartwright's great love for the river and for steamboating on it.

Unlike Captain Wallace, who never wanted a boat of his own, Bohannon Cartwright will strongly want his own boat. He will thoroughly enjoy, take great pleasure in, piloting for the "Company" but he will be far too independent in temperament (he is Tattie Cartwright's grandson) not to want to be his own boss. The power of the pilot, which begins only when the captain has given the order to proceed and stops when a landing is made, will not be strong enough for him. His great dream will be to run his own boat on the river. All his efforts, when he has served his apprenticeship, will be directed toward that end. He will be satisfied, he says, with a small boat to begin with, even a one-decker, but someday he means to have a real steamboat, "with feathers on the stacks, and a gold insignia swung between, and cornices on the pilothouse, a three-decker, maybe, with a texas. Double engines, with three-feet strokes . . ."

"God," Foss said, "you don't want much, do you?"

"Just the prettiest damn steamboat on the river is all. Just the prettiest that ever run the river."

The time is from just before the outbreak of the Civil War to about 1880.

The state of Kentucky appropriated moneys to build a system of locks and dams on Green River (the first inland waterway to receive state attention) in 1833. The five locks and dams were finished and slackwater navigation was possible from the mouth of the Green to Bowling Green, head of navigation, by 1842. For twenty years the state of Kentucky operated the locks.

The Civil War intervened and all navigation on the river was halted because both armies blew up the locks and dams to keep the other from making use of the river. When the war was over, the locks were so badly damaged that the state was reluctant to repair them. It leased them, instead, to a private corporation formed by Evansville and Bowling Green men, most of them rivermen, and all of them with river interests through ownership of boats and/or land contiguous to the river.

The Company was not corrupt, nor did it ever operate illegally in any way, but because it held the lease on the locks it did, in a quite businesslike way, raise the lock tolls to such a figure that few private owners could afford to run the river. The Company's boats, not having tolls to pay, could operate freely. The Company's downfall came when they overplayed their hand. Because of their almost total monopoly they could charge whatever the traffic could bear in the way of freight rates. Not satisfied with a moderate rate, they slowly raised them to the point where shippers all along the river were angered and antagonized, took them into litigation, complained so loudly and so often to the state that eventually the state tired of all the fretfulness and tried to recall the contact. The court of appeals upheld the Company and it was not until 1888, when the federal government took over control of river navigation, locks and so on, that there was real relief on the Green.

Bohannon Cartwright will have his first old boat just before the outbreak of the Civil War. He finds an old, very small boat, a one-decker, that has been in the boneyard for a good many years. With the help only of Foss, a boyhood friend from Cartwright's Mill, he builds a new hull and mounts the machinery of the old boat on it. The first *Rambler* thus came into being.

He is just beginning to pick up a little freight and a very few passengers, just beginning to pay off his debts, when the war breaks out. He cripples along for a while, but in early 1862 the lower Green River locks are destroyed by Union troops and later that year, in September, Johnson and Bragg make their foray into Kentucky and destroy the upper Green River locks. Bo has had to go more heavily into debt and is now threatened with attachment of his boat. He "runs it off" to save it and on a high tide brings it upriver to hide in Russell Creek, just above Greensburg.

He and Foss go to war. In this area the sympathies were strongly Union, but having steamboated so much in and out of Bowling Green, which was the Confederate capital of Kentucky, Bo's sympathies are just as strongly Southern. His own family, at Cartwright's Mill (his father is a son of Cass Cartwright, dead by now, of course), are Union. There is no angry feeling at Bo's choice, but some sadness.

Bo's war is lightly sketched and very brief, for I don't want to get away from the river. When he comes home, in 1865, the *Rambler* has been found and burned by Union sympathizers.

The Green is not yet open and will not be open for another four years. But Bo Cartwright, his dream undamaged, thought feckless by his family because he will not give it up, stays in whatever ways he can on the river. Because of his Southern sympathies during the war, he can't get a job on the Ohio, which is open. So he rafts logs down the Green for a while. Then, the mother-of-pearl button industry having begun around 1850, centered in New Orleans and the Mississippi, he builds and outfits a mussel boat and goes to "grabbing" mussels on the Green. Mussel shells provided "mother-of-pearl" almost entirely in the U.S., incidentally.

Bo has a break, finally, when he is at the wharf at Evansville with a load of shells and a steamboat goes aground and can't be got off. The line superintendent, angry at the pilot, whom he thinks was drunk, has hauled him off the job. Bo offers to get the boat off, on the condition that he be given a job if he is successful. "Who are you?"

"Bo Cartwright."

"Hummph. You're the fellow had that dinky little single-decker on the Green. Why should I let you at the wheel of my boat?"

"I've been at the wheel of that boat. She's an old Strader and Gorman boat. Used to be on the Cincinnati-Saint Louis run. I run her regular between Cincinnati and Louisville."

Bo waited. "I get a job?"

The man thought about it. "Well," he said, then, "you can't do her any more damage than that fool has done."

Bo knows that the *Lindley* was built from a Billy King design, her wheels a little aft of center. It was a Billy King-designed boat, the *J.M. White*, built for Pierre Chouteau of St. Louis, that made the famous record run from New Orleans to St. Louis in 1844 of three days, twenty-three hours, nine minutes, which was not broken until 1870. Billy King would never show his design or give away his secret, but many boats thereafter tried to copy the set of the *J.M. White*'s wheels in the hope of imitating her speed and lightness of balance.

The pilot has been trying to back the boat off the bar. Knowing how shallow the *Lindley* draws, and knowing the buckets of the wheels cannot be damaged by plunging (they are too far aft) Cartwright boldly rings for full ahead, which plows the nose deep, but loose. He orders stop and back and she comes round, floating. The superintendent keeps his word and Bo is once again in a pilothouse.

For two years, lightly sketched, he is on the Ohio, then the Green is opened again and he goes with the Green and Barren River Navigation Company, headquarters at Bowling Green.

He has never faltered in his determination to have his own boat again. He hoards his money. He is never out of a job for he is a bold, but safe, pilot. He has a good reputation with the Company.

Bo's father dies about now and he receives his part of the estate — land at Cartwright's Mill. He promptly sells every acre of it, the first Cartwright ever to sell an inch of land. To Cartwrights, land is wealth. The family are incensed. He is a fool, an idiot, especially when he uses every penny he has saved, plus what he receives from the sale of the land, to buy another boat. This one is an ancient side-wheeler that has been laid up for years. He quits the Company and, with Foss again, spends a happy six months reconditioning the boat. When he is ready he names her *Rambler II* and hires a crew on credit.

Caught in the Company squeeze, he is barely able to keep going from one trip to another. Since the boat is under 100 tons he can, by law, be his own master as well as pilot. He cannot afford a relief pilot, nor can he afford a mate. Foss, nominally the engineer, must often double as mate and even as roustabout. Running, Bo has to tie up when he is so tired and sleepy he knows his judgment would be bad.

The Company won't credit him for his lock tolls. They raise the wharf fees on him at both Evansville and Bowling Green. He has trouble with his crew frequently because he can't pay them. Only one man, Foss, the burly, corpulent, illiterate friend of his boyhood, is always and unquestioningly faithful. To Foss, Bo Cartwright is just this side of the Lord Almighty. Foss is too slow-witted ever to be critical. All his life Bo has been the leader, has said what they were going to do and Foss has followed and wants it no other way. During this time, Foss is invaluable to Bo. He licks mutinous crews into submission, does every hard job that needs to be done, and on one unbelievable run downriver when there is no crew but Foss his oxlike strength and endurance are enough for him to fire the engines, load and unload the cargo, and go without sleep until the run is made.

Bo's triumph comes when a spring flood wrecks the walls of the lock "crib" at Rochester, Lock #3. The Company is caught without a single boat upriver. Bo, because he can't pay the lock toll at #2, Woodbury, is laid up there. *Rambler II* is the only boat on the Green above the wrecked lock. The Company is forced to approach him and make a contract with him to meet their upriver boats at Rochester and to allow them to transfer both freight and passengers at that point to his boat.

Bo drives a hard, but not unscrupulous, bargain with the Company and, since it takes the best part of a year to rebuild the lock, he "cleans up."

The book ends on his triumph when he has paid off his debts, has money in the bank and the *Rambler II* has been overhauled and put into top condition. He sends word home that he is bringing her up to Greensburg on the next tide. Only once before has a steamboat come upriver as far as Greensburg. The *Rambler*'s coming, therefore, causes great excitement. A gauge is set out and watched carefully and when the word is sent around that the rise is nearing the necessary level, people come from miles around to watch the *Rambler* come in.

Long before they can see her, they can hear her whistle, a three-bell chime, sweet and throaty. Then they can see black smoke pluming up, and then she comes round the bend (forgive it — at Greensburg there *is* a big bend!), almost dancing on the water. She is all fresh white paint and gilt and the sheer of her decks is swaggering. Bo has got his feathers on the stacks, and he has got his cornices on the pilothouse, and he has got his texas, and between the stacks he has swung his gilded insignia — a replica of the first *Rambler*. But best of all, he has set *Rambler II*'s wheels a little aft of center, and her balance is good and she moves like a lady dancing, light and swift and free.

There is little made of the love interest in this story, because Bo Cartwright's deep love is for the river and for steamboating. Rivermen were married to the river. Bo has a girl in Cartwright's Mill, but he is away for months at a time, and the girl does not understand his consuming passion for the river and for boats. Nearly every time they are so briefly together, in joy at first, their encounters end in her failure to understand and her wish that he would "get off" the river and stay at home, as decent and normal men do, as all other Cartwrights do. Tend the land and increase it, is their way. But to be a "dry-lander" would be death to Bo.

At the last, still not understanding, but proud, finally, of him, reluctant, but more reluctant to give him up entirely, and facing the unalterable fact that she must either go with him or give him up, she meets him at Greensburg and goes downriver with him. Henceforth her life will be on the river, too. The book ends.

Realistically, this is a temporary triumph, for, of course, as soon as the lock was mended the Company would be in the saddle again. But Bo has a good stake now. He can sweat it out. And there is beginning to be enough dissatisfaction among shippers that he can be certain to stay on the river. He can't see the end, but he has faith.

* * *

The other hero of the book is the river itself. The book must be wet and drowned with it, flow with it, be liquid. It must be borne and carried by the Green's slow-winding course. The face of the water must always be seen, its depth felt, its bends taken, its vining tributaries accepted into its water and swelled by them, its long, long drainage of one-fourth the land mass of

Kentucky felt, its snags and bars and slides and low, striated cliffs, its islands, its willows and above all its goodness to boats with its depth and slow current (except when it is rampaging on a rise) and its ice-free harboring, its beautiful bottle green color. Bo knows, as I do, every bend of it from its rise in cold springs thirty-five land miles, sixty river miles, above my home (and his) to its mouth, 380 river miles west.

I have run the river, every mile of it, by skiff and motorboat to Mammoth Springs, by motor cruiser from there to Bowling Green, by towboat from Bowling Green to Rochester Lock. Below there the river has changed so much there was no point going.

Two of the ancient locks, built in 1839, are still in use, at Rochester and Woodbury. On the towboat trip we locked through these only by breaking the barges loose and locking them through one at a time. Upriver traffic is very slight these days, for this reason. These old locks are too short. But they are to be rebuilt soon. Below Rochester the locks have all been rebuilt and the lower river is humming with more traffic than it ever saw before. T.V.A. has built a plant at Paradize, Kentucky, on the lower Green and it will require endless amounts of the fabulous coal that has been lying waiting along the river for just such an event. Sixty-five million dollars worth of coal was taken downriver by barge last year.

There are three books envisioned in this Green River series, with three generations of Cartwrights. The glamorous era of steamboating on the Green came after 1888, when the government took over the locks and dams. It became true free navigation, every man and every company having a chance. The railroads, the L & N, the Illinois Central and the Southern, had not yet made inroads into the territory.

This was the day of the showboats, the photographic studios, the shantyboats, the grocery boats, up and down the river, the day of the plush boats with full orchestras and luxurious cuisine. This was the romantic era on the Green; it had already passed its peak on the Mississippi. *It did not end* on the Green until 1931!

This would be the second generation.

The third generation would see the coming of the towboats and the passing of steam. River business was not good but it was practical and sensible. To stay in business, companies and rivermen had to make the inevitable adjustment to diesels. Some, like Captain Wallace, were already too old and either couldn't or wouldn't. I think my third generation Cartwright would. He would be young on the river; it would be just as much in his blood as it was in his father's or grandfather's.

I went downriver on the towboat *Maple*, Jim Nasbitt, owner and master, Buddy Nasbitt, his son, pilot. Both of them loved the river. While Buddy was off watch and sleeping, Jim Nasbitt took the helm. I asked him if he thought Buddy would stay on the river. He pondered the question, then grinned. "He may try to get off of it. I think he may try to get it out. But I don't think he will. Once the river has got you, she's got you for life. There's no other way you want to live. I tried it once. My wife hated it. So I got off. Like to died. A riverman can't turn into a dry-lander. I don't know why. I don't know what there is about it. It's hard work and no end to it. You wring yourself dry every run you make. There's a thousand easier ways of making a living. Trouble is, the only time you're really living is when you're on the river."

I know just what he means, because I'm more alive myself when I'm on Green River. There's a joy and lift in your heart that is an exultation. Every sense is acute and perceptive, eyes, ears, taste, smell . . . how can my Cartwright generations fail to have it?

The first book will be *Write Me the River*
The second, *The Face of the Water*
The third, *Green River Line*

(This story was written for the *Atlantic Monthly*.)

RUN ME A RIVER

" 'Be at the old wharf at five-thirty in the morning,' he said,
'if you want to catch the *Maple* for your towboat trip.' "

Around Our House

It was five-thirty in the morning. In late September in Kentucky it is barely daylight at that hour.

It was cold and raw and a sluggish fog lay thickly over the river. My artist friend, Pansy Phillips, and I sat on rocks on the bank of the Barren River at Bowling Green and huddled into our coats and felt the fog on our faces and tasted it on our tongues. In the half-light we looked like sleepy ghosts to each other.

We had been deposited a few minutes earlier by a skeptical taxi driver. "I haven't seen a boat on the river in three years," he said. It was his only hint that he believed two middle-aged women expecting to hitch a ride downriver on a towboat were mildly mad.

We felt a strong sense of unreality ourselves, on the bank of this strange river, at this hour of the morning, in a spectral sleaving fog. We chattered nervously for a while, then a silence developed, in which Pansy tried to sketch the island that almost filled the bed. It was no good. Her pad grew damp and her pencil wouldn't work. She put them away and, chin on her palm, pondered the fog-screened river.

"Why," she said suddenly, "did he tell you the old boat landing? This isn't a boat landing. This is just a pile of rocks."

241

"The cab driver said this was the place," I replied.

"But why here? Don't the Hines people have a wharf, or a dock or something of their own?"

"I don't know," I said. "All I know is that Warren Hines said for us to be at the old boat landing at five-thirty this morning. He said the boat would pick us up here."

"What are we supposed to use to flag him down? I think we should have come equipped with foghorn and signal light!"

I giggled. "Pansy, Warren Hines has made the arrangements. The towboat owner knows we are to be here. He *knows* to pick us up."

Pansy rose to her full and impressive height of five-feet-nine. From too many unfortunate experiences she has no faith in her ability to catch trains, planes, buses and, for the first time in her life, a boat. "I don't believe it," she said. "It's the silliest thing I ever heard of." She mimicked my instructions. " 'Be at the old boat landing, somewhere between the ice house and the country club, at five-thirty in the morning. A towboat will come round the bend and slow for a landing. It will put in and you will go aboard.' No," she went on, "there is no boat on this narrow little river. It has sunk. Or it has gone off and left us. Or it will not stop for us at this godforsaken place."

Looking about me at the desolate, lonely, fog-bound place, I felt some qualms myself. It did seem most unlikely that any riverman with good sense would bring his boat into this narrow bend.

And yet . . . I knew that this very place had once been a busy wharf. In the old steamboat days this wharf at Bowling Green had been the head of navigation on Green River. There had been regular and daily runs of steamboats from Evansville, Indiana, up the Green to the mouth of the Barren, then up the Barren to this narrow bend and back again. Beginning in 1828, this river traffic had continued for one hundred and three years.

A constant stream of freight and passenger boats had unloaded at this very spot. An immense freight warehouse had stood here.

Now the cobblestones of the landing were overgrown with weeds. The gaping maw of the huge warehouse was closed forever. It had burned with the *Evansville*. Nothing was left of the landing but this pile of rocks on which we sat and some pieces of twisted iron. Were they, I wondered, struts and braces of the *Evansville* itself? I felt a personal interest, for her last master, J. Frank Thomas, was one of the retired river captains with whom I had had so many talks. He had told me how busy this wharf used to be, round the clock.

But it had been the nice, courteous voice of Warren Hines that had told me over the telephone the day before to be here in this place, at this hour. "If," he added, "you want to go downriver on the *Maple*."

I desperately wanted to go downriver on the *Maple*. It was the last leg of research for my novel. All the background reading, all the study of the history of steamboating on all rivers, had been done. All the study of Green River navigation had been done. As many rivermen, pilots, captains and navigators and engineers as I could track down had been interviewed for countless hours. It was all behind me. Now, one way or another, I *had* to sit in the pilothouse of some kind of boat and see for myself how Green River was navigated. I had, in a sense, to become a Green River pilot myself.

The *Maple* belonged to the Nasbitt brothers. "I can arrange a trip downriver for you," Warren Hines had said, "but it may be pretty rugged. Those little boats don't have accommodations for passengers."

"That isn't important," I had assured him. "It doesn't matter. I'll camp on the barge if necessary."

He smiled at me. "Oh, you can be made more comfortable

243

than that. But I'm afraid you can't stay aboard overnight. There's only a double-deck bunk for the crew."

Sensing my disappointment, he leaned across his desk. "They can take you as far as Rochester. That's an eighty-mile run, about twelve hours. And that will give you the old river, all there is left of it. Below Rochester and Lock Number Two the new locks have changed the river so much you couldn't find any of the old landmarks. They have even changed the river so much with new channels it isn't the same river. But from Bowling Green to Rochester it's all exactly as it was in eighteen forty-two."

It was a piece of the greatest good fortune to have this opportunity to see the upper Green. Though rivermen loathe those old locks at Rochester and Woodbury, for my purposes it was wonderful that they had not yet been rebuilt. I was grateful to Warren Hines and said so.

He fiddled with a pencil. "Well, then, the Nasbitts will be bringing up a barge of gasoline next week. I'll call you in plenty of time."

Now it had come to pass and here we were, fog-bound and becalmed, cold and ill-nourished on two cups of coffee each. I tried to make the passing of time less tedious by detailing something of the history of navigation on Green River.

The first steamboat came upright on a high tide in January of 1828. It was a small, side-wheel, one-stack boat owned and piloted by James Garrard Pitts, but it opened a great hope for the big, rich, land-locked Green River country. Heading up in a spring under a mountain in Lincoln County, the Green winds 380 miles westward before it joins the Ohio near Henderson, Kentucky. With its thousands of tributaries it drains one-fourth of the land mass of the entire state and, along its lower reaches, is the deepest river in the United States. Near its mouth, where it empties into the Ohio, it is said to be around two hundred feet deep.

Flatboats, keelboats and log rafts had been the only way of shipping for the farmers and merchants along its length until James G. Pitts proved a steamboat could come upriver as far as Bowling Green. Now an exciting era lay just ahead.

Until the locks and dams built by the state and completed in 1842 were finished, however, boat passages were very irregular, having always to be timed to rise in water. But when the locks were opened there were 180 miles of slackwater navigation available and the real era of the steamboat, with regular schedules, began. For ninety years the Green carried the burden of all shipping and most of the passenger traffic on its bosom.

Steam has gone, but river traffic did not end with the steamboats. The age of the diesel towboats began. Today the lower Green, with its fine new hydraulic locks, is humming with river traffic such as it has not ever seen before.

By contrast, the upper Green is almost deserted. On it there are still two ancient, too-short locks, #3 at Rochester, and #4 at Woodbury. Completed in 1939, they are manifestly barriers to modern-day navigation. No boat or barge longer than 138 feet or wider than 35 can pass up the river beyond Rochester, Lock #3.

In the event, we didn't get to see the *Maple* come round the bend, which I had longed to do. Instead, Warren Hines came to report a delay and to take us to breakfast, which earned him Pansy's profound gratitude. His thoughtfulness was wasted on me. I was far too excited to eat.

When we returned to the wharf, the *Maple* was tied up and waiting. She didn't look very small to me, with her eighty-foot length and twenty-five-foot beam, but by the standards of towboats on the Ohio and Mississippi she was a pygmy. She was squat in the water, plump-looking but smart with white paint and her new pilothouse atop the deck housing. She looked businesslike and sensible, like a rather battered old lady with her head up high and her face powdered for the occasion.

We met Jim Nasbitt, the owner. He was a broad-shouldered, sturdy man of perhaps forty-five, with a laugh and wrinkled blue eyes. "Make yourselves at home," he said. "The boat is yours for the day."

"No place we shouldn't go?" I asked.

"Nope," he shook his head. "Only, if you go up on the barge, don't smoke please." His grin widened. "It's empty of gasoline now but full of fumes. We wouldn't like to be blown to kingdom come."

Pansy and I didn't allow we'd like to be blown to kingdom come, either, and besides we didn't think my research required me to inspect an empty gasoline barge.

We met Jim Nasbitt's son, whom he called Buddy. "He's the pilot," Jim said. He was a slim, blond, willow switch of a boy who later admitted to twenty years. He looked sweet seventeen and not a day older. Privately, I was of the opinion that if my fate was in this child's hands, I might never return from this voyage. I ate my opinion later and did it gladly!

We met the deckhand, "Peanuts" Ray, a solid, broad-shouldered chunk of man who was the cook. He offered us coffee immediately. I was to learn that rivermen, like writers, drink coffee all day long and that, like writers, this writer at least, never know whether it's hot or cold. The habit is simply a cup of liquid at the elbow.

We met Paul Johnson, the engineer, and looked briefly at his engines. We didn't see much of Mr. Johnson anymore because he was always with his engines.

This was the crew. Normally the *Maple* ran with only three

and tied up at night, but because the Hines people needed gasoline in a hurry Jim Nasbitt had come along on this trip so they could run straight through.

Seats had been provided for us in the pilothouse. They were boxes upended with life preservers for cushions. We followed Buddy Nasbitt up the steep metal companionway and occupied the boxes while the crew cast off.

We drifted downstream for perhaps a quarter of a mile, then picked up the empty barge. When we saw the long pipeline climbing the face of a sheer bluff and counted the hundred and eighty-six steps leading down to a small platform, we understood why Warren Hines had asked us to board at the old boat landing. It would have taken a bosun's chair to swing us onto the *Maple* at this place.

Some towboats actually tow, but most of them push. The *Maple* was a pusher. The barge, riding very high in the water, was now made fast to the head of the boat. It was 130 feet long. It was done only by backing, going ahead several times. It reminded me of the effort required to get a car out of a tight parallel-parking place. If we had ever swung broadside we would have been wedged between the banks, probably stuck there for hours.

The Barren was low and although the *Maple* drew only four and a half feet of water she churned mud in this backing and filling necessary to come round. But it was accomplished eventually and we headed downriver.

Except for brief periods, never more than five minutes each, that was the last time I sat down for twelve hours. I found my box too low for watching ahead well, and since I had to "pilot" this boat, I stood.

The Corps of Engineers provides detailed, blown-up charts of all navigable rivers. Divided into sections of only a few miles each, they are bound in book form. Buddy Nasbitt's chart of

247

Green River was open on the chart table to his right. Studying it, I saw that he had penciled in many details — slides, bars, snags, shallows, narrows, even a baby island lately formed and the place where he had seen some deer.

The names of the charted landmarks fascinated me. Hobson's Towhead. "What is a towhead?" I asked. Mark Twain mentions them constantly in his *Life on the Mississippi* without once telling what they are.

"A towhead," Jim Nasbitt said, "is a spit of land projecting into the water. Most islands are formed by the channel swinging around behind a towhead and cutting it off."

There was Big Eddy, Stephen's Bart, Sibert Island, Boat Island, Thomas Landing, Slim Island, Whitehouse Bluff . . .

Barren River coils its way downstream to the Green like a great snake looping back upon itself. The channel is always narrow and the beds are always short. Bearing up on some of them, I didn't see how the boat and barge could maneuver around, and I became absorbed in how it was done.

It was done a little, I thought, like skidding a car around a curve on ice — in slow motion of course. Buddy Nasbitt would throttle down and nose the head of the barge close inshore, as close as he dared thrust it, then he waited and watched to see if the stern of the boat would swing too wide. Sometimes it eased past the opposite bank, by inches, and we had it made. But twice, at Slim Island where the river makes a sharp horseshoe bend, the island bending with it, we had to stop, back and try again. Buddy said he had made both those bends on the first try and he was apologetic that he didn't now, but I needed to know what you did when you couldn't make a bend on the first try and was glad for the two opportunities to watch.

These bends and loops make it thirty-four river miles to the mouth of the Barren, whereas it is only eighteen miles by land. All along the way the river was lined with fishing camps and small craft tied up at private docks. There were houseboats, motorboats, cabin cruisers and skiffs, even a few canoes. Where there were people, they waved in friendliness and were delighted when the whistle answered them. To this day a big boat on the Barren creates a lot of excitement.

About twenty-five miles downstream is the Barren River Lock #1. There are no other locks on the Barren, but this lock needed to be named to distinguish it from those on the Green.

Before we reached the lock, however, Peanuts called us to lunch. The big meal on boats, their "dinner," is eaten at midday, in this case eleven o'clock. Peanuts had been distressed when we came aboard by the state of his galley. "Don't put in your book," he warned me, "that my galley was dirty. I meant to have it cleaned up for you, but we run aground on a bar last night and had to work all night to get off. I didn't have time to clean up before you come aboard."

Ordinarily he must have kept his galley as neat and clean as a good housekeeper's kitchen and it was perfectly clean as far as I could see. But his apologies told us what had caused the delay in picking us up that morning.

"Haven't any of you had any sleep?" I asked.

Peanuts shrugged. "Well, Jim and Paul are sleeping now. Me and Buddy'll sleep this afternoon."

He gave us a feast of good roast beef, mashed potatoes, fresh green beans, sliced tomatoes, pumpkin pie and coffee and milk. A tradition on the river is good food. In the heyday of the steamboats they vied with each other to provide the best food and the widest varieties.

Mrs. Thomas, wife of my retired steamboat captain, had told me that on the *Evansville* there was always offered at dinner at least three meats — ham, fried chicken, roast beef or pork — and there were never less than three desserts — watermelon, in season, blackberry cobbler, in season, ice cream all the time and pies and cakes. Since towboats carry no passengers, their food is plainer and heftier, meant for a working crew, but it is always plentiful and well cooked.

Barren River Lock #1 is one of those that have been rebuilt. I don't know why it received attention before the Green River locks, but it did. It is both long enough, 350 feet, and wide enough, 56 feet, for comfort and it is operated with hydraulic power. Locking through was automatic and took only ten minutes.

We chugged on down the Barren, past the little village of Greencastle, past Jones Hole, Snowbird's Point (where we saw only hawks lazily circling), past the Narrows, on to Sally's Rock, of which I had heard so much.

In the early 1900s, a farmer's daughter, Sally Beck, had loved steamboats so much that she had run to stand on this point of rock to wave at each one passing. It began when she was a child but continued through girlhood into womanhood. Rivermen knew to watch for the girl and to whistle in answer to her wave. One form of the story has it that Sally's father became postmaster of their village and the boats carrying mail delivered it into a basket Sally lowered.

Captain Thomas did not recall that as being true. He does say that during his day (1912 to 1931) the Beck store had the only telephone between Bowling Green and Woodbury, Lock #4, and that any riverman wishing to send a message up- or downriver used her lowered basket to get the message to Sally for her father. Ruefully, Mrs. Thomas admitted that the wives of the rivermen unanimously loathed Sally Beck. "That Sally Beck," they would sniff, "trying to get herself a riverman!"

Ironically, Sally did not marry "on the river." She married a dry-lander and went to live, first, in Illinois, and then in Lakeland, Florida. The point of rock eventually fell into the river, fortunately at a time when no boat was passing. A government dredge boat had to blast it out of the channel.

Reinforcing her sketches with photographs, Pansy had been busy all morning taking pictures and her artistic soul was delighted with the whitened, bleached sycamore snags thrusting up from the river. She had, also, been sent into raptures over the coloring of the low, striated rocks of the cliffs. I saw their beauty, too, but, piloting the boat even harder than Buddy Nasbitt, I dreaded them for the boat's sake.

Each one of those gaunt sycamore snags, so startlingly beautiful in its nakedness, was a hazard. Any one of them could rip a hole in the hull of the boat and there was so little room in which to avoid them. The striated rocks were a double hazard, especially on a bend, and they seemed to occur most on bends. There is absolutely no give in a rock and the hull of a boat caught in the current and slammed against a low cliff would have to do the giving in a disastrous way.

I had no fear of this, but, getting into the skin of the pilot as I was, becoming the pilot, I liked neither the snags nor the rocks. They were the reason Buddy Nasbitt never took his eyes off the face of the water. One moment of carelessness might mean death to his boat.

Nine miles below Barren River Lock #1, we came out into the Green, and almost immediately bore up on Green River Lock #4 at Woodbury. In contrast to the ten minutes it took us to lock through at Barren #1, we took forty-five minutes at Woodbury. This lock was finished in 1839, is 138 feet long and 35 feet wide. The barge had to be broken loose and locked through ahead and it was a close fit even so. The gates of the lock were wooden and operated by hand with a sort of windlass.

As the *Maple* was on its way, the lock chamber was full and Buddy nosed the barge in. The crew broke it loose and he backed the boat away so the upper gates could be closed. It took four men to close the two halves of the gate, two to each windlass set on either side of the lock walls. The men moved down then and opened the lower gates in the same manner. When the barge was down, it had to be hand-towed out of the lock crib. Then the lower gates had to be closed and there was a wait while the water level rose. Buddy nosed the boat in. The routine of closing the upper gates and opening the lower was repeated. Six times, four men had to walk around and around four windlasses, closing and opening the gates. I thought forty-five minutes a relatively short time for locking through, under the circumstances.

Since we locked through Woodbury Lock the dam gave way under flood waters several years ago, so nothing can come up the Green now except fishing boats, shanty boats and the mussel boats.

We found the Green a much lonelier river than the Barren. We had seen the last of the fishing camps and there were comparatively few small craft tied up. The Green is a rampager in flood and it's best not to build too near her.

It was a much wider river, and deeper, and in our prejudiced eyes a much more beautiful river than the Barren. The Green is our own river. In its upper reaches it flows practically through my back yard. Pansy Phillips grew up on it and has fished and boated on it all her life. We were proud of its beauty and its stillness and its goodness, in width and depth, to the boat. There were fewer bends and they were rounder. There were long, quiet stretches of comparatively straight water.

Buddy Nasbitt marked his log, now, and went below to sleep. His father, Jim, also a pilot, took the helm. There was a forty-six-mile pool of good water ahead of us before we would reach the Rochester Lock, about a six-hour run. Buddy must use this stretch of water and in this six hours make up his lost night's sleep.

Jim Nasbitt has been on rivers all his life and he is a good pilot. But this was his second run up the Green. The Ohio is his home. He says frankly, besides, that even on the Ohio Buddy is the better pilot. "He's as good as they come," he told us, "and better than most. Anybody can learn to be a river pilot but Buddy was born with it in his bones." He laughed. "He likes a little more water than he's got on the Green, but it don't really bother him like it does me. He can make this boat do anything he wants."

Rivermen speak of making a run up the Cumberland or Green or Kanawha, or down the Ohio or the Mississippi, but they speak of themselves as being "on the river." Wives of rivermen have a hard time of it, for their men are really married to the river. Some wives hate it and never quit trying to get their men off. Some wives accept it and make the most of their portion. Some, the blessed and the happy, learn to love the river themselves and go with their men constantly, and make the river their home. Mrs. Thomas was one of those. "It nearly killed me," she said, "when the *Evansville* burned and we left the river. I was raised on the river. My father was a towboat pilot and then I married Captain Thomas. My whole life was spent on the river. And nothing since has been as good." It was Mrs. Thomas who had showed me the coonjine step the roustabouts used to do when loading and unloading cargo.

All real river people feel the same. Nothing else is as good. They are a breed, a clan, set apart. They are an aristocracy of their own creating, holding dry-landers in faint contempt for the dull and deadly sameness of their lives. There is always something different on the river, they will tell you. No two runs are ever the same. The river is the heart of their lives and they talk about it constantly. They talk with their hands, as airplane pilots do. You can watch a boat nose into a bend as an old pilot talks you around. Or you can feel the spread of high water from his flattened palms. You can sense the beauty in the unfaded dream of their eyes.

"You should have seen the *Evansville*," Mrs. Thomas mourned to me, "all lit up, ready to back out from the wharf. Clear in the channel the pilot always played 'My Old Kentucky Home' on the wildcat whistle, to signal we were leaving Evansville for Kentucky. You should have seen the rousters unloading, singing and doing their coonjine step. You should have seen the passengers dancing in the evening at night, the prettiest women and the nicest, handsomest men. I tell you, it was the best and finest life you could have."

And my old pilot, Mrs. Thomas's father, had said to me, "In forty years I never took the wheel that my heart didn't beat up faster."

"Custom did not stale?" I asked.

"Not ever. Not ever." He added slowly, "If you cut me, I'd bleed river water instead of blood."

So, I do not think Buddy Nasbitt will ever get off the river.

Although the Green was wider and deeper here than it is up where Pansy and I know it, its banks looked familiar. As on our own headwater river, there were inroads of shale and gravel, there were drowned logs and bleached snags, there were slides cut off from the bank and there was the same lining of huge, overhanging willow and sycamore trees.

One of the willow trees provided a moment of tense excitement in the afternoon. Jim Nasbitt was nosing the barge into a long swinging bend. He was cutting in near the shore. We drifted around easily; then just ahead I saw an enormous willow hanging very low overhead. I said nothing, however. Jim was steering the boat. I didn't doubt but that he saw the willow and knew what he was doing. When the head of the barge began to pass under the willow, however, it seemed to me we could in no way avoid hitting the top branches, and every branch was as big as an average tree. River courtesy could not keep me quiet any longer. "Jim, you're going to hit that tree with the pilothouse," I said, and I *believe* I said it quietly.

He raised startled eyes. "By George," he said, "I sure am!"

Several things seemed to happen all at once. First there was a thrashing of water at the stern as Jim throttled down; then the crane on the barge hit the tree with a crashing impact and sheared off one limb as big around as a man's thigh and sent a dozen smaller limbs falling like rain over the barge deck. Next we swung sharp right and the head of the barge plowed aground. Although we were jostled considerably by the impact, it is to our eternal credit that neither Pansy nor I screamed. I couldn't have screamed for I was holding my breath. I remember thinking that right here was where we wrecked!

But the reason Jim had plowed the rake of the barge into the bank became evident immediately. With the head fast on the bank, the stern of the boat began to swing around, slowly, slowly, all too slowly it seemed to me. We waited to see if it would swing wide enough for the rest of the tree to miss the pilothouse. You could have heard a pin drop as we waited. We're going to miss, I told myself, and then, no, there isn't time. Still the stern swung about, and about, and then, ducking a little in spite of myself, I saw, and heard faintly, the brush of the willow tips as they swept harmlessly down the side of the pilothouse.

Jim Nasbitt blew out his breath. "Lord, I'm glad you spoke up! I didn't see that tree at all. I was watching the water depth."

A little weak-kneed, I sat for a moment while Jim backed off the bank and went ahead. "Suppose there hadn't been room for you to swing wide enough there?" I asked, when he had the boat straightened out.

"We'd have lost the pilothouse," he said. He grinned. "Scare you?"

"Yes," I confessed, without any shame.

He shook his head. "I oughtn't to have done that. Just shows you can't *ever* overlook a thing. You got to watch for *everything*." He sighed. "Always something on the river."

Farther down we passed through a small fleet of mussel boats. Mussel shells are still used in the button industry, though plastics have replaced them to some extent. I believe mussels are eaten in some places. We never eat them on Green River. Too many people have tried and been made ill.

The mussel boats were built like small scows and had a frame of hooked rakes attached to one side and a great, saillike seine attached to the other. The rakes swept the mussels into the seines. The boats pulled to shore at Jim's whistle toot and watched us pass. I had seen both Nasbitts take up the binoculars often during the day to peer ahead at what looked like a rock or bleached stump to the naked eye. Sometimes it was. Occasionally it was a small boat. Then the whistle was blown immediately. "If you're ever on the river," Jim warned, "and a barge boat whistles, get to the bank as quick as you can. The suction can draw you down and wreck your boat."

I didn't think a barge boat would ever come up over the shoals to our Beaver Hole, but I tucked the information away. I *might* be fishing sometime on the lower Green or even the Ohio.

We had a long peaceful afternoon, closing up the landmarks on the chart. Both Nasbitts had entered with much understanding into my needs and had tried eagerly to help me identify the old landings and abandoned ferries. We didn't have much luck with the landings for they were usually nothing but clearing on the banks and in thirty-one years they had grown over. Most of the ferry roads showed up plainly, however. They had been cut too deep to grow up completely yet.

When the sun went down the barge lights were set out: a green light on the starboard side, a red light on the port and an amber light dead-center. The white light on the stern of the boat was also flicked on, and the headlight centered under the pilothouse. But Jim did not yet use the powerful searchlight mounted on top of the pilothouse.

All through the twilight we ran through a wide, silent stretch of river, the utter peace and tranquillity making us silent, too. Jim flicked on the tiny nightlight over the chart from time to time, but quickly flicked it off. A pilot's night sight is extremely important and marine law requires that all lights, his own as well as those of other boats, be shaded at certain stated degrees to protect him.

When full dark came, Jim began to use the two searchlights that are atop the pilothouse. They are operated by handles that protrude into the ceiling.

All day, in the long stretches of the river, each Nasbitt had sat much of the time. But now Jim Nasbitt kicked the high pilot's chair out of the way and stood. I was suddenly conscious of great tiredness in myself and of great tension. No fear entered the feeling at all. I simply knew that running a river at night calls for absolute and undistracted attention and just as Jim Nasbitt girded himself up for it, so did I.

There are queer illusions, after full dark. The reflections of the tall dead snags seem to double their length and you want to veer too far around them. The water shimmers and you want to steer by the shimmer. The river seems to narrow dangerously. You have a feeling that the banks are closing in and that you are creeping down a little creek. And the sense of movement is slowed. Looking ahead, you wonder if you are moving at all. You have to look alongside, watch the banks flow steadily by, to realize you are still chugging along at a fairly good pace.

I recalled that Mark Twain, when he was a cub pilot on the

Mississippi, was at the wheel one night. His pilot was resting on the long bench behind him. Suddenly Mark Twain couldn't believe his eyes. The ripple of shoal water lay dead ahead. He knew it shouldn't be there. He knew he had good, deep water in that place. But the illusion was so strong that, bearing down on it, he could not make himself hold the boat on the ripple. He swung dangerously aside and the pilot jumped for the wheel. "What the devil are you doing?"

"There's shoal water ahead!"

The danger of the swing aside now averted, the pilot said, "What made you think there was shoal water there? Don't you know it's good water?"

"Yes, sir, but it looked . . ."

"You," the pilot said crushingly, "won't make a pilot until you learn to steer by what you *know,* not by what you see."

Jim Nasbitt nodded. "It's the living truth. Many a boat has been wrecked because a pilot forgot that."

We were due at the Rochester lock at eight o'clock. At seven-thirty Jim sent Peanuts below to waken Buddy. I knew why. Jim had said he wouldn't take a boat through that lock at night for all the money in the world and Buddy had said it always scared the living daylights out of him in the daylight.

The Rochester lock is built in a short, right-angle bend in the river, with the dam on the outside of the bend. It is even smaller than the lock at Woodbury . . . only 135 feet long and 35 feet wide. It is a ghastly place for a lock and dam, and one can only speculate as to why it was chosen. In the 1830s, as now, politics and private interests played a big part in all public works. Somebody with power and pull had owned the land contiguous to the river at this place, and had got a nice fat price for it as a dam site, probably. For that matter, not a lock on the river was located with a first consideration for the convenience or safety of the boats that would use it.

Buddy came up. "Where are we?"

His father pointed on the chart. "About a mile and a half to the lock."

Buddy took a few moments to study the chart and get his night sight; then he took the helm and his father went below. I saw him walk out onto the barge and take his stand at the starboard side on its head. Peanuts was already on the port side and Paul Johnson was in the middle. They were ready to break the barge loose when she had been safely cribbed.

Buddy flicked off the searchlights and ran dark for fully a mile. "Watch the tops of the trees," he told me. They were clearly outlined against the starlit sky. He was steering by them. In this stretch of full, deep water just above the dam there were no hazards, and in the dark the river kept its proper proportions and there were no distorting reflections.

We came round a wide slow bend and saw the lights of Simmon's Ferry. The ferryboat was pulled into the right bank. Buddy kicked his chair away and blew, both for the ferry and for the lock . . . one long and two short blasts for we were a double lock.

Now he turned on the searchlights, for the lock was just beyond. We passed the ferry. Both searchlights playing constantly now, sweeping ahead, to the sides, on the water, around, first one hand then the other turning their handles near the ceiling, his free hand maneuvering the rudder, reaching to the throttle, keeping the boat steady in the channel, Buddy eased along.

It was a solo dance in a ballet of precision; it was stylized, slowed and infinitely graceful movement. The boy was still so young that he could not have made a graceless movement. His slim body swayed as he reached for the lights, played them, bent again over the controls, reached again, as he felt his way into the bend.

To the left was the dam and we could now hear its roar and
see the glare of its white water. The slightest miscalculation
could have sent us over with the rush of water. If this boy did
not bend in close enough, or if he swung too wide, the current
could catch us and take us over. If he lost power too much,
throttled down too much, the boat wouldn't steer and we would
be helpless against the strong current. I knew all this and yet
I felt absolutely no fear. I knew the boy had said it scared the
living daylights out of him, and my absence of fear was not
wholly faith in him. It was simply that there are times when
danger does not frighten; it exalts instead. And this was one of
those times. I was caught up, and lifted, by the fantastic beauty
of the whole drama.

Well into the bend, the lock lights showed up. The gates
were open. The head of the barge found them, nosed past them
noiselessly. The whole length of the barge crept by inches into
the crib, slid past the walls, was swallowed and pocketed. The
barge was in. Without scraping so much as a flake of rust off
the barge, or a mossy lichen off the old rock walls, the boy had
put his barge precisely where he wanted it. I expected it, but it
was still a miracle when it happened.

Oh, I know steamboat pilots did it for ninety years. But they
weren't pushing a barge ahead of them. And I know towboats
pilots did it for a long, long time. But they tied up at night. This
boy had done it with the face of the water shimmering with reflections, distorted almost beyond recognition, full dark on all
sides, the narrowest measure of safety between him and the dam.
I was suddenly as limp as a tired old dishrag.

But the boy only hooked up his pilot's chair to wait for the
barge to be broken loose. He grinned. "Well, here you are."

I tried to tell him what the trip had meant to me, how invaluable it had been and how fine he and his father had been. He
waved it away. "It's been our pleasure. You have turned a

routine trip into something special. We'll never forget this day and you'll always be welcome on a Nasbitt boat."

Pansy and I clambered up the ladder of the lock wall, my husband, who was meeting us, and Jim Nasbitt giving us a hand. I tried to tell Jim, too, what the trip had meant. Like his son, he waved it away. But he laughed, and then said to Henry, "If she writes a book as hard as she pilots a boat, she ought to write a damned good book about the river. She sure as hell did run herself a river today!"

I certainly had run me a piece of the river, and the title for my book was given to me now, too. It had to be *Run Me a River*.

L'ENVOI

Life — so beautiful, and yet so fraught with tears,
I have not asked the easy way.
As I've gone down the road of years
You have not heard me say,
Spare me distress, or pain, or fears.

I've only asked to keep for mine
A few rare things;
The beauty of a rose, the shadow of a tree, and stars that
    shine;
The plane of light that darkens on a small bird's wings;
The stormy race of water down gray fingers of the rain;
The still sweet hush of evening as it closes on the plain;
To laugh with friends, and hold them dear.
To love a child, and know its clear
Look of abiding trust.
These things I ask, somehow, because I must.

But Life, I could have used so well
The greater gift you have in store;
That you'll not loan, nor barter for, nor sell.
(Be quiet, be still, you cannot ask for more).